"You and Mildred best head for cover."

"Ryan, they'll only hit us by accident with those oversize muskets," Mildred replied.

"Mebbe, but it looks like some smaller craft are heading this way. Krysty, Mildred—*git*!"

"Come on." Krysty grabbed Mildred's wrist and dragged her toward the cabin.

She heard Ryan open fire, accompanied by staccato bursts from J.B.'s submachine gun. Given the range, the bobbing of the approaching war craft on the water and the complex movement of the *Queen*—pitching fore and aft as well as heeling to her right from the centrifugal force of the fastest left turn the vessel could manage—she doubted he'd be lucky to hit anything significant. Much less score another shot through a forward port to take the helmsman.

She and Mildred had almost reached the cabin when the return fire hit, roaring like an angry dragon. Stout planks suddenly erupted into fragments, almost in the redhead's face.

And then the world vanished in a soundless white flash.

Other titles in the Deathlands saga:

Pandora's Redoubt	Eden's Twilight
Rat King	Desolation Crossing
Zero City	Alpha Wave
Savage Armada	Time Castaways
Judas Strike	Prophecy
Shadow Fortress	Blood Harvest
Sunchild	Arcadian's Asylum
Breakthrough	Baptism of Rage
Salvation Road	Doom Helix
Amazon Gate	Moonfeast
Destiny's Truth	Downrigger Drift
Skydark Spawn	Playfair's Axiom
Damnation Road Show	Tainted Cascade
Devil Riders	Perception Fault
Bloodfire	Prodigal's Return
Hellbenders	Lost Gates
Separation	Haven's Blight
Death Hunt	Hell Road Warriors
Shaking Earth	Palaces of Light
Black Harvest	Wretched Earth
Vengeance Trail	Crimson Waters
Ritual Chill	No Man's Land
Atlantis Reprise	Nemesis
Labyrinth	Chrono Spasm
Strontium Swamp	Sins of Honor
Shatter Zone	Storm Breakers
Perdition Valley	Dark Fathoms
Cannibal Moon	Siren Song
Sky Raider	End Program
Remember Tomorrow	Desolation Angels
Sunspot	Blood Red Tide
Desert Kings	Polestar Omega
Apocalypse Unborn	Hive Invasion
Thunder Road	End Day
Plague Lords	Forbidden Trespass
(Empire of Xibalba Book I)	
Dark Resurrection	
(Empire of Xibalba Book II)	

JAMES AXLER
DEATHLANDS®
IRON RAGE

A GOLD EAGLE BOOK FROM
W❂RLDWIDE®

TORONTO • NEW YORK • LONDON
AMSTERDAM • PARIS • SYDNEY • HAMBURG
STOCKHOLM • ATHENS • TOKYO • MILAN
MADRID • WARSAW • BUDAPEST • AUCKLAND

Recycling programs
for this product may
not exist in your area.

First edition July 2015

ISBN-13: 978-0-373-62633-5

Special thanks and acknowledgment to
Victor Milan for his contribution to this work.

Iron Rage

Printed in U.S.A.

Now and then we had a hope that if we lived and were good, God would permit us to be pirates.
—Mark Twain,
Life on the Mississippi

THE DEATHLANDS SAGA

This world is their legacy, a world born in the violent nuclear spasm of 2001 that was the bitter outcome of a struggle for global dominance.

There is no real escape from this shockscape where life always hangs in the balance, vulnerable to newly demonic nature, barbarism, lawlessness.

But they are the warrior survivalists, and they endure—in the way of the lion, the hawk and the tiger, true to nature's heart despite its ruination.

Ryan Cawdor: The privileged son of an East Coast baron. Acquainted with betrayal from a tender age, he is a master of the hard realities.

Krysty Wroth: Harmony ville's own Titian-haired beauty, a woman with the strength of tempered steel. Her premonitions and Gaia powers have been fostered by her Mother Sonja.

J. B. Dix, the Armorer: Weapons master and Ryan's close ally, he, too, honed his skills traversing the Deathlands with the legendary Trader.

Doctor Theophilus Tanner: Torn from his family and a gentler life in 1896, Doc has been thrown into a future he couldn't have imagined.

Dr. Mildred Wyeth: Her father was killed by the Ku Klux Klan, but her fate is not much lighter. Restored from pre-dark cryogenic suspension, she brings twentieth-century healing skills to a nightmare.

Jak Lauren: A true child of the wastelands, reared on adversity, loss and danger, the albino teenager is a fierce fighter and loyal friend.

Dean Cawdor: Ryan's young son by Sharona accepts the only world he knows, and yet he is the seedling bearing the promise of tomorrow.

In a world where all was lost, they are humanity's last hope…

Chapter One

"It looks pretty," Ricky Morales said.

"Bad country," Maggie Santiago replied. "Worse comin'."

She was a small woman, with jaw-length brown hair that was held off her face by a headband. She had a slight build and was decidedly flat-chested. Ricky was sixteen and noticed that kind of thing.

He wiped sweat from his forehead. The approach of the Yazoo River to its confluence with the Sippi was unquestionably beautiful, with tall green grass to either side, crowned by the shattered ruins of what he was told was Vicksburg rising above it to the south, and the brown expanse of the great river itself ahead. The Yazoo rolled by the hull of the *Mississippi Queen*, brown and slightly greasy in the hot sun, which threw eye-stinging darts of morning light at the slow, slogging waves.

A great blue heron, with its beautiful gray-blue plumage shining in the sun and a crest of feathers sweeping back from its head, stalked majestically through the shallows of the northern bank. It was hard to believe the green reeds lining the flow, and the green heights to the left, harbored any kind of wickedness or ugliness.

"I don't know," Ricky said, holding up a toothed

washer to the near-cloudless sky to squint through it, looking for lingering grit or crud. The slight machinist and mechanic was teaching him to disassemble the *Queen*'s bow winch. It was just the sort of thing the youth found fun. "It looks double-peaceful to me."

Krysty Wroth, her flame-red hair tossed by the slow afternoon breeze—moving, in fact, rather more than the light wind could account for—joined the pair. She stood gazing out of the blunt round prow of the river tug with one boot up on the gunwales. Ricky tried hard not to stare at the tall, statuesque woman. As usual. She was one of his companions, and one of the most beautiful women he had ever seen. He had a crush on her, even though she was the lover of the group's leader, the one-eyed Ryan Cawdor.

"It's hard to imagine anything so beautiful could be so deadly," Ricky told Maggie.

A sliding brown ridge appeared in the water near the wading heron. A pair of big, broad jaws burst through the surface in an explosion of spray. They snapped shut on the majestic bird. A savage shake, a roll, a wave, and the bird was gone beneath the water with nothing to show that it had ever been there, except for a heavy roll of greenish water slowly diminishing to become one with the flow, and a blue-gray feather swooping down to light delicately on the river and be carried away downstream.

Ricky jumped to his feet. "Whoa!"

"Hey," Maggie snapped. "Mind the parts, kid! You kick them in the Yazoo, and I'll kick you in right after."

She referred to the components of the winch, which

they had spread out on oiled canvas. Though she was only an assistant to the vessel's chief engineer, Myron Conoyer—also known as husband to the captain of the *Queen*, Trace Conoyer, with whom he co-owned the boat—she took her task seriously. So did the rest of the crew who worked for the pair.

"What was that?"

Maggie glanced that way. Ricky hadn't thought she'd noticed the commotion, but she had.

"Nile crocodile," she said matter-of-factly. "These waters are lousy with them."

She gave him a gap-toothed smile.

"One of the reasons this is a nasty stretch of river," she said.

Ricky looked at Krysty. "Didn't that bother you?" he asked. He was still freaked out about seeing the bird snatched below the lazy, deceptively innocuous water so precipitously, and he needed someone to validate him.

"What?" she said.

"The bird—the heron. A big old croc grabbing it just like *that*—that doesn't bother you?"

Krysty shrugged. He tried to keep his eyes off the fascinating thing that did to the front of the plaid shirt she wore, and failed.

"It's just the circle of life," she said.

"What's the problem, Ricky?" a voice asked from behind him. "We're not getting paid to sightsee."

He turned. There was no mistaking that voice.

"He was alarmed because a Nile croc took down a heron, right over there, Ryan," Krysty said, as her man approached with the captain and her husband alongside.

Ryan came up and put his arm around her. He was a tall rangy man, narrow-waisted and broad-chested, with shaggy black hair and a single pale blue eye. His other eye was covered by a black patch, and a scar ran from brow to jawline.

"I just don't want him kicking any parts of my winch overboard," Maggie said.

"Don't worry," Krysty told her. "He loves his machines far too much for that."

"Nile crocodiles," Ryan grunted. "Great."

"Don't mind them," said the short, potbellied, curly-bearded man in the glasses next to him. He wore grease-stained tan coveralls. "Everything else here is *much* worse."

"You and your exaggerations, Myron," Trace Conoyer said. She was taller than her spouse, with a hawk nose and piercing dark eyes to match, and dark blond hair worn short. "Though for a fact, I'd just as soon people keep their eyes skinned proper until we're well out in the Sippi stream and heading south."

"Start with the worst thing, then," Ryan said. "After that, it'll only be good news."

"Don't be too sure of that, my friend," Myron said. As the *Queen*'s chief engineer, he was Ricky's nominal boss while aboard the vessel. Although in Ricky's mind his boss would always be the group Armorer, and his mentor, J. B. Dix.

And Ryan, of course.

Most of them had abilities that were useful to the vessel and her crew—even Doc, with his weird, eclectic old-days knowledge.

As a general rule, Ryan Cawdor did not hire his group out for sec work, unless survival was at stake, for one reason or another. When survival for himself and his small, loyal band of friends was concerned, anything and everything were always on the table.

The companions had been hired on the *Queen* as crew. There was always plenty of work to be done. Captain Conoyer was grateful for fourteen extra hands to do it, and willing to pay with room and board and a share in the proceeds of every transaction—the same deal she and every other member of the crew had. With differences in percentage, of course.

One of the conditions of the companions' employment was that if—more likely, *when*—there was fighting to be done, they would be required to defend the ship. It just so happened that the new crew members were all ace at that particular skill.

But then again, that was pretty much an unspoken condition of every job, including just living day to day. They lived in the Deathlands, after all.

"Stickies," the captain said. "Been colonies of them around the confluence of the Yazoo and the Sippi for fifty years, the old river folk say."

"Do they ever attack boats?" Ricky asked, as he settled back down by the tarp on which the winch parts rested.

"Not if they keep well clear of the banks," Trace said.

"What if there are snags on the river?" Krysty asked. "Or mebbe sandbars narrowing the channel."

"Like I said—if they keep clear of the banks. Otherwise all bets are off."

"Don't forget the rads," Myron said helpfully.

"Rads?" Krysty and Ricky said almost simultaneously.

"Oh, I was getting there," Trace stated. "Not just rads, but heavy-metal pollution, big-time. You know how you always hear talk about strontium swamps? Well, they actually got stretches of that around here."

Ricky eyed a flock of ducks starting noisily from some reeds on the right bank. "Does that mean those birds are muties too, if they can live around here?"

Trace shrugged. "Many of the creatures seem less affected by the rads than we are," Myron said.

"Sounds like a double-bad place for shore leave," J.B. said, approaching from astern.

"It's not my idea of a vacation spot," added Mildred Wyeth, who walked by his side. She was taller than he by a slight margin, which the battered fedora he wore tended to disguise.

"The rads won't kill you," Myron said. "Not right away. The swampers who live in these bogs will likely get you first."

"Swampies?" Mildred asked.

"Swampers," the engineer repeated, with added emphasis on the second syllable. "Not muties. People."

"Of a sort," his wife told them.

"Wouldn't they have to be muties to survive if the rad count's that high?" Ricky asked.

"They're too mean for the rads to chill," Santiago offered.

"How about them?" Ryan asked. "Do they go after vessels that are underway?"

"Not much when they stay clear of the banks," the captain said. "Like the stickies. Like most things, come to that. That's another reason we stay out in the middle of the channel when we can. The river's lethal enough. We don't need the grief that comes from *land*."

"Which is her typically sour way of saying the river is our home, and we feel safest here," Myron said. "Right, my love?"

That got a lopsided grin from the captain. "Anything you say, Myron."

Ricky picked up a sprocket and held it up to the sun to be examined.

"I get it," he said glumly. "Everything's dangerous. Especially everything beautiful."

Ryan winked at Krysty and grinned. "Pretty much."

"The real danger is the darkness in the human soul," said Nataly Dobrynin, the *Queen*'s first mate, emerging from the superstructure and walking up to join the others. She was on the tall side, taller than either Conoyer, and skinny. She wore her long, dark brown hair pulled back in a ponytail that emphasized the austere bone structure of her face, and her slightly angled gray eyes. She never smiled, and intimidated the hell out of Ricky.

Surely that can't be right, Ricky thought. Stickies are double dangerous, for one thing. Rads and heavy-metal poisoning, for another.

He looked to Ryan for confirmation. *He* sure as nuke wasn't contradicting the somewhat-scary mate.

But Ryan frowned thoughtfully.

"That's true enough," he said. "That's what blew up the world, after all."

"Some would blame the cold hearts of the white-coats, lover, never mind the darkness of their souls," Krysty said drily.

"That 'some' being you."

She grinned; he shrugged.

"Well, 'some' aren't wrong," he said. "But they still had their reasons, which fieldstripped down to that."

"I'd say it was the madness of shutting themselves off from the natural world in order to try to control it," the redhead said.

"Sounds like the same thing, to me," Nataly said. She turned to Trace. "Captain, we're coming eight up on the confluence."

Trace nodded. "Right. Everybody, get to your stations. Break time's over. The big river's mood doesn't look bad today, but wrestling this bitch of a barge through the turbulence where the streams join could get triple ugly triple fast."

"You best put your toys away and step lively too, Ricky," Ryan said. "I think we need to have weapons in hand when we hit the Sippi. With the captain's permission, of course."

"Why's that?" Myron asked. The bespectacled engineer sounded more curious than challenging.

"Junctions are good places for bad things to happen," J.B. stated, settling his fedora more firmly on his head. "Like crossroads. Reckon rivers aren't any different."

"They used to say the Devil hung out at crossroads," Mildred said. "Back in the, uh, day."

Ricky turned his face down to hide his grin. The "day" she meant was back in the long-dead twentieth century, where Mildred had lived most of her life. She had undergone a routine abdominal surgical procedure and something had gone wrong. She'd been frozen in a cryogenic procedure and shipped to a cryocenter in Minnesota just as the balloon was going up on the Big Nuke.

Trace nodded. "You're right, Ryan. Take your people to full alert. But stand ready to lend a hand if it turns out the river's what we really need to be worried about."

Ryan nodded.

"Get that winch back together double quick," Myron said, all business now.

"But we haven't finished cleaning it," Maggie protested.

"Yes, you have," Myron told her, his tone at once gentle and commanding. "You'll just take it apart again and clean it after we're headed up the Sippi for Feliville."

"Aye-aye, sir," she said glumly. Then she sat back on her heels, looked at Ricky and suddenly grinned.

When she did that she was positively cute, he thought.

"All right, champ," she said. "Show me what you've got."

THE DECK ROLLED beneath Ryan's boots as the Mississippi Queen chugged into the joining of the Yazoo with the Sippi.

His Steyr Scout Tactical longblaster in hand, he stood at the bow, with Krysty at his side. The rest of the companions were spread out around the eighty-foot-long vessel's perimeter, interspersed with armed members of the *Queen*'s regular crew. Doc Tanner, his LeMat combination handblaster and shotgun at the ready, held a position to Krysty's right. J.B. was to Ryan's left, holding his Uzi, and Mildred flanked him farther astern. Jak Lauren, their young scout, stood in the stern. He was ready to run down the thick hawser by which they towed a hundred-foot barge stacked high with lumber and bales of cloth and leap aboard to repel any would-be boarders with his knives and .357 Magnum Colt Python revolver.

Finally, Ricky Morales, having reassembled the power-winch to his stern task-mistress's approval, lay on his belly on the flat roof of the main cabin, ready to snipe with the DeLisle replica carbine he had helped his uncle make by hand, in happier times on his home island of Puerto Rico. Although it couldn't really be called "sniping," since the weapon lacked a scope, the boy could consistently hit his mark with whisper-quiet shots out to a hundred yards.

In the event Ryan's people had to reach out and touch somebody—as Mildred put it in her quaintly anachronistic freezie way—any farther than one hundred yards, Ryan's Steyr, which did have a scope, could do the job.

Not that Captain Conoyer believed there'd be any trouble. But she hadn't batted an eyelash when Ryan suggested turning out as many hands with blasters as possible to wait for it, just in case. Having hired him in part as a sec consultant, as she put it, she had the sense to listen to him on the subject.

Over a third as wide across the beam as she was

long, the tug was surprisingly stable as she chugged confidently out into the crosscurrent from the Sippi. As ballast she carried tons of big metal scrap chunks, plus crates of weapons and ammo that were the actual prizes from this current voyage up the Yazoo. The cream of the crop was a Lahti Model L-39: a bolt-action antitank rifle firing 20 mm armor-piercing rounds, in cherry condition, consigned to a wealthy baron up the big river. Or so Ryan was told; sadly, Captain Trace had refused to open the crate despite the near-drooling entreaties of J.B. and his apprentice armorer, Ricky.

The *Queen* began its turn to starboard almost as soon as it cleared the banks to the north. Ryan glanced back over his right shoulder, along the vessel's length toward the barge. He knew that getting it safely around the corner would be the trickiest part. But Trace had taken the helm herself, and just in their brief time aboard Ryan and his friends had learned she was expert in piloting the boat.

The one-eyed man was just as glad the *Queen* wasn't a pusher-style Sippi tug, of the sort her crew told Ryan had dominated the river before the nukeday. Bigger and of all-steel construction, they used to push not just single barges, but sometimes two or more in series—each many times larger than the wooden one the *Queen* was dragging toward Feliville—with their square prows. He didn't even want to try to imagine how pulling off a maneuver like this would have worked in such an arrangement.

He was unlikely to find out. Nukeday had triggered colossal earthquakes that had started shaking up the continental US even before the warheads stopped detonating. None was worse than the quake caused by the New Madrid Fault Line that ran by the Sippi from north of Memphis to St. Louis. The blasts, quakes and seismic water surges had smashed most of the vessels on the river into twisted junk, left them high and dry when the great river actually changed channels, and even tossed them inland, sometimes even into the hearts of major cities.

They had become mother lodes of fabulous scrap for generations of especially intrepid scavvies. Or for barons willing to enslave the people of the villes they ruled to the arduous and dangerous work of ship-breaking. These days most of the river traffic was wood-hulled, driven by steam engines or, as the *Queen* was, by scavvied Diesels. And when they hauled barges they were content to pull them.

As Ryan turned his face forward again, he scanned the seven-foot weeds that obscured the Yazoo's north bank and the east bank of the Sippi. He wasn't sure what he expected to see, but he expected to see *something*. His gut told him that trouble was coming.

But it gave him not the slightest clue as to what that trouble would actually be. Nor where it would come from.

He looked back out across the Sippi and saw a geyser of water shoot up into the air, fifty yards ahead and a little off the port bow of the turning tugboat. A heavy boom hit him with an impact as much felt as heard. It was a sound he was all too familiar with.

He spun to look south. Steaming up the river from the

south came four boats, a quarter mile away and closing slowly. They were a ragged assortment, no two alike, and none as large as the *Queen* herself. They had a strange, ugly, bruised glint to them in the afternoon sun, and were gray mottled with red. Black plumes billowed from their smokestacks and were swept away east by a crossing breeze.

Yellow light flared from the bows of the nearest two, accompanied by giant puffs of dirty-white smoke.

"Red alert!" he turned and shouted toward the *Queen*'s cabin. "Cannon fire! We're under attack!"

Chapter Two

Ryan heard a rushing roar pass overhead. Then a fresh column of water blasted up from the river right in front of the left side of the bow, drenching him.

A hand-cranked siren was winding from the tug's cabin. Ducking reflexively behind the rail—as if that would offer protection from a cannon shot, either shell or solid ball—Ryan equally reflexively looked back to Krysty.

His lover was likewise crouched, her Glock 18C blaster looking especially futile clutched in her white hands. Her hair had retracted itself to a tight scarlet cap on her skull.

He felt the vibrations of the hull through his boot soles change. At the same time the growl of the Diesels grew louder and slightly higher in pitch. Trace had ordered full throttle. Her husband was doubtless belowdecks now, babying the powerful marine engines to keep them churning at maximum power. Ryan could feel the propellers straining to drive the vessel and the burden she towed faster. But there was no way to give hundreds of tons jackrabbit acceleration. Their accumulation of speed would go painfully slowly.

And the pursuing vessels already had a speed advantage, even though their steam engines were powering them against the Sippi's sluggish but immensely powerful flow. If this was a race, they couldn't win it.

And if this was an artillery duel—well, Ryan thought, the *Queen* was nuked, as the tug had no artillery. Accommodations were tight aboard the tubby vessel as it was—he and his companions slept on deck, when weather permitted, as fortunately it had most nights they'd been on the *Queen*. And every pound counted when your entire living was based on hauling cargo. The Conoyers could have mounted a black powder cannon, but they chose not to.

Even if they had, they would have been outgunned. The enemy cannoneers hadn't yet hit the lumbering tug, but it was a matter of time.

Something cracked above Ryan's head. He ducked even lower, instinctively. The crack was repeated, slightly less loud.

I know that song, he thought. Someone was firing a blaster at him—not a charcoal-burner nineteenth-century replica, but a smokeless-powder high-powered longblaster.

The longblaster shots, in their way, concerned him more than the cannonade. Most black powder cannon weren't rifled, and therefore weren't accurate, even though a metal ball weighing just a couple of pounds could do a shocking amount of damage to a body. While most blaster-shooters weren't particularly accurate, either, there was always the chance that their pursuers would have a marksman in their ranks.

On the other hand, the *Queen*'s complement most definitely did. And his name was Ryan Cawdor.

He laid the Steyr's foregrip on the rail and sighted through the low-power Leupold variable scope. He didn't need much magnification to confirm what he already suspected: the weird, dully metallic stuff covering the oncoming boats looked that way because it was weird and metallic.

The vessels had been covered, at least up front, in plates and pieces of scrap metal.

"J.B.," he called. He didn't take his eye from the scope. "Get over here. I've got work for you."

The attacking vessels were steaming in a V formation, with the lead boat on Ryan's right. As he panned his scope across the vessels, he noticed activity on the bow of the one to his left. Men were swabbing out the barrel of their blaster with what looked like a wet mop and probably was, so that the fresh charge of black powder they were fixing to put in wouldn't cook off the moment they inserted it.

Ryan sighted in on the nearest gunner and drew a deep breath. As the sight lined up he let half of it out, bit back the rest and squeezed the trigger.

The carbine bucked and roared. Automatically Ryan's right hand left the rear grip to work the bolt, jacking out the spent case and slamming home a fresh cartridge from the 10-round magazine in his longblaster. The empty brass clinked off the deck boards and rolled out one of the scuppers, which was a shame, since the things were valuable for their metal, even if they were bent or otherwise unable to be reloaded.

But spilled blood wouldn't go back in the body, either. All that mattered to Ryan now was lining up the next shot.

As he expected, the four-person crew was hunkered down and frozen in place. A brighter smear on the improvised-armor plate above them and to the left showed where Ryan's bullet had hit and knocked away a path of rust the size of his palm.

Also as expected. Like any master marksman, Ryan knew pretty well where a bullet would go when it left his longblaster—not an option except in aimed fire, of course. Though neither the Yazoo nor the Sippi were exactly racing today, the interference of their currents meeting did cause some chop, which in turn made the *Queen* wallow in a not-entirely-predictable way. But it wasn't hard to compensate for the motion. And while she was still turning to starboard, into the bigger river's flow, the enemy ships were coming pretty straight on, and not fast, either. That meant Ryan didn't have to lead his target much to speak of.

The second shot wasn't perfect, either. Because of the *Queen*'s motion he still pulled slightly off, though he reckoned the shot would take the swabber in the right shoulder. When the scope came back level, Ryan saw that his target was out of sight, and the short, skinny kid who'd been just to his right was spattered with red and visibly freaking out about it.

The other two shooters dived for cover behind the armored rail, which unlike the *Queen*'s wooden hull would reliably stop most bullets, possibly including his pointy-nosed, high-powered, 7.62 mm full-metal-jacket slug. It depended on the hardness of whichever chunk of scrap he happened to hit.

A quick examination showed all four boats carried but a single bow blaster each. It also showed a shocking bright flash of yellow fire from the one on the left-most craft, followed by a vast gout of smoke that instantly began to blow back over the hunchbacked, ironclad shape of the cabin in the breeze of its passage, as well as overboard in the crossing wind.

This time, the projectile's moan punctuated with a shattering crash from somewhere astern.

"Is everybody fit to fight?" Ryan shouted. He still kept his eye to the glass. He was getting an idea.

"Everybody's fine," J.B. replied, crouching at his left side. "The shot blew a section of the starboard rail to glowing nuke shit, just aft of the cabin."

"Reckon you can hit anybody with the Uzi at this range?"

A beat passed while J.B. considered that. Ryan continued scrutinizing the closing craft.

"Be easiest firing single shots, with the folding stock extended, like she was a big fat carbine. I could hit one of those boats, anyway, I'm pretty sure, but wouldn't promise anything more precise. Nor even how much damage a round would do if it hit somebody at this range."

J.B. paused again.

"But I reckon you mean full-auto?"

Ryan grinned behind the Scout's receiver.

He actually sensed the Armorer's shrug. Perhaps because he knew the little man so well. They had been best friends for years, ever since they'd served together in the war wags headed by the enigmatic—and legendary—character known only as the Trader.

"Reckon I could bounce a few off their...what? They got some jury-rigged armor, don't they?"

"Yeah and yeah. I'm about to throw a real scare at them. I want you to make sure they get the message."

Another loud noise—this one was definitely an explosion, though without the terrible sharp sound and shockwave of *high* explosive. Immediately the hand-cranked siren atop the bridge—the front part of the cabin—whined out three staccato yips, a pause, followed by three more, and then repeated. It was the Conoyers' signal for *fire aboard*.

"Looks like Baron Teddy's going to have to make his harem's underthings out of something other than that fine muslin we were taking to him," J.B. stated. "The shell burst in the barge and set some of the cloth bales on fire."

That was neither man's problem. Trying to prevent another shell from landing smack in the middle of the cabin—or blowing a hole at their waterline—was.

In his observation of the enemy vessels, Ryan had noticed that the helmsman of each was plainly visible through an ob port, above the bow cannon, although shadowed. He couldn't tell if the port had glass. Since he knew the odds of its being bulletproof were slim, he discounted the chance it would turn a longblaster bullet.

It wasn't an easy shot. Realistically, Ryan didn't think he had to hit spot-on, but he lined up the shadowy head on the lead boat's driver as carefully as he could, and fired.

"Head shot," J.B. reported. He had whipped out a handy little 8-power Simmons monocular he'd bought off a scavvy a few weeks back and was scoping out Ryan's target.

"Ace on the line," the one-eyed man said. And indeed, when he could see his target again, there was an indistinct flurry of activity on the boat's bridge, and no head visible behind the spoked wheel. "Light 'em up."

As J.B. began to rip short, controlled bursts of 9 mm rounds at the other craft, Ryan saw that, without a hand at its helm, the lead vessel had already began to slew to his right. A second shot through the front ob port helped discourage anyone who might think of trying to regain control.

Ryan swung his scope in search of new targets. He heard cheering break out from behind him and realized the pursuing craft were losing way against the slow, heavy Sippi current.

"Looks like they had enough for now," J.B. remarked, as he eased off the trigger. "Want me to continue firing them up?"

Ryan lifted his head from behind the scope.

The distance between the lumbering *Queen*, which had almost completed her turn to the north, and the other craft was visibly increasing now. Blasterfire from that direction had ceased.

"Don't waste the bullets," he said.

Chapter Three

"What the nuke did you do?" Trace Conoyer called.

Ryan looked around to see the captain striding toward him from the cabin on her long, jeans-clad legs.

Her tone of voice had demanded a response, but it wasn't hostile or challenging.

"I left Nataly at the helm," she said. "How did you make those New Vick frigates sheer off?"

"Frigates?" J.B. echoed.

"New Vick?" Ryan asked.

"They like to call them that. They're just glorified blasterboats and muster two, three cannon. Four, five at max. But they are ironclad. They're part of the fleet the barony of New Vickville has been building for a generation now."

The barge began to obscure Ryan's view of the so-called frigates. The cloud of brown-tinged white smoke told him that the fire there wasn't serious.

"I sent Moriarty and a damage control party aft to put out the fire," the captain said. "I sent the white-haired kid and Doc along. It was obvious they weren't going to have anything to shoot at, and they seemed antsy for something to do. Got the kid perched up top of the cabin, keeping eyes skinned for trouble from landward. He's still at it. He's a strange one."

"That he is," Ryan agreed, although Jak was no longer a *kid*. Then again, he was slighter and smaller than Ricky Morales, who was a kid. It was a natural mistake.

"Were those boys shooting at your tow barge, for some reason?" J.B. asked.

Trace shook her head. "They weren't aiming for anything in particular."

"Must be triple-bad shots," J.B. said. He had slung his Uzi and now took his glasses off to polish them with a handkerchief.

The captain shrugged. "Mebbe. But those cannon aren't anywhere near accurate at that range. They're smoothbores. Usually four-pounders, in boats like those. Six for the broadside cannon, mebbe."

J.B. nodded. That was his lingo, even if charcoal-burning cannon without rifling were pretty far out on the fringe for him.

Krysty and Mildred approached them from around the starboard side of the cabin.

"No injuries, Captain," the shorter woman reported. "That was some lousy shooting, thankfully."

"Any orders for us, Captain?" Krysty asked.

"Stand ready if you're needed."

The statuesque redhead gave her lover a wink as he straightened from the rail. He kept his blaster in hand, just to be sure.

"So what's the deal with this barony of New Vick?" J.B. asked. He settled his wire-rimmed spectacles back in place. Behind them Ryan could see a gleam in his eyes. "Why are they building up a fleet?"

"They're in an arms race with Poteetville," Trace replied.

"Captain."

"What have you got for me, Edna?" the captain asked.

This time it was Edna Huang who was approaching from astern. A short, bespectacled Asian woman who inexplicably liked to wear her shiny black hair all wound into circular pigtails, she was the *Mississippi Queen*'s chief purser.

"Arliss reports the fire is controlled and he'll soon have it out," Edna said. "There's no sign of structural damage to the barge that he can find."

"Ace on the line," the captain said.

The purser seemed less than happy at the very news she brought.

"What's eating at you?" Trace asked.

"There's not *much* damage to the textiles, ma'am. But there's still some. We may need to write off as much as ten percent, adding in for smoke damage."

"It's the cost of doing business on the river," the captain said.

"Baron Teddy's not going to be triple pleased."

"You leave him to me. He knows how the world works today."

"Yes, ma'am."

"Now run along and send up Avery."

"Already here, Captain."

Avery Telsco, the *Queen*'s chief shipwright, was a long, lanky black dude with short dreadlocks. He wore a monocle, of all the nuking things, screwed into his right eye. Although having seen him work repairing the ship and fighting off the ever-present danger of rot in her wooden meat and bones, Ryan gathered it wasn't wholly an affectation. He did make use of it on detail work and inspecting for damage.

"Ace. Report."

"The shot that hit us just busted a chunk of rail all to nuke. Mebbe ten feet. I can have it fixed in twenty minutes with a spare spar from stores. Or, if you'd care to send a boat ashore we could cut down a sapling—"

"Nuke, no!"

"It would be cheaper, Captain," Edna said.

"Getting people killed by stickies would not be cheaper," Trace replied. "And I doubt your crew mates would like to have all their hair fall out and have their skin get all gross with rad blueberries and stumble around like zombies for a few days from even a mild rad dosage. Now git!"

The purser turned and hurried back into the cabin as fast as her legs would propel her.

"Do the badlands extend a ways?" Ryan asked. The view astern was completely hidden by the barge now. Under Nataly's firm hand, the *Queen* was churning steadily north up the big river. Ryan could see activity at the stern of the barge, including glimpses of Doc Tanner's disorderly white hair, past the stacked lumber as the damage control crew pitched still-smoldering bales of Baron Teddy's expensive, recently spun muslin overboard.

"A couple miles in all directions, pretty much," Trace admitted.

"So if you got a minute, Captain," Ryan said, "tell

us about this arms race between Poteetville and, uh, New Vick."

"New Vickville is just south of the hot spot that includes the ruins of old Vicksburg, on and around the bluff, down there to the south. The ville got pretty rich off scavvy from the ruins, not too long after skydark."

"Seems like that would be pretty dangerous, what with all the fallout around here," Mildred commented.

"The first baron believed in ruling with what you might call an iron hand," Avery said in a dry drawl.

"Avery here's our history bug," Trace stated.

"Poteetville lies about five, six miles north of here," the shipwright said. "It started out as a camp for people scavvying flotsam on the Sippi, of which there was a drek-load, right after skydark. Eventually both Poteetville and New Vick turned into pretty big river trading ports. And natural rivals, being so close together."

"Yeah," Ryan said. "I wouldn't think they'd both be able to get rich."

"Well, Poteetville naturally gets first dibs on traffic coming down from the north," Trace said, "while New Vick is the stop-off spot for ships from the south. Plus there's a fair amount of traffic coming off the Yazoo, like us."

"Things started to heat up between them mebbe thirty, forty years ago," Avery said. "Baron Poteet sent his daughter to marry Baron Vick, and she promptly died under mysterious circumstances. It seems she committed suicide, but that didn't mollify Poteetville any. Both villes started building up their fleets. Each already had one or two improvised-armor vessels apiece, to repel river pirates."

"And do a little pirating themselves," the captain added.

"But both sides decided they needed full-on iron-clad fleets. Or mebbe flotillas. So they started building them like crazy. And expanding and consolidating their holds on the countryside surrounding, making lesser villes either pay them tribute or just absorbing them. That kind of thing."

"Building pocket empires," J.B. said. He looked at Ryan. "There's a lot of that going around this days."

Ryan shrugged. "It was one of the things that kept Trader in business, back when we ran with him."

"Yeah."

"Now both sides got, what? A dozen or so apiece of what you might call ironclad warships. They've got three or four big vessels that they call 'capital' ships, some smaller ones they call frigates, and a shitload of unarmored little patrol boats. Some of them don't amount to much more than a canoe with a trolling motor, truth to tell."

"And those that we just had the run-in with were frigates," Ryan stated.

"Like I said, they're what pass for frigates," Trace replied. "The capital ships run up to a hundred and fifty feet long, and can mount up to ten blasters on the *Pearl*. That's Baron Vick's flagship. Baroness, some people would say, though no one would say that to her face. We can be glad we didn't brush up against them."

"Any rifled blasters?" J.B. asked. Ryan didn't think his friend needed to sound quite so rad-blasted *hopeful*.

But the captain shook her head. "All smoothbore, like the smaller ships carry. But that many weapons can put a *lot* of metal in the air in a hell of a hurry. It was lucky that we didn't run into them."

"I notice you people seem to use the words *ship* and *boat* pretty interchangeably," Mildred said. "In my experience, nautical types tend to get pretty sticky about the distinctions between them. They can be real assholes about it. Pardon my French."

"'French'?" Avery asked, blinking in confusion made comical by one eye being magnified to double size by his monocle. "Wait, that was French? I don't speak French, but I understood what you said—"

"She's not from around here," Ryan said by way of explanation.

"This isn't the Cific," Trace said drily. "You may have noticed. Not even the Gulf. Back before the Big Nuke there may have been craft working the river big enough to be worth making a fuss over which were ships and which were boats. Not these days."

"I take it we're not close to this New Vick," Ryan said. "Any idea why they'd have their ironclads this far north?"

"Well, things have been coming to a head between them and Poteetville the last few years," Avery said. "Fifteen years ago they were having a bit of a thaw between them. Then the old Baron Vick, Silas Krakowitz, took a new wife after his first one died. And I mean the old baron—the one who started building up his ville and its ironclad armada in the first place. His wife was much younger, late twenties or thereabout. Then Baron Harvey J. Poteet's Senior's wife, Maude, insulted Krakowitz's young wife, Tanya. That started things off. Then, after old Silas croaked, Tanya became the baron. She was still hot past nuke red over Maude's slight. Not long after Harvey Junior became baron of Poteetville, he refused to recognize Tanya's legitimacy as baron. So the shit has been seriously headed for the fan between them ever since."

Ryan frowned.

"That suggests we might just find ourselves running into the Poteetville fleet," he said.

"Ships!" Jak shouted from atop the *Queen*'s cabin. "Lots! *Big ones!*"

"We just did," the captain replied laconically.

Another rushing roar like a young tornado passed overhead.

Chapter Four

Krysty felt her gut clench and her eyes widen as the roar ended in a colossal splash to the west of *Mississippi Queen*, so close that the tubby tug rocked perceptibly.

The redheaded beauty looked north. A line of ships, ominously dark in the shadows of chem clouds crossing the afternoon sun, seemed to stretch across the mile-wide river, side-on to each other. Thin lines of dark smoke rose from their stacks, diffusing rapidly as the breeze began tugging it toward the west bank. A puff of lighter smoke, also drifting to her left, stood out from the rest. That was from the cannon that had fired at them.

Yellow lights flashed from all along the line.

The first boom rolled over them like thunder. Ryan knelt and laid his longblaster across the railing. J.B. knelt by his side, his fedora jammed tightly on his head and his Uzi in his hands. Krysty knew he was by Ryan's side for support only. His blaster didn't have the range to do any damage to the hostile ironclads, which were at least a quarter of a mile distant.

Captain Conoyer was already sprinting for the cabin, shouting, "Hard to port, now! Redline the engines!"

She paused at the pilothouse doorway. "Everybody

whose duties don't keep them up top, get belowdecks now!" she bellowed. "Barge damage party, get back aboard and under cover!"

Most of the attackers' volley dropped into the water at least a hundred yards shy of the *Queen*'s bow, sending up greenish-brown columns of water that burst into white froth before opening like flowers and falling back again. A couple shots splashed closer, but wide to the right and left.

"At least it'll take them a while to reload," Mildred said, wincing as the multiple *thumps* of cannon shots reach them. She had reflexively hunkered down behind the front rail. So had Krysty.

"Bigger boats are already turning broadside to bring their side blasters to bear," Ryan reported, peering with his scope through falling spray.

"I'd say it's just about ready to get serious," J.B. said, sounding more interested than alarmed.

Krysty looked back. The people who had gone on board the barge to fight the fire in the fabric bales were scrambling back across the thick hawser that connected the hulls. She was relieved and pleased to see Doc trotting right across, as spry as a kid goat, holding his arms out to his sides with his black coattails flapping. Despite his aged appearance, he was chronologically but a few years younger than Ryan. The bizarre abuse and rigors the evil whitecoats of Operation Chronos had subjected him to after trawling him from the late 1800s had aged him prematurely, and damaged his fine, highly educated mind. But he could still muster the agility and energy of a man much younger than he appeared to be.

Ricky came last, straddling the thick woven hemp cable and inchworming along, but he did so at speed.

Avery had vanished. "You and Mildred best head for cover," Ryan said.

"They'll only hit us by accident," Mildred replied, "shooting oversize muskets at us."

"They're going to have a dozen or two shots at us, next round," J.B. said. "That's a lot of chances to get lucky."

"Looks like some smaller fry are heading this way," Ryan reported. "Krysty, Mildred—*git*!"

"But what good will a wooden hull and decks do against iron cannonballs?" Mildred asked.

"Splinters!" Ryan exclaimed.

"Come on." Krysty grabbed the other woman's wrist and began to run for the cabin. Though Mildred was about as heavy as she was, Krysty was barely slowed, towing Mildred as if the woman were a river barge. She was strong, motivated and full of adrenaline.

Krysty heard Ryan open fire. Given the range, the bobbing of the approaching lesser war craft, and the complex movement of the *Queen*—pitching fore and aft as well as heeling over to her right from the centrifugal force of the fastest left turn the vessel could manage—she doubted he'd be lucky enough to hit anything significant.

The women had almost reached the cabin when the next salvo hit, roaring like an angry dragon. Krysty saw stout planks suddenly spreading into fragments almost in her face.

And then the world vanished in a soundless white flash.

RYAN'S HEART ALMOST imploded in his chest when he heard the shell crash through the roof of the bridge and detonate. *Krysty!*

He stood, pushed off from the rail and spun.

The forward port corner of the cabin—his right—had been smashed. Smoke streamed out. He heard screams, smelled burned flesh, and burning horsehair from padded chairs.

Krysty lay on her back on the deck, her head in Mildred's lap. Her hair was curled close to her head, though not tightly, and was waving feebly. Her face was a ghastly mask of gore and char.

"Krysty!" he shouted.

Mildred waved him off.

"Her forehead's just nicked," she said. "The rest is just smoke."

"She's not hurt?"

"She's concussed," Mildred said. "But she's tough. She'll make it. There's nothing more to do for her right now. Ow! *What?*"

The last was directed at J.B., who had taken off his fedora and was swatting her on top of the head with it.

"Your hair's smoldering up top," he said.

"Oh," she said sheepishly. "Something made me dive for the deck. Since Krysty was hanging on to my wrist it was easy to take her down with me. But she still caught more of the blast than I did."

"Help!" somebody yelled from inside the cabin. "Somebody help the captain!"

Ryan and Mildred looked at each other. "Look out

after Krysty, John," she said. Easing Krysty's head to the planks, she extricated herself and stood.

As soon as he saw Krysty's head laid gently down, Ryan moved ahead of Mildred to the door and looked inside.

A dense haze of greenish smoke filled the bridge, lit poorly by afternoon sunlight slanting in through the hole, and a few oily flickering yellow flames. The stink of burned gunpowder, hair and overcooked flesh was intense. Ryan had to clamp his jaw shut against acid vomit that shot up his throat.

Nataly Dobrynin stood at the wheel. Like Krysty's, her face was a black-and-crimson mask. She was craning to her left to peer out the front port. The polycarbonate there had been blasted free by the explosion. The right side, though intact, was smoke-smudged, partially melted and tricky to see through.

"I'm fine," she said. "Scalp cut and smoke damage. It's not as bad as it looks." Despite her words, she seemed to be as much holding herself upright as steering the *Queen* through its hard left turn.

She jerked her head toward the cabin wall to her right. "Help the captain."

Ryan looked the way she indicated. Trace Conoyer was slumped against the bulkhead. Her right arm was missing from above the elbow. Avery knelt beside her, frantically trying to tie off the wound with a handkerchief. He didn't seem to be making much headway against the blood spurting all over him, and rendering the floorboards slippery.

"Mildred," Ryan rasped.

"Already on it," the predark doctor said. She actually shouldered him out of the way as she entered the bridge and went to the captain.

When she had been studying to become a doctor, Mildred had discovered she enjoyed research more than tending to the sick and injured, so she chose the field of medical research and focused on cryogenics. Ultimately, her research had saved her life, as it allowed her colleagues to freeze her after the botched surgery. Her sleep lasted longer than a hundred years, and when she awakened, the world had drastically changed. And to survive—emotionally as well as physically—she had to change, as well. She had thrown herself wholeheartedly into the role of healer, bringing real medical skill and knowledge to a world that almost completely lacked them. And when she went into full-on healer mode, she would turn aside for nothing.

Not even Ryan Cawdor.

To the right of the entrance, at the bridge's rear, was a hatch leading to the deck below. Just short of it lay a body. At one time it had been human, but now it was hard to tell. It seemed to have been blown open, with entrails scattered on the deck. A string of intestine was draped over a chart table lying on its side. The chill was still smoldering.

"I had just gone below," Avery said over his shoulder. He was now helping the dazed captain hold her stump upright while Mildred tied it off properly. "Edna was headed down right behind me."

"She had to have taken the brunt of the blast," Nataly said. "She never had a chance. Poor woman."

Another salvo landed around the vessel. From the sounds they made, Ryan gathered the Poteetville iron-clads were firing a mix of solid shot and explosive shells. Probably whatever was closest to hand.

Ryan stepped up alongside Nataly and began piston-ing the butt-plate of his Steyr into what remained of the windscreen. Even damaged as it was, the tough poly-mer resisted his jackhammer blows. But he managed to pop it out of its framework.

Nataly nodded her thanks as she straightened, show-ing a quick flash of teeth, bright white against her hor-ror mask of a face.

"What about you?" he asked.

"I was right beside the captain," she said through gritted teeth. "The blast didn't do much to me. I thought I was chilled for sure."

Seeing that both the tall, thin woman and Mildred both had their respective situations well in hand, Ryan went back outside. He found Krysty sitting up against the remains of the cabin's front wall, while J.B. tried to daub the blood and soot from her face with a wet rag.

She was awake, and she smiled as her emerald green eyes met his.

"You were worried," she said. "That's sweet."

"We're not out of the woods yet," he said. She was clearly still dazed.

He looked around. The *Mississippi Queen* had al-ready swung its bow past due west and was continuing to turn back south. In the process it had moved most of the way to that shore. Most of the barge was visible to port behind the tug.

Suddenly the rest of the companions were gathered around. "How's Krysty?" Ricky asked. "*Nuestra Señora*, please let her be okay!"

"I'll be fine," Krysty said, more in the tone of voice of a person agreeing with someone who had just said something she didn't really understand than as an actual affirmation.

"What are you all doing here?" Ryan demanded of the boy, Jak and Doc.

The old man shot his cuffs with elaborate unconcern. "There seems to be a dearth of jobs for us to do at the moment."

A shattering sound erupted from aft of the cabin. Pieces of the roof flew off in a big gout of smoke. Yellow flames began to flick just above the jagged edges of the bulkhead.

"Dark night!" J.B. exclaimed, as voices began shouting in alarm. "It must've set bedding on fire."

"We've got a job now," Ryan said grimly. "We'll man the hoses and try to get the fire out. J.B., help me carry Krysty into the cabin."

"Just leave me here, lover," Krysty said. She still sounded out of it, but was clearly pulling her blast-scattered wits back together. "Be as safe here as anywhere."

"No way," Ryan said, gathering her in his arms for the briefest of hugs, then pulling her away from the bulkhead so he could hoist her by the shoulders while J.B. lifted her feet. "It's at least some protection. Better than none."

"You know what old line about lightning not striking twice in the same place?" Krysty asked, her head loll-ing. "It's not true. Lots of times lightning hits the same place a dozen times in the blink of an eye."

"I know that," he said. "Stay with me."

He managed not to say, *You're starting to sound like Doc.* Although it probably wouldn't have mattered because the old man had already led the two youngest members of the team back to where several of the crew were unrolling canvas hoses to fight the flames.

Inside, Mildred was letting Trace Conoyer lower her arm, gingerly, to see if the pressure bandage she had taped over the wound would hold. The dirty-rag tourniquet had already been removed and discarded.

Myron Conoyer and Arliss Moriarty hunched over the captain. Avery hovered in the background, uncertain as to how to help.

The captain had already recovered her senses.

"Go tend the engines, Myron," she ordered in an almost normal voice. "We need to keep them on full power, and we can't have them blow up on us."

"But—"

"If you think Mildred would do as good a job taking care of the Diesels as you would, by all means swap places with her. But somebody needs to be down with those engines, and not just Maggie. She's ace, but doesn't have a third of your chops."

Myron bobbed his balding head. "Aye-aye, uh, Captain." He turned and hurried back below, shaking his head at the sad mess that was all that remained of Edna.

Ryan and J.B. had settled Krysty on the floor, as clear as they could of the still slightly smoking Edna, the captain, and—most important, in Ryan's view—the helmswoman's feet. He had folded his long black coat and propped her head up against it. Her hair lay limply across it, as if eager to give up the fight.

"Thank you, lover," she said as he kissed her cheek and straightened. "I'll be back on my feet before you know it."

"Not before *I* tell you you're ready," Mildred said sternly, not even looking around from examining the captain's dressing.

"Let's go, J.B." Ryan jerked his chin to the door. Though the *Queen* sported powered pumps, at times like this they used hand pumps to allow the engines to devote full power to driving the vessel and her burden. From the way the deck shuddered beneath his feet, he knew that Myron had followed his wife's initial order to redline them and keep them there, regardless.

Ryan approved. His own team worked that way: if he told them to do something that pushed the envelope, or even seemed flat crazy—and their own judgment told them it might actually be worth a try—they did it. And they usually pulled it off.

"Ryan." Trace's voice rasped as if she'd been gargling lye. "Stay. If you will."

That latter part was one of the shipboard niceties the captain liked to maintain, and Ryan knew it. He turned back. Aboard the *Queen*, she was his boss. And in this case what she was calling him back from was adding the strength of his back and arms to saving her ship.

"I need you...to advise me," she said. "We've had more than one run-in with people who want this cargo, and I've seen that you know something about tactics."

"You're the authority on ship-handling," he said. "I can't pretend to know nuke about it."

"We put our…heads together, then," she said, managing a wan smile.

She was triple tough, there was no question. When her ship and crew were on the line, she would do her job and die doing it. For their part, the crew knew it, and responded accordingly.

Even Ryan and his people knew that. Good, honest bosses were hard to come by.

"I'm fresh out of ideas, now," he admitted, as another volley came rushing in with a hurricane sound.

He felt a tremor beneath his feet, accompanied by a thunderous bang from astern. Immediately voices began screaming, "Fire! Fire on the barge!"

A moment later, Suzan Kenn appeared in the door, her gray-shot brown hair in more than the usual disarray.

"A shell hit the barge right where the lumber meets the cloth bales, Captain!" she exclaimed breathlessly. "She started burning like Billy Jesus right off the mark. The only hope we've got of dousing the blaze is turning on the power to the pumps."

"We can't do that," Trace rapped. "Cut her loose."

Suzan blinked. "Captain?"

"Are you sure, Trace?" Arliss asked.

He was the *Mississippi Queen*'s master rigger, which meant he kept the steering linkages in top shape, among other duties. A little guy, somewhere between J.B. and Jak in size, he had a short frizz of graying hair and a beard, prominent ears, and a missing right front incisor. He was the second-best financial mind on board, after the now-deceased Edna, and usually advised the Conoyers in negotiations, a job Edna had been too shy to do well. Like everybody aboard the *Queen*, he was ace at his job, and Ryan knew that part of his job was to keep his captain's eye on the bottom line.

"The price—"

"Probably won't buy us a new ship, Arliss, and definitely won't buy a new us. We can't die for the load."

"But Baron Teddy—"

"Will have to—" she winced at a twinge of pain as Mildred adjusted the bandage "—deal with his disappointment. We can send him a nice note from upstream. He knew the risks when he ordered the goods. Cut her loose, Suzan."

"Wait," Ryan said.

Everybody looked at him. "You sound like a man with a plan," Trace told him.

"I don't know if I'd dignify it by calling it that," he said. "Yet. Give me a minute to look outside."

Suzan started to pull back away from the door as he headed for it. Then she ducked hastily inside at the thud and shudder of another impact.

Ryan's nut-sack tightened in anticipation of the following explosion, which didn't come. He poked his head outside.

The middle-aged deckhand had not been lying. Great clouds of white smoke were pouring out of the barge. He could see flames leaping to a height he judged to be higher than his head. He doubted their ability to put out the fire, even with power to drive water at good pressure through hoses stretched far astern. That wasn't anything he knew much about, but his gut told him he was right. He trusted it.

The wind was still blowing out of the east and freshening slightly as the sun headed for the horizon behind the tall weeds of the western shore. There was already a respectable wall of smoke extending across the wide river in that direction.

The *Queen* was almost turned clean south. Ryan glanced upriver. As he feared, the half-dozen or so smaller craft giving chase were closer now, and at least three of them were big enough to be what he took for the so-called frigates, and armored.

They had one bit of luck: when he stepped briefly out to the rail to look astern, he could only see the easternmost of the bigger Poteetville ships now lying broadside to their fleeing prey. The rest were completely blanketed by a brown-gray haze of their own gun smoke. That was the thing about black powder weapons: unless you had a wind blowing up double brisk, you only had a few good shots before you were nigh-on blinded by a smoke screen of your own creation. The only bonus to that was that if your enemy was similarly armed, they had the same problem.

Good to know, but not particularly significant, Ryan thought. They were getting close to the point at which there was no sense wasting the powder and ball in hopes of scoring some lucky hits. In fact, he couldn't see any muzzle-flashes from the stationary capital ships and frigates, even the one that was mostly clear because the breeze blew its gun smoke away. But the pursuing vessels all had bow cannon, even the patrol boats, and they were all banging lustily away as soon as their crews could reload them, which wasn't fast, fortunately.

But now Ryan had his plan. He smiled and stepped back inside.

"It's about time to straighten the rudder to run downstream, Captain," Nataly said as he reentered the bridge. She had gotten her strength back and stood tall.

Trace had her eyes shut and her head back against the bulkhead, but she was awake and alert.

"You still have the helm," she said, wearily but firmly.

"Keep us turning counterclockwise," Ryan said. "Uh, to port."

Nataly looked at him, shocked.

"Captain?" Arliss asked, sounding as if he thought the shock and the pain of her blasted-off arm had robbed her of her senses. "That'll take us back toward their cannon."

But Trace had raised her head upright and was gazing at Ryan with clear, brown eyes.

"Go on, Ryan," she said. "I like where I think this is going."

"Captain," Arliss said, sounding pained that she was taking a landlubber's advice, when it ran dead counter to every bit of his own riverman's lore.

"Yeah," he told the captain. "I got a plan. Bring the *Queen* as close as you can to the east bank and still safely sheer south. Then cut the barge free before you start your turn. I don't know if that's the right lingo, so I put it as plain as I know how."

She managed a smile, albeit a thin one, and fleeting.

"Close enough for getting on with. Nataly—"

The helmswoman had subtly straightened her shoulders. "Aye-aye, Captain!" she said smartly. She had clearly grasped Ryan's intention.

Arliss frowned, then he nodded and showed a gap-toothed grin.

"Good one," he said. "If we've got to write off the barge, we can use her to lay us a smoke screen. And give those Poteetville bastards something to think about to get around it. You *do* know your shit, Cawdor."

Ryan nodded once, briskly.

HE HELPED THEM beat down the fire. Fortunately only one of the rooms—which the Conoyers and their crew rather grandly called "staterooms"—was gutted. Sadly, Suzan had shared it Edna, and all their possessions were write-offs. That didn't matter a bent shell case to Edna anymore.

It took Ryan, his friends apart from Krysty and Mildred, and the *Mississippi Queen*'s crew only minutes to reduce the flames to smoldering char. But they were intense minutes, and when they were done even Ryan had to find a cable coil to sit on while he caught his breath.

Krysty sat next to him, still seeming subdued. Though mostly concerned with keeping an eye on the captain, Mildred had not neglected to watch her concussed friend. She only let the redhead out of the cabin when the fire was out.

His friends found places to flake out on the deck or railing, as did the regular crew they'd been helping: Jake Lewis, tall and saturnine, Avery Telsco, Suzan Kenn, the cheerful bear of a South Plains Indian, Santee, a medium-sized dude named Abner MacReedy, who looked way too much like a rabbit, although he wasn't particularly shy or skittish, and finally Arliss Moriarty, leaning back against an intact wall of the cabin smoking a corncob pipe. For some reason that gave Mildred the uncontrollable giggles every time she looked at him.

Jak, meanwhile, scrambled back onto the cabin roof. Unable to engage in his usual wide-ranging scouting, he settled for perching up there like a pelican, keeping watch at all hours of the day or night. He even slept up there. Aside from the fore and aft ends, both to portside, where shells had struck, the roof seemed pretty sound structurally. Ryan declined to worry about it. Jak of all people knew how to be careful where he put his feet, and not venture out on anything that wouldn't support his slight weight. And anyway, it was his stupe neck.

"By the Three Kennedys!" Doc exclaimed.

He had been squatting on his long, skinny shanks, facing aft. All that was visible behind the tug was churning green water. Arliss and his red-haired crony, Sean O'Reilly, who was back helping Myron and Maggie nurse the engines as usual, had cut the barge loose at what Trace Conoyer judged the optimum moment.

By that time it was fiercely ablaze from one end to the other. Enough so that Ryan could feel the heat beating off it as he helped work the pumps. Had the wind not been blowing the sparks away from the *Queen*, they might well have set the tug alight too.

Now Doc drew himself up to his considerable height

and flung out a long arm to point dramatically over the taffrail.

"The blackguards have found a way around the burning hulk, and are emerging from the smoke!"

J.B., who was sitting just aft of the cabin near a boat hung in davits with his back to the stern, barely tipped his head back and turned it to glance over his shoulder.

"Nothing shaken, Doc," he said.

Ryan was surprised that J.B. could see over the stern, as short as he was. But the Armorer was the last person in their group to say more than he knew. "We knew it was going to happen sooner or later. They're way out of range now, anyway."

"Their frigates can't keep up with us now," Arliss said. No longer weighed down by the massive barge and her currently burning-to-nuke-shit cargo, the tubby little tug was making surprising time downriver. "They're slow and handle like pigs, with all that armor. Unarmored patrol boats likely can't catch us, even."

That last bit of information was delivered with a note of unmistakable pride in his voice.

He shook his grizzled head.

"It's lucky we got off as light as we did," he said. "Except for poor Edna. We're lucky, and that's a fact."

"Count no man lucky before his death," Jake said.

Arliss put his hands on his hips and stuck his elbows out to the sides. "Well, aren't *you* Captain Gloom 'n' Doom? What, are you taking lessons from Nataly now?"

"It's an old Viking saying. From my Viking grandmother, Freya."

"She weren't no Viking."

"You didn't want to tell her that."

"Where are we going, anyway?" Ricky asked.

"Captain says she means to head back up the Yazoo," Arliss said. "From there we'll play it by ear."

"So we're basically in the clear?" The youth sounded relieved.

Krysty lifted her head and gave him a wan grin.

"Don't ever say that, Ricky," she said teasingly. "It's only tempting fate."

"Ships ahead!" Jak cried out from above. "War boats!"

Chapter Five

"It's the New Vick fleet!" Arliss exclaimed. "And they got their big tubs with 'em!"

Krysty climbed to her feet in alarm. Without even looking, Ryan stood up beside her and reached an arm to steady her.

Ryan gazed south, along the length of the cabin. Out beyond the prow of the *Mississippi Queen* a V of five blasterboats was steaming toward them with little mustaches of water by their bows. He knew that meant they were driving hard, although the slow but strong Sippi current's flowing against them slowed them.

Behind the blasterboats came the main New Vickville fleet, darkened by the long shadows that stretched from the low bluffs on the west bank of the big river. It was still well beyond blaster range, but the ironclad ships looked huge, like a distant range of mountains.

"Fireblast," Ryan said, almost conversationally. Another person might have taken it for resignation. Another man saying it under the circumstances might have meant it that way.

But not Ryan. Krysty knew that his tone meant he had already accepted the situation—and begun to plot how to beat it and survive, as he had a thousand times before.

"Blasterboats have already cut us off from the Yazoo," he said.

"And the big boats are squatting right in the river mouth," said Jake, who among other duties was an assistant navigator, though pretty much every member of the *Queen*'s crew could do pretty much everyone else's job.

Krysty and her friends were exceptions, of course, although they were willing hands. All had been aboard ships a number of times. They did what they could and nobody complained. When it came to fighting, it was the river-boaters who were second string.

And she already knew that it would come to fighting. Because if the patrol boats or heavy ironclads didn't sink them with their blasters, they would wind up having to seek shelter somewhere in the deceptively green, rad- and mutie-haunted countryside around them.

Plus it *always* came down to fighting, sooner or later. These were the Deathlands.

Ryan was already half carrying her forward at a good clip. Several of the crew raced on ahead, maneuvering carefully past to avoid jostling the pair. They were on good terms, along with being nominally on the same side, but none of the *Queen*'s complement was eager to cross any of the newcomers. Least of all their tall, one-eyed wolf of a leader. Or his woman.

The rest of the companions followed Ryan and Krysty. They were never eager to race toward danger, at least when that wasn't called for. Except Jak, who scampered forward along the cabin roof like a white two-legged squirrel.

On the bridge Trace Conoyer was standing determinedly on her own, next to the wheel, where Nataly was still piloting the boat. The captain's right arm had been safety-pinned to the captain's shirt to discourage her from waving it around. Mildred hovered next to her, watching her like an anxious mother. "They've opened fire," Nataly said in her flat voice. She never seemed excited.

A waterspout blew up out of the river right in front of them. Droplets struck Krysty in the face, without much force.

"Steady as she goes," the captain said. She shouted into a speaking tube down to the engine room to maintain full speed.

"But, Captain," Nataly said. For the first time her voice betrayed emotion. She sounded worried now. "We're heading right into their cannon!"

"Poteetville patrol boats aren't that much farther behind us," J.B. called from the open door. The door-slam sound of the shot that had produced the splash hit Krysty's ears.

"Steady as she goes," Conoyer repeated. She was leaning forward, gripping the lower sill of the now-vacant front port with her left hand so hard her knuckles whitened. "On my word, turn her hard aport, smartly as you can."

The mate glanced nervously aside. Her steely veneer was showing serious cracks now.

"Aye-aye, Captain," she said.

Ryan, J.B., Doc and Ricky had pushed onto the bridge with Krysty. Jak was doing whatever he was doing, as he usually did. Under the circumstances, he was as helpless as the rest of them. Arliss had come in with them. The rest of the *Queen*'s crew had dispersed elsewhere.

Flashes flickered from the bows of the oncoming craft. "Get down!" Ryan commanded.

He did as he ordered, although he stayed just high enough to peer out the front port. Krysty did likewise. She realized he had likely ordered his people down to reduce the targets they offered. She doubted the wooden front of the cabin would offer any resistance to a solid cannonball. It had not been built for that.

"You too, Nataly," Trace ordered. After a dubious glance her way, the mate hunkered as low as she could and still see to steer.

The captain stayed erect. "Mildred, stay hunkered down too, but please help me stand. I need to see."

Mildred reached out and grabbed her hips to steady her.

A shot whined overhead, then the ship was racked by a shuddering crash that seemed to come up through the deck by way of Krysty's knee and boot sole. Another crash came from somewhere astern.

"Captain," Maggie called, coming up the hatch from below, "the bow's been holed below the waterline. We're taking on a lot of—"

Something moaned by Krysty's head, between her and Ryan. A hot breath blew across her face. She saw a lock of her lover's curly black hair tweaked briefly out from his head as by invisible fingers.

From behind she heard a strange squelching noise,

followed by another sound of rending wood. Something like hot rain fell on her shoulders and back. She heard a sizable amount of liquid hit the planks of the deck.

She and Ryan both turned. His lone blue eye was wide.

Maggie stood a step away from the hatch below. Or rather her slight torso did. Her head was missing entirely. A pulse of blood shot up from the terrible vacancy between her shoulders, then her headless trunk toppled down the ladder.

Ricky puked. The stink of vomit, added to the reek of fresh blood, excrement, burned flesh and lingering peppery gunpowder smell, made Krysty's head spin.

"Arliss," Trace snapped without turning, "get every hand available to work the bilge-pumps."

His wrinkled, sunburned face was white beneath his beard, but he bobbed his head. "Aye, Captain."

He vanished below, slipping slightly in Maggie's blood.

"Captain," Nataly said in a strained voice, "those blasterboats are getting mighty close—"

"On my mark, start your turn to port," the captain said. Nataly stood back upright, her hands white on the wheel.

"Don't see much of a break, up ahead," J.B. murmured.

Krysty didn't, either. The summer-green reeds and rushes on the left bank waved in the breeze in a line unbroken as far as the eye could see. She realized Ryan was gripping her arm, tightly enough to hurt, but she didn't say anything. It reassured her more than it felt bad.

"Three," Trace said. "Two…"

"Captain, I don't see—" Nataly began.

"Now! Hard aport!"

"But it's just land!"

"Now, nuke it, *do it now*!"

Ryan let go of Krysty's arm. He started to grab for the wheel.

But Nataly, her normally narrow eyes now saucer-wide, began to crank the big spoked wheel counterclockwise for all she was worth. The *Mississippi Queen* began to heel to the right as her bow swung left.

They were curving toward what indeed looked to Krysty like solid land at a good rate of speed. She gripped the sill in front of her with her right hand and Ryan's arm with her left. Bracing was the only thing she could think of to do.

The vessel shuddered to another hit.

The land rushed toward them. Krysty held her breath.

"By the Three Kennedys!" Doc crowed from behind them. "I see it!"

Then Krysty did, too. The weeds were thinner directly in front of them, stretching twenty or twenty-five yards to either side. The *Queen*'s bow slid smoothly among them, right into a channel Krysty would have bet her life a few seconds ago was not there.

"Ladies, gentlemen," Trace said, "welcome to Wolf Creek."

An explosion came from behind. It was as loud as rolling thunder, and made the stout little vessel rock violently back and forth. Instantly Krysty's keen nostrils smelled fresh smoke, and not just of burned black powder.

"There's another fire in the cabin," Avery yelled from the hatch in the aft bulkhead.

"Get anybody who's not pumping out the hull to fight the fire, Avery," Trace ordered. Her voice was getting as thin as hope.

"That's us," Ryan said, straightening. Krysty went with him.

"Ryan," Trace called. Krysty saw her sway despite Mildred's strong hand supporting her. "Have that albino scout of yours keep his eyes skinned. Stand ready to repel boarders."

"Right," Ryan said.

"Nataly, take us up-channel at least a mile. Then look for the best place to ground her."

The first mate had the steel back in her spine. "Aye-aye!"

"Mildred, help me...lie down. Then you're relieved from tending me to join your friends. I need to pass out now."

"Then let us help you out on deck to get you laid down," Mildred said, working her hands professionally up the captain's solid body as she stood up. "I'm not laying you down in this slop, no way."

Trace's short-haired head lolled on her neck. "What... ever."

Her eyes rolled up in her head. Mildred was ready, but still had to bend her knees to hang on to the woman when her knees sagged.

"I'll help you, Mildred," Krysty said. She went to

support the now-unconscious—or perhaps semiconscious—captain from the left.

It feels good to be able to do something, she thought. Even if we're nowhere near safe yet.

"FIREBLAST!" RYAN EXCLAIMED as the sound of cannon fire echoed between the banks of Wolf Creek.

But when he paused in chopping away burning planks from the starboard side of the *Mississippi Queen*'s cabin to look astern to where the dull booms came from, he saw nothing but clear green water on Wolf Creek. They had rounded enough of a bend in the stream that the original screen of weeds that had shielded the creek's mouth had passed out of sight. But he could clearly see two big banks of smoke like riverhugging fog, off above the flat land with its tall grass. The tops of the smoke clouds were already tinted gold by the rays of the sun sinking into the horizon.

"Poteetville and New Vick," Arliss said grimly. The ship rigger was perched perilously atop the weakening roof of the *Queen*'s cabin forward of the fire, directing water from a canvas hose into its hungry red heart. "They found better things to play with than us. Meaning each other."

"Think they'll follow us this way?" Ricky asked. He was taking a break from manning the deck pumps, which worked on a teeter-totter sort of principle, like a railway flatcar. Although now that they were in a side channel, and out of the line of fire, Myron had throttled back the Diesels and diverted some power to pumping out the water gushing in through the breach. Instead

Ricky and Jak were kicking the burning planks chopped free overboard.

There wasn't enough power to spare for the above decks pumps too. Myron clearly reckoned that if the boat sank, it would take care of the fire, anyway. So his priority was keeping her afloat. His prime enemy as he saw it was *water*, and Ryan couldn't disagree.

Avery laughed. He was pointing out to Ryan where to cut with the ax, plus helping out with one of his own.

"Not triple likely, kid. They probably forgot all about us. The only stuff we had worth stealing's burned to the waterline. Least as far as they know."

"The only reason either bunch really had for shooting at us," Arliss pointed out, "was that they're both plain mean. They've been rival king-ass fucks lording over this stretch of river for generations, each with only the other to give them any kind of check. And it went to their heads."

"So are they meaner than the countryside hereabouts?" Ricky asked.

"Unless the stickies or the swampers got themselves some cannon," J.B. replied, "I'd reckon yeah."

"Too slagging right," Jake said. He was handling the portside hose, where Krysty and Mildred worked the pump, while J.B. and Doc operated the starboard one that fed Arliss's.

Ryan wasn't pleased about Krysty working as hard as she was so soon after her concussion. But since the concussion wasn't literally life-or-death, but putting out the fire might be, he knew better than to try to order her to sit this one out.

"But we gotta beach her soon," Lewis said. "Then everything changes."

It was the longest speech Ryan had heard the lanky man make. His tone carried a sense of doom. And if Ryan had any doubt the *Queen* was doomed—at least so long as she stayed in open water—Arliss chilled it at once.

"She's riding lower in the water as every minute passes."

"At least we mostly got the fire beat down," Avery stated.

"What happens if we go down?" Ricky asked.

"Nile crocodiles," Jake said with doleful satisfaction.

Ricky emitted a yelp of terror. Everybody laughed. He blushed.

Suzan came back aft. "Captain's compliments, Ryan, and she asks that you present yourself on the bridge at your earliest convenience."

Obviously under the inspiration of their captain, Ryan had noticed the crew was partial to the use of old-timey-sounding nautical talk on formal occasions. "She requests your advice picking a spot to ground the vessel."

"Right," he said. Just because he knew the game didn't mean he had to play. Their employers didn't seem to expect it of him or his people, anyway.

"We got the fire controlled," Arliss said. "Jake, Avery and I can take it from here. You all can go."

"You heard the lady," he said, passing the hose down to Krysty and clambering from the roof of the mostly gutted cabin. "Let's shift on out of here."

Jak looked at him with eagerness written on his face. "Go up top, watch?"

He nodded. Jak scrambled up to the roof.

"Man doesn't talk much," he told the *Queen* crew members.

"Noticed," Jake said.

"WAIT," MILDRED MUTTERED. "How did I wind up carrying the lower end of this freaking coffin when the dude on the other end is like eight feet tall?"

Santee was not, in fact, eight feet tall, although he *was* six-six, minimum, or she was the Pope, Mildred thought, and he was indisputably on the end higher up the staircase. Or "ladder," as the boat people insisted on calling it. That struck the much shorter Mildred as markedly unfair.

Of course what they were carrying could only serve as a coffin for a child or a very short adult. It was no more than five feet long and felt as if it were packed with lead ingots. Or maybe she felt burdened because it was sweltering hot there in the cargo hold, and she had to breathe through a wet handkerchief tied around her face to filter out the smoke. And then there was the stench of rotting blood from poor Edna and Maggie, although their bodies had been taken ashore.

"What's in it, anyway?" she demanded as she struggled up the stairs with her unbalanced burden. "Shouldn't we only be carrying, like, food and other vital supplies off the boat?"

The big man smiled down at her. "Treasure," he said cheerfully. Nothing seemed to get to Santee.

She managed to make it up the rest of the way and onto the deck, where the two of them handed the long wooden box over the rail to a quartet of workers stand-

ing in shin-deep shallows. Then she propped her butt
on the rail to catch her breath. Santee said nothing,
only drank deeply from a canteen and handed it to her.

He didn't seem offended when she wiped the mouth
with her hands. Even on short acquaintance, the *Mississippi
Queen*'s crew had learned that she had her ec-
centricities. Fortunately, they were inclined to take folk
at their own value, and not sweat that kind of thing unless it slopped over into their own personal lives. They
weren't outlaws, these people who made their livings on
the river—certainly not by the standards of the day—
but they were pretty clearly out*casts*, who had trouble
fitting into the more settled societies ashore.

Which is probably why we and they get along like
bosom buddies, she thought.

Her companions and the crew worked without particular urgency to unload the boat of whatever was deemed
necessary, and prepare a camp on the riverbank, which
was as flat as a board and barely higher than the water.
The sun wasn't going to set for some time yet, and it
wasn't as if they could hide their presence.

Ryan and the captain had chosen a decent spot to
ground the boat. It was a mostly clear area of dry, firm
soil. The radiation in the immediate vicinity wouldn't chill
them too quickly, according to Ryan's coat-lapel rad counter. As for the amount of heavy metals—brutally toxic—
they might be taking in, there was no way to tell, which
didn't make Mildred any too happy. But what mattered
was immediate survival. In the absence of that none of
the other stuff would matter anyway.

The one slightly alarming aspect was the presence

of a dilapidated railroad bridge barely a quarter mile upstream. The rusty steel structure had fallen into the creek from roughly one-third of the way out from this bank almost to the far side. Likely there was still a rail line, long overgrown by weeds, leading to and from it. The problematic part was, this region was alleged to be crawling with stickies, and that derelict bridge would provide an ace nest for a major stickie colony.

Still, she thought, we take what we can get. As usual.

Ryan was hacking back the long grass and scrub surrounding their landing point with his panga. Jake was helping out with a scythe that they seemed to be carrying to trade at some point. He mowed the stuff down far faster than Ryan, and likely could have done as well by himself. But Ryan clearly felt the need to do *something*, especially after the enforced helplessness when they were trying to run from a bunch of boats shooting cannon at them.

At least Ryan and Mildred had prevailed on Krysty to take it easy, once they got ashore. She had insisted on carrying her own backpack off the vessel—fortunately all their gear had survived the fires and general smashing. Then she went off to the side and sat down on her jacket, spread out on the dirt. She was acting normally, aside from her not being in the thick of all this activity.

Mildred smirked. *Sometimes* she got her companions to stop acting as if they were superhuman, and to take some regard for their health. If you didn't take care of yourself some, your performance degraded. There was no way around that. And especially given the way they all lived, that was a fast ride to a hole in the ground, with dirt hitting you in the eyes. Such was life in the Deathlands.

Sadly, the captain would not listen to Mildred's urging that she rest after her terrible injury and blood loss, though in fairness she wasn't listening to her own people, either. She was wading around in the water with Avery and Nataly, inspecting the pierced hull to see if it could be repaired. Or if it even had the structural integrity left to be worth repairing. After sharing a brief, impassioned hug with her, her husband had retreated below to the engine compartment with J.B. and Ricky, doing something to take care of the engines, which Mildred understood not at all and cared about less.

She decided to watch Trace closely. Strangely, aside from her losing her lower arm, and Edna and Maggie losing their lives, no one was seriously hurt. Pretty much everybody had gotten cut, scraped, bruised and burned. Even Nataly looked as if she'd just gotten a bad sunburn on the left side of her face, once the grime and gore got washed off. Mildred guessed it hurt like bloody hell, but the first mate was stoic about it.

Well, great.

She heaved herself to her feet. Suzan and Abner MacReedy were carrying a crate of scavvied canned goods out of the hull. They were prime trade goods, too, as whatever the few-spoken Santee termed "treasure" presumably was. But if their day-to-day survival depended on consuming them—well, they were cheap at the price, as long as they weren't spoiled. She reckoned she needed to get back and pitch in.

We're all exhausted, she thought. Surely I can take my eyes off Trace and Krysty for a few minutes…

From his perch atop the cabin, which was the most intact roof section of the largely burned-out cabin, Jak yelled out, "Crocs! Lots!"

Chapter Six

Ryan knew their scout Jak didn't cry wolf. But what really ripped his attention away from hacking at the weeds surrounding the camp—and keeping his eye scanning in all directions inland, mindful of all the reasons he was trying to clear the tall grass and brush away—was that Jak's falcon-scream warning was followed promptly by the cracking, booming blast of his .357 Magnum Colt Python handblaster.

Unlike the rest of them, who were extremely handy with a blaster—even Mildred had been an Olympic-level pistol shot in her day, and carried a competition-quality Czech-made ZKR 551 revolver to prove it—Jak was all about blades. At any given time he had a dozen or so knives hidden on his body, both for close-quarters fighting and throwing. He was ace with them all, and he loved getting the chance to use his skill.

Ryan's head snapped around in time to see the grounded *Mississippi Queen*'s first mate and chief ship-wright pick up their captain by the elbows and carry her onto the bank, sending big splashes of water into the twilit air. There were four or five others in the shallow water that he could see, including Doc and Ricky, helping unload the boat of whatever Arliss deemed necessary.

Another thunder crack ripped from Jak's Python. Ryan saw a plume of water spurt up about ten yards downstream of the boat. The craft was beached at an angle of about forty-five degrees, with the keep of its prow driven into the soft soil of the beach, and its stern pointing west. Trace had ordered Nataly to bring her in that way to facilitate loading and unloading. The actual channel of Wolf Creek got steep fast, they told Ryan, who had no reason to doubt them.

They know their trade, and we know ours. There wasn't a nuking thing any of us could have done to stop us from winding up here, stranded on some forsaken shore in the middle of a nuking strontium swamp, he knew.

The one-eyed man hated the feeling of helplessness their bombardment had pounded into him. Into all of them, he knew, crew and companion alike.

He was already running toward the shore, transferring his panga to his left hand and drawing his SIG Sauer P226 handblaster with his right. His boots wanted to sink into the firm but moist soil. It was just this side of being straight-up mud. Out in the stream, Ryan could see what looked like random snags disturbing the water's oleaginous flow, except that they hadn't been there before. They were strangely bumpy. Some of those bumps showed glabrous gleams. And they were *moving*.

"Fireblast!" he burst out. There had to be a dozen of the bastards. More. How did so many get so close without Jak noticing them? he wondered.

Then he saw what seemed like a mostly submerged log, but with eye-bumps on the near end, slide out of the lower weeds in the water by the far bank, sculling with faint side-to-side strokes of its tail.

The bastards were cunning, he thought. They snuck up on them.

"Mildred!" Ryan yelled. "Stay in the nuking boat!"

The physician froze with one leg over the rail. The last of the stragglers in the water had made the sanctuary of the bank. Clearly, Mildred didn't realize the big Nile crocodiles could swim quite easily in water as shallow as that surrounding the hull.

Jak fired again. Ryan could see thrashing in the water this time, and he spotted a pink tinge in some of the splashes. A couple of the "snags" diverted toward it. Apparently these bastards weren't above making a meal out of one of their buddies.

But the others headed for the bank like starved ville rats offered a feast by their tyrant baron. Blasters were coming out among the people onshore, although they hesitated to waste ammo on such dubious targets.

When she was about four feet from the water, Trace shook off her helpers. Then she turned back to the creek.

"We should be clear as long as we keep away from the water," she said. "We just need to figure out how to drive these bastards off so we can work on getting the *Queen* under way again."

"At least we've got plenty of ammo," Arliss said. Though the *Queen*'s crew preferred black powder blasters—indeed, preferred fleeing to shooting, whenever the option offered—they kept a hefty store of all kinds and calibers of ammunition in the hold. It was something they could always trade, and be pretty sure of catching a profit, too, almost regardless what they traded for it.

"Right," the captain said. Despite her horrible wound, she seemed strong and in command of herself. Ryan knew what it felt like to step up in emergencies, disregarding your own wounds. If he hadn't shown that knack early on, he'd never have made it out of Front Royal alive, after his brother Harvey's treachery cost him his eye and left him with a scar down his face.

"I saw," Doc said, stepping toward her tentatively with his outsize LeMat wheel gun in his knobbly-knuckled hand. "I am not sure it is safe to stand so close to the water, Captain. These Nile crocodiles have a reputation as being quite aggressive."

She waved him off with her stump. "Light some torches," she commanded. "I bet they don't like fi—"

In the midst of a big wave of water a huge, pebble-scaled form erupted from the creek. Tooth-daggered jaws opened what seemed a whole yard wide. Before anyone could react, they snapped shut on the captain around her waist.

"Hold fire!" Ryan shouted. He tucked the SIG back in its holster and charged.

The croc was a monster, at least twenty feet long. It was shaking Trace in its jaw like a dog with a rat as it backed toward the water.

Ryan reversed his panga. Gripping the hilt with both hands, he took a running dive toward the immense reptile.

The wide-bladed panga was not meant for stabbing,

especially, but it did have a point. He aimed to bring that down on the spine behind the horror's triangular skull.

But the croc was heaving too much. The panga sank into its neck a full six inches as Ryan landed half on the croc, half in the water.

The croc whistled in pain and fury, but it did not open its mouth and release its prey. Instead it started to roll away from Ryan, either in a premature death roll meant to drown its captive, or more likely as a simple animal reflex to get the injured site away from the thing that had caused it unexpected pain.

Trying to mute his own awareness of the scaled, toothy horrors that could be wriggling toward him with their bulging eyeballs fixed on his legs, Ryan maneuvered himself to straddle the beast. He wrenched the broad blade free with the same effort it would have taken him to deadlift an engine block.

The croc had made a tactical mistake. Its back was armored well enough to shed bullets that hit at any kind of angle, if the crocodiles and gators he'd tangled with before were any guide. But its pale belly was vulnerable. As soon as Ryan saw the flash of yellow hide, he plunged the panga down again.

It sank into the beast's chest, between its scrabbling forelegs. He twisted the blade, hoping he'd hit the heart. Then again he didn't know where the nuking thing was located.

The crocodile roared. Meaning at least it opened its jaws—meaning it let Trace go. Ryan was in no position to confirm that fact, though, because before he could yank the panga free, or even let go of the handle, the monstrous creature had sped up its roll—dragging Ryan right along with it as if he were a rag doll.

For a moment he felt the crushing sensation of incredible mass on top of him. The thing had to have weighed a ton or more, at that size. The air was blasted out of his lungs in an involuntary yell. Had the mud beneath not been so soft, taking him into its slippery embrace and cushioning the weight, the behemoth surely would have crushed him to death.

The beast kept rolling. When the unendurable weight came off Ryan, he managed to let go of the panga's hilt and somehow get one boot and one knee planted into the muck.

He was also able to draw his handblaster. He pressed its muzzle almost into the croc's throat, right at the base of the long, triangular head, and started cranking off rounds. He figured if anything would cause handblaster rounds to penetrate the croc's notoriously hard skull—not a triple-big target as well—it was a lot of them, from below, at near-contact range. The fact that the copper-jacketed 147-grain 9 mm bullets had a lot of penetration for a handblaster didn't hurt.

The croc began to thrash from side to side. The water around it was maroon with blood except when its visibly diminishing efforts churned it to froth. That was pink.

Ryan flung himself away from the monster. It was still strong. A death-throe crack of the tail could pulp his hips or snap his spine like a baby's arm.

Trace was on her feet but bent over and staggering in knee-deep water. She had her good arm pressed to her gut where the jaws had closed, but she waved her stump, its compress now soaked red with blood from her struggles, at the shore and the stunned watchers.

"Thanks," she croaked. "I'm all right, all right, I'm fit to fight—"

She was yanked right out from behind her words and under the water in a flash. There was surprisingly little disturbance on the surface where she vanished. It was as if she'd never been.

Even Ryan was shocked immobile by the suddenness of her disappearance. But being Ryan Cawdor, he didn't stay that way longer than a heartbeat or two. Instead he hightailed it for solid land. He was not diving into a river full of nuking killer crocs to wrestle with one big and strong enough to make the captain, who was no small woman herself, simply disappear like that.

If he was going to commit suicide, he'd pick a better way.

As he reached land, though, he turned. Long-practiced habit kicked in. Even as he scanned the creek's surface for some sign of the captain—or where the next attack might come from—he kicked the magazine free of the handblaster's well, stuck it in a back pocket and slammed a fresh one home. He had no idea how many cartridges he'd fired, but he wanted *all* of them if he needed to shoot again.

For a moment the creek's surface was peaceful and even seemed free of crocodiles, at least in the stretch Ryan was watching with laser focus, past the *Queen*'s stern.

Then Trace burst out of the water, head back, arm and stump thrown high, but not under her own power.

She was well out from the bank, where soundings by means of a predark weighted line said the channel was more than eight feet deep.

She spun counterclockwise, hitting the murky water in a shower of spray that dwarfed the one that had accompanied her brief reappearance. Then two separate waves sloshed upward on opposite sides of where she'd gone down again. Tall tails thrashed the water into curtains of spray.

Ryan took his SIG in a two-handed grip and blasted off the whole magazine, plus the cartridge up the spout. He reckoned if he chilled the captain by accident now, with two of the monsters fighting over her, it would just be a mercy chill. The spurts kicked up by the bullets striking were barely noticeable against the effects of their titanic struggle.

The farther croc reared out of the water. In its jaws was clamped one of Trace's legs. Red flew from the ragged end, past the yellow knob of her femur head. The commotion ceased.

Dead silence reigned. It was as if time stopped, though Ryan's pulse continued to pound in his ears. The violated water subsided into the usual ripple of its undisturbed flow so swiftly and smoothly it almost seemed to be trying to erase the horror that happened upon and inside it just moments before. The suspended moment was broken to pieces by a wailing wordless cry from Myron. The chief engineer was tackled by Santee just shy of the monster-haunted water as he tried to run to his doomed mate's aid.

Ryan realized he needed to follow the advice he

been given when he was a boy learning to hunt: shoot enough blaster. He holstered the SIG, which he'd already reloaded, and ran for his Steyr. The longblaster was propped against his pack thirty paces inshore, muzzle-up to keep muck from getting in the barrel.

"Everybody, get big blasters or big sticks," he shouted. "The bastards tasted blood! They're going to come swarming—"

His words were drowned in a sudden cacophony of blasterfire.

He grabbed the Scout and spun, dropping to one knee for better aim, even on the fly. His companions and the late captain's crew weren't just busting caps at empty water.

It seemed as if dozens of crocs were rushing toward the shore and up onto the bank, tooth-fringed mouths wide.

Ryan picked the nearest open pink-and-yellow maw and blasted a 7.62 mm round into it. It snapped shut. The creature behind it rolled onto its side and kicked air.

As Ryan jacked the bolt of his Steyr, he saw a croc leap clean out of the water toward where Mildred stood by the rail. She danced aside, panic-firing at it as she did. Jak stood with legs braced on the cabin roof, firing down at the beast as its jaws snapped shut on the rail. For moment it actually hung there, all four legs out of the water, hanging on with its teeth buried in the wood. Mildred took the opportunity to take quick one-handed aim, arm fully extended as if she were at the target range, and put a .38 slug through its right eye. It let go and slid back into the creek.

Santee rolled over and over in the shallows, with his legs around the middle of a croc at least two feet longer than he was tall, holding its jaws shut from beneath with one hand while his other plunged a big Bowie knife repeatedly into its exposed belly.

Krysty and Ricky, flanking Myron, fired their handblasters. Nataly sat astride the engineer's hips, pinning him facedown to the ground while she coolly reloaded the chambers of a cap-and-ball revolver from a red leather flask. Ryan was concerned the man might drown, but his face was not in the water, and by the motion of his shoulder he was sobbing uncontrollably.

Doc blasted a lunging croc in the snout with the short shotgun barrel affixed beneath the pistol barrel of his LeMat revolver, shattering its upper jaw. Then he deftly stabbed it through the eye with his rapier as it wagged its ruined upper jaw back and forth, shedding dislodged, jagged teeth and sheets of blood.

Sean and Suzan pinned a croc's head to the soil while Avery whaled on the creature's head with an ax.

Targets were already getting scarce as Ryan peered across the iron sights of his Scout. He fired at one charging at Ricky from an angle, smashing its shoulder so that it collapsed writhing and snapping its jaw. Ricky turned and without batting an eye emptied the .45 ACP rounds in his Webley's cylinder into its jaw when it opened. The croc subsided on its side with blood drooling from its whole snout onto the short, beaten-down grass.

The smell of blood, digesting fish liberated from crocodile bellies, and burned powder of both the smokeless and ultra-smoky blasters filled the air. The crocs decided they'd had enough of eating lead—or of eating their own brothers and sisters that had been chilled or badly injured. They turned and vanished into the water with contemptuous flicks of their tails, some dragging still or feebly struggling crocs with them.

"Cease-fire!" Ryan yelled. He stayed on one knee with his longblaster held ready in case the monsters decided to make another try.

All the shooting stopped. He realized the *Queen*'s crew had obeyed his order as well as his own people, to whom the command was directed. Even Arliss, who had been laying into the attacking reptiles with fire from a lever-action Marlin carbine, lowered his weapon.

Nataly rolled off Myron. Then, with her reloaded Ruger Old Army revolver ready in her right hand, she reached down and gently shook the grieving man's shaking shoulder.

"Come on, Myron," she said gently. "It's over. You need to get up and get away from the water now. We don't know if or when those *things* will come back."

A shudder passed through her long, lean frame. Apparently man-eating crocodiles attacking en masse could do what unanswerable cannon fire, even when it was striking down her friends and coworkers around her, could not: shake her iron self-control.

"Right, Mildred, Jak," Ryan called. "Looks as if it's safe to come back to shore now. Don't hang around to hunt for crawdads, though."

"Is there any more unloading to do tonight?" Mildred asked.

"I'd advise against it." Ryan glanced at Nataly. The mate had managed to get Myron to stand and shuffle back a few yards from the water. Then he had promptly collapsed to his knees, sobbing uncontrollably once more, while Nataly stood beside him patting his shoulder uncomfortably. He seemed locked up double tight in his grief.

Ryan couldn't say he blamed him.

He slung the Steyr. There were still eight croc carcasses on the beach, plus two injured too badly to pull themselves off the shore into the water. Avery quickly finished them with neck-blows from his ax. He wrenched Ryan's panga from one of the corpses and returned it to him.

"Let's pick out some of the likelier-looking chills and butcher them. Some fresh meat wouldn't hurt us. And does anybody even know if crocodile jerky is possible?"

Everybody shook their head. Even Doc, which mildly surprised Ryan. Doc knew a lot of seemingly random facts about the natural world.

"What about the others?" Sean asked.

"Shove them back in the water. Given what lives around here, we don't want to be attracting scavengers. Remember, those crocs may not be the worst things that live in the area."

Chapter Seven

"So, where do we stand?" Myron asked.

The crew and companions were sitting around their driftwood campfire. Sitting across from him, Krysty studied the man's face. To all appearances he was back in control of himself.

But he was still a man who had watched his beloved ship—his home, his livelihood, to all intents his life—reduced to a wreck, and seen the love of his life torn limb from limb and devoured alive by crocodiles.

"Well," Mildred said, "we already know we won't die from radiation poisoning. Not right away."

Myron's jaw tightened briefly under his beard. Krysty's friend Mildred tended to deal with severe stress through sarcasm. And what she said was actually both true and responsive to the question. But put that way—well, it probably didn't sit too well with the poor man.

"We have food for a couple weeks, easy," Arliss said. "More if you don't mind living on nothing but that hundred pounds of jugged sauerkraut we picked up in Moellerville. We'll see how bad the croc jerky we've got drying turns out to be."

"We can also fish, and mebbe catch some more crocodiles," the rigger went on.

"If they don't catch us first," Jake said.

"Yeah, thanks for the reminder." Arliss flicked his eyes to Myron, the acting captain. He had his head down with his beard on his collarbone and seemed too sunk in his own misery to register what the perpetually gloomy navigator had said. "We can also try hunting, trapping and fishing for fresh meat."

"We want to be triple careful of that," Ryan said. "Especially if stickies are in the area."

"Of course, if they are, we'll likely find out about it when they come calling," J.B. stated. He sounded way more amused at the prospect than the *Queen*'s crew looked.

Ryan scratched his right ear. "That's why Jak's prowling out in the weeds beyond the perimeter. That, and we'd have to chain him to the boat to keep him from patrolling on his own."

"Will he be okay out there?" Suzan asked. "I mean, if there's stickies and all. Not to mention other wild animals."

"If stickies reside in the vicinity," Doc said, "it is highly unlikely that any other predators of any size do. Many muties are not highly tolerant of competition."

"Not to mention just plain mean," Abner added.

"What about the rads?" Nataly asked. "And the toxic metals Mildred talks about? I mean, in the fish and game, if we eat any of it."

She dabbed at some crocodile grease at the side of her thin-lipped mouth. The fresh croc flesh had been altogether tasty, roasted on driftwood spits over open fires.

"If we stay away from internal organs, especially the liver, we shouldn't get hurt by heavy metal toxicity any more than from environmental exposure to the fallout. Same for the radiation, actually. The fact there's no real hot spots right close by, and we didn't land smack-dab in the middle of a strontium swamp, is a hopeful sign, at least."

Her broad, normally smooth forehead creased in a thoughtful frown.

"Still, as long as we don't spend more than a week or two here, the rad and metal poisoning shouldn't shorten our lives by more than ten, twenty years."

Everybody had a good laugh at that. None of them would have called the prospects of their all living to see the sun come up again particularly prime.

"What about those two fleets full of ironclads that almost did us in today?" Sean asked.

Arliss looked at Myron, who was still sunk in his despair. Then he looked at Ryan.

"That's a fighting matter, I'd say, more than a river boatman's. Where do you guys stand, anyway? You signed on for the duration of the voyage down to the Sippi Delta baronies, which would appear to have come to an end, at least for now. And you hired on to accept the, ah, the Conoyers as your bosses while actively employed. But it looks to me like you're free agents now."

He grimaced. "It's not like there's anything we could do to stop you if you decided to leave us high and dry."

"It's not like we have a better way out of here than you do," Mildred said, sounding almost as if she were talking to herself.

Ryan shot her a hard look, then he cast his lone blue eye over the rest of the group, which aside from Jak was scattered among the other survivors around the fire.

"You're right, Mildred," he said. "On land or not, we're all on the same boat still, so to speak. And our best shot at surviving this mess seems to be sticking together."

He turned to look Krysty straight in the eye. A mutie of the nonobvious stripe, pretty much the opposite end of the spectrum from the barely humanoid likes of stickies or scalies, or even the more common deformed norms, she had a touch of the power of a doomie—the gift of prophecy, which right now was hinting that the future was double bad, and likely to get triple bad before it got better. If it did. She also had a way of feeling things, which may have been no more than an unusually intense sense of intuition.

She was no mind reader, yet on such occasions she could look at Ryan's rugged yet handsome face and plainly read the words he didn't speak: *for now.*

He, and therefore the rest of the companions, would abandon their fellow survivors in a heartbeat if it upped their chances of survival. It made Krysty's heart ache to think of that, but that was just the way the world worked, if you wanted to put off taking a dirt nap as long as possible.

She also felt, as if the pain was hers, what it would cost him to make such a choice. He was a hard man, hardened by the brutal decades he'd lived since fleeing Front Royal. But he wasn't heartless.

Ryan just did what he had to do to keep the companions alive. He would never show his own pain or hesitation. To show weakness was to die. "But to answer your question," Ryan said, turning back to the others from what had seemed a lengthy if wordless conversation but really passed in a cluster of heartbeats, "I think we don't have much to worry about from the splendid little war going on down at the mouth of the creek. As somebody pointed out when it was clear they were shooting at each other rather than keeping after us, they've got better things to do than chase a random tugboat. Especially one that when last seen was afire and sinking. We were never more than a side dish to them. To each, the other is the main course. They've forgotten about us—most likely."

"And if they remember?" Suzan asked.

Ryan shrugged. "We run, we fight, or we die," he said. "Or some combination of those three. Or all of them."

"Usual day, in other words," J.B. added.

His friends laughed more loudly at that, and less nervously then the crew did.

"I think we need to get out of here as fast as we can, however we can," Krysty said.

"On-target as usual, lover," Ryan stated.

Arliss grunted. "I don't think you'll get much argument here. But the 'however we can' seems to be the sticking point, right now."

"We've got all of exactly one functional power launch," said Abner, who served as mate to Avery, and was an expert in small boats. "It'll hold mebbe six of us. Eight if we was all friendly. Meaning we don't mind capsizing and drowning together."

"So, half of us," Sean said.

"Say six, you stupe," Arliss chided his friend. "Unless you're volunteering to be one of the ones to drown?"

"We could draw lots," Ricky said.

Everybody stared at him. He blushed.

"I mean—I read about that in a book… I…"

"Your best move now is to just stop talking," Mildred said gently.

Ricky shut his mouth firmly.

"Nuke that," Ryan said. Again, Krysty could tell that his main consideration was that the boat would likely not accommodate all seven of *them*.

"We could raise her."

Now the whole group turned their faces to Myron as if he were a magnet and their noses, iron.

"Uh, Myron," Arliss said reluctantly, "I don't mean to reopen any recent wounds, but you know as well as I do—"

"The *Queen*," Myron said.

Arliss slumped so hard he almost fell over against Sean in his relief that the acting captain wasn't talking about his wife, now almost certainly residing in the belly of one or more crocodiles in the stream. Or stored in handy chunks in burrows beneath the banks for later consumption, as Krysty seemed to remember was a habit for gators and crocodiles.

"We need to raise her," Myron stated. "She brought us all here. She can get us out."

"We did keep the engines from flooding," Sean said.

"Then there's the little fact she's still almost as good as sunk," Sean pointed out.

"We've got some plankage on board we could use to patch her," Avery said. "If that's not enough, we've got plenty of canvas. We could fix a couple layers over the hole on the outside of the hull. Be enough to get us a dozen or two miles, anyway, although we might have to keep the bilge-pumps going."

He looked at Ricky.

"I read that in a book, too."

Myron had raised his head now. His shoulders were back. His cheeks showed signs of color above his curly beard. But Krysty thought the gleam in his eye was more than a little unhealthy.

"We can do it!" he said, too brightly. "We can get her up and running again in a day! Two, max!"

"No," Ryan said.

Myron jerked his head back, blinking as if the tall man had slapped him.

"Excuse me?" Arliss said, in a less-than-friendly tone.

"Run where?" Ryan asked.

"Well, down Wolf Creek, then along the Sippi!" Myron said, rallying.

"We tried that already. And this is where it got us."

Most of the *Queen*'s crew had bristled at a man who was still an outlander flatly contradicting their acting captain. But that drained the tension right out of them, as well as the hope that had begun to fill their faces.

But Myron wasn't ready to let go so easily. "We can steam upstream, then," he said.

"To where?" Ryan asked.

"Why—" Myron blinked again. He gestured vaguely west with his hand. "Upstream."

Nataly sighed heavily. "*Where*, Captain?" she asked gently. "We don't know what lies upstream. How far the creek is even navigable or how far the badlands extend. We don't want to find ourselves aground to stay in the middle of a true strontium swamp nuke hot spot."

"And that's if the swampers don't take us," Jake added.

"We don't know that they won't take us here," Arliss said. But he sounded as if he were just pointing out facts, instead of still staunchly supporting Myron's scheme. "There's that rad-blasted derelict bridge practically on top of it. It's likely crawling with stickies."

"Won't it also block the channel for a boat the size of the *Queen*?" Krysty asked.

"Well," Nataly said, sounding reluctant but compelled by sheer professionalism to steam on, "that shouldn't be a problem. We can sound the channel first to make sure we have clearance under the keel, and hunt for sunken snags. But there should be plenty room abeam for her to pass below the intact part on this side of the creek."

"What about attempting to escape overland?" Doc asked. "It would at least spare us the attentions of the vying armored war fleets."

J.B. shook his head.

"Triple-bad odds, Doc. We might stumble into a hot spot that way. And even if we found game trails to follow, and kept our eyes skinned, we'd be begging to get ambushed. We wouldn't make it a mile, if this country lives up to its rep."

It was the old man's turn to sigh.

"Sadly, it appears to have done so thus far," he admitted.

"Just because the rads and the fact everything we eat is seasoned with plutonium salt won't chill right away, it doesn't mean we can just dawdle here," Ryan said. "To me, trying to fix up the *Queen* enough so she won't sink and kill us before something else does, all so we can steam blindly upstream to where as far as we know there won't be a *way* out, is nuking near a last-chance measure. Like, right exactly above trying to hike out with stickies likely to sucker the flesh off our faces before we go a quarter mile."

"But I *can't* leave her!" Myron wailed.

Krysty wasn't entirely sure he meant the boat. Or only the boat.

Nataly moved to the stricken man's side. "I'm with the captain," she said. Krysty thought she didn't sound particularly happy about it.

The other members of the crew traded uneasy looks among themselves. Even Arliss failed to leap up and join her, though he looked guilty about it. But Krysty sensed the rest would stand with the tall first mate, come the crunch.

Ryan's craggy features tightened. He was getting ready to blow them all off for glowing night shit. She didn't need mutie ESP to see that.

"We can come back and salvage her," she said loudly. "Afterward. I mean, once we all get away, and those two crazy baronies sort out their differences. Or at least get tired and go home."

J.B. chuckled. "It's not like a lot of scavvies are going

to find her and come swarming to salvage her themselves, here in the middle of a strontium swamp."

"Especially not if the stickies have been at it," Mildred said, "shitting and sliming on everything the way
they do."

"Quit helping, Mildred," Ryan growled.

"Has anybody read *The Adventures of Huckleberry
Finn*?" Ricky asked. "We had a lot of books back on
Monster Island."

That shut everybody up and let all the air out of the
rapidly inflating confrontation.

Arliss raised a hand. "My ma had nearly the whole
book when she was a young'un, and she told me the
story."

Doc raised his hand, which given the time he came
from didn't surprise Krysty. She raised hers too, as
did Mildred.

"Yeah," Ryan said. "Me, too. And what does this
have to do with rad-blasted anything, Ricky?"

"Well, it gives me an idea…"

Chapter Eight

With a sluggish, brackish-water-and-dead-fish-smelling breeze blowing out of the east, Ryan heard the chug of the motor launch returning downstream before Ricky, sitting sentry on the *Queen*'s largely intact bridge roof, called out that he saw it.

Ryan stood up out from under the shade of the crude lean-to where he was working. Similar structures were dotted around the cleared space, which had been cleared out considerably more as they gathered tall grass to make into rope to lash rafts together.

Even though twisting together yard-long stems of the smooth saw grass that grew in crazy profusion in the area, nukes or no, was sitting-down work, the sheer amount of concentration it required made it tiring. And although he had the hard, skilled hands of a man who did frequent piecework, rather than using them just to pull triggers and the stoppers from jugs of Towse Lightning, he was getting a series of blisters, cuts and cramps in brand-new and unexpected locations.

At the sound of the motor launch approaching, everybody stopped what they were doing to get a drink of water and gather by the shore. But not too close. They hadn't seen any more of the big, killer crocs. Likely the surviving local crocodiles had gorged themselves and were sleeping it off in their dens. But the castaways had seen how they could approach the land underwater, and were in no mind to go making assumptions. They came under the still-standing part of the red steel bridge, Jak crouched in the prow, with J.B. and Nataly behind him. The rabbity-looking Abner MacReedy steered the boat in the stern. In a few moments he was backing the engine deftly as the launch slid into shore just upstream of the grounded wreck of the *Mississippi Queen*.

"Any luck?" Arliss sang out. He was wearing only his grimy, blood-splashed dungarees. He'd washed them in the stream that morning, as most of them had their clothes, faces, and bodies. You didn't have to be fastidious, the way Mildred was, not to be keen on spending any longer with your former friends' blood and bits of flesh stuck on your face and clothing and starting to stink. Nor to be covered all over with old smoke and crocodile grease.

The master rigger was the one who was teaching them to weave rope out of the tough local grasses. He didn't want to use up too much of the rope they carried aboard the *Queen*. Among other things, they needed enough to lash the rafts to one another for towing. He said they could make rope strong enough to hold planks or logs together, for long enough and far enough to get clear of the New Vick fleet. And Avery, who apparently had grown up making rafts in Defianceville, near the rubble of Cairo on the Ohio just north of where it met the Sippi, agreed. They knew more about the subject than Ryan or any of his companions, including Ricky whose idea this whole plan was. And the two were ready to trust their own lives to the rafts with their homemade rope, which Ryan always found powerfully persuasive. At least when the folks doing the trusting had an actual clue about what they were doing.

"None," Nataly said, standing up and stepping from the boat into the shallows with barely a rock. She moved briskly during the two steps it took her to get out of the water, and took several more inshore for good measure.

Jak sprang onto the bank, which made the boat wallow side to side ferociously. J.B. clung to the sides tightly until it steadied somewhat, his jaw set and brow ever so slightly furrowed, which for a more expressive human—most of them—would be the equivalent of a furious scowl. Nonetheless, the Armorer quickly recovered his composure, and shook off Abner when the grinning man offered his hand from shore.

"You were right, Ryan," J.B. said. "About four miles upstream the Wolf turns into a true strontium swamp, just like in the stories. There's a lot of channels through it, but the rads are near the red zone on the counter. Depending how big far it goes, we might make it through without anything worse than our hair falling out in clumps and our getting nuke blueberries all under our skin."

Ugly and alarming as those effects were, Ryan knew a body could get over them. "But if we get stuck there…" J.B. shook his head. "We'd go into convulsions and die of the bloody shits in one day. Two if we're too tough for our own good, and too stubborn to eat a blaster first."

"How long would it take to get through?" Krysty asked. She had been cutting grass, and her beautiful face glowed with sweat in the late-morning sun.

"No idea," J.B. said.

"There are a number of channels winding through the swamp," Nataly said. "But all of them were shallow. Every one we tried ran stretches no deeper than three feet."

Ryan glanced at the *Queen*. Ricky sat huddled atop the largely burned-out cabin with his DeLisle across his legs, too dutiful to try to leave his appointed lookout post, but not too much so not to make it abundantly clear how much he hated being left out of whatever news the exploring team brought back from their crack-of-dawn expedition up Wolf Creek.

Inside the hull, Myron was hard at work on his beloved engines, with Sean assisting him. Ryan didn't know how much of that was necessary for the big Diesels—and how much for the man.

"So she wouldn't make it, huh?" Ryan asked, turning back to the tall brunette and rubbing his chin. His beard rasped at his palm. He hadn't shaved for a couple of days. Another twenty-four hours and he'd start looking like the grizzle-bearded Arliss. "The motor launch could," Abner said. "One of them little unarmored patrol boats the two fleets got, mebbe. Not the *Queen*. Not even stripped."

"I wouldn't care to risk going aground, given the dangers our friends discovered," Doc added. He had been weaving the braids of grass such as Ryan had been making into what master rigger Arliss called "plain-laid rope," winding them together in three strands in such a way as to make the individual lengths hold together strongly. Ryan was none too clear on that part of the process, but Doc was, and he proved to better even than the river folk at doing so.

"It's not an option," Ryan said flatly. He looked at Arliss, not quite challenging him to disagree, but not hiding the fact that he wasn't open to debate.

Arliss shook his head and heaved his powerful shoulders in a sigh. "I'll break the news to Myron," he said.

"How about carrying out Ricky's plan, but with the motorboat towing the rafts and the unpowered boat upstream instead of downstream, and trying to sneak past a whole assload of heavily armed ironclads?" he asked.

"Aw, no," Abner said. "We don't want to go through that in small boats. No way."

"Saw stickie," Jak said. "Chilled stickie."

"We saw more than one," Nataly stated. "It looked as if we disturbed a whole nest of the monsters." She shuddered.

Ryan cocked his head at J.B. "Didn't hear blasterfire."

"Jak used his knives."

Ryan jutted his jaw and nodded. It was tough to chill a stickie with a knife. The blade would have to be thrown hard enough to penetrate the mutie's brain. Body strikes were useless.

"And Abner used the motor."

"You bet I did!" The normally quiet mate was animated. Apparently his brush with the dreaded muties had pumped him high on adrenaline. "Why fight those monsters when we can run?"

"Too true," J.B. said, then shrugged. "I didn't see the need to waste cartridges."

"Good move," Ryan said. "Still game to try escaping upstream, Mildred?"

"Let's go just right on through that big old fleet," Mildred said. "I love this plan."

As if to try to persuade her otherwise, the booming of cannon fire, dulled by distance but audible and unmistakable, drifted to them against the slow breeze. It was only a few shots, sounding to Ryan as if they mebbe came from both sides.

"Big boomers," J.B. said. "Not any of the kitty-cat crap blasters the patrol boats carry in their bows."

"Still love the plan to try creeping past all those big old cannons in the dead of night, Mildred?"

"Compared to sitting on a bundle of sticks tied together, floating at zero-point-five miles an hour through a maze filled with lethal radioactive sludge, waiting for a tribe of stickies to wade out and eat us? Well, yes."

"Right. Is there time to hit up some of the places where you found suitable timber, cut it and make it back here before dark?"

Nataly thought, then nodded. "We'd have to move fast."

"You and Abner up to going out again?"

The two said yes.

"Jak?"

Jak only grinned. Ryan didn't think it was necessary to point out to the *Queen*'s crew that meant he reckoned they were likely going to have trouble, probably of the stickie kind, and he was eager to get stuck in some.

"You both ready to chop wood?" he asked the pair.

"Yes," Nataly said. The coxswain just nodded again.

"Two boats should be fine carrying four people each, right?"

"Sure enough," Abner agreed.

"Pick five more people you reckon can use an ax or that two-man saw we got. Avery, are you up to coming?"

He drew in a deep breath. "I can't say I'm eager to move toward a nest of riled-up stickies," he said, "and speaking of them, I still don't double like the looks of that old bridge. But yes, and I can swing an ax with the best of them. Or use a saw of any description."

"Ace. We'll need to pick out trees that are the best compromise we can find between too small to work and too big to cut down fast. Can we do that?"

The boatswain's teeth were bright in his dark face when he grinned. "We can. And I can pick out just the ones."

"Pick four more, then, Nataly. J.B., will you swap longblasters with me? I think that riot gun of yours will be more useful in the kind of scrape we're likely to get into than my Steyr."

"Sure, Ryan. And I'll swap your Scout out with Ricky. He's better with a longblaster than I am, any day. And that little homebrew carbine of his is better for hitting stickies with, if it comes to that."

"How likely is it that the stickies around here have

learned we're here from their kinfolk upstream?" Kenn asked.

Jak laughed softly. "Know here," he said.

The crew frowned at him. They hadn't begun to have a chance to learn to decipher his oddly clipped speech. His companions had a hard enough time figuring it out.

"He means, the stickies around here already know we're here, Suzan," Krysty said. "Whether or not they live under the railway bridge."

"How likely are they to rile up the whole country and come down on our necks, is what she's trying to ask," Arliss said. "Right, Suzan?"

She nodded, looking even more wild-eyed than usual.

"Can't rightly say," J.B. replied. "There's no telling with stickies."

"Like humans," Doc said, "different bands of stickies vary widely in intelligence and social organization. At the very least they display a form of cunning. In general they do have some means of communication in the way they hoot and shriek, and if they can communicate, the mood of the band can shift with astonishing speed."

"You folks know fighting better than me," Arliss said, "but isn't it supposed to be a bad idea to divide your forces in the face of the enemy?"

"Yeah," Ryan agreed, "but I don't see that we've got a choice. We can't leave the supplies unguarded. Mutie bastards'll trash the whole lot, mebbe even burn everything if they have the means start a fire."

"They do love them fire," J.B. agreed.

"That is so strange," Jake said. "I associate them more with the element of water. Not its opposite."

Ryan looked at the navigator in surprise. He was pretty sure that was the least gloomy thing he had heard the man say in the past few days. It also was exactly not the sort of thing Ryan would ever expect him to say.

There's just no reading people, he thought with grim amusement. I can see why J.B. and Ricky would rather work with machines. You always know where you stand with them.

"The more people we take with us the slower we go," Nataly said. "We couldn't safely carry the whole party in the two boats, anyway, Arliss."

"Aye," the rigger said. "You're right."

"How will you get enough wood for the rafts back here?" Mildred asked.

"They float," Ryan said. "We tie them up in big bundles, lash them together, toss them in the creek and tow them downstream with us. Easy as taking jack from a dead man."

OH, WELL, RICKY thought as the water slogged around the raft being slowly towed behind the motor launch. It's not as if it's hard keeping noise discipline with Jak for a raft mate. Overhead, what looked like a million stars had no trouble staying silent at all.

Five of the rafts were strung out behind the lead boat, followed by the unpowered dinghy from the *Mississippi Queen*. Ryan and Krysty rode in the tow boat, with a morose Myron.

At least he's piped down, Ricky thought, less charitably than he would have liked. When they'd started out, about one in the morning by J.B.'s chron, the acting captain had wailed like a lonely puppy as they pulled away from the abandoned tug.

Piloting the boat, and by extension the whole waterborne caravan, was Abner. Ryan, Krysty and Myron were his passengers. Ricky and Jak were on the second raft with their packs, behind the one carrying Arliss and Sean. They lay on their bellies, because Avery had warned them in bloodcurdling terms not to try sitting, much less standing, on the lumpy bundles of tied-together logs. Ricky didn't trust theirs anyway, so he had little trouble obeying. Jak would go ahead and get up and dance on the horrible thing if he took a mind to. But he was so coordinated he could probably get away with it without making the raft come apart or tipping it over. Ricky was not that coordinated, and was painfully aware of the fact.

Doc rode on the raft immediately following theirs with Jake. Avery and Suzan rode the fourth. The fifth raft was loaded with supplies, mostly food and extra ammo. In the trail boat were J.B., Mildred, Nataly and Santee, primarily because none of the rafts would safely carry him.

Ricky moaned, but softly, as the turbulence of the Wolf Creek waters blending with those of the mighty Sippi rocked the raft. He saw Jak laughing silently at him.

A killdeer flew overhead, low but invisible, its passage marked by its shrill staccato tweets. It was one of the few mainland birds Ricky had learned to recognize by sound, simply because they were so common and distinctive. The smell of water was thick in his nostrils, emphasized by actual water slopping over the cut-up saplings of the raft to hit him in the face or soak his clothes. He could also smell the tang of burned black powder, and the more appealing smells of food cooking.

The lead boat was turning south. Its engine purred on low RPM, barely audible even this close by. The sloshing water was louder. Ricky had been told it was a tricky maneuver, towing a series of rafts around a turn like that. He looked back nervously, but the other craft seemed to follow in an effortless arc.

They rode toward the New Vickville fleet. Lights burned among the ships, enough to show there were about a dozen sizable ships there, two or three of them scary big. He couldn't tell for sure because it looked as if their silhouettes overlapped. From somewhere ahead he heard a fiddle being played.

Ricky wondered what time it was—how long until dawn, mostly. Nataly and Abner had calculated they needed about three hours to reach the New Vick fleet. Maybe less, probably not much more. They planned to slide in close to the western shore and hug it as close as possible to reduce their chances of being seen.

Arliss had expressed surprise that they'd set out so early. "I thought half an hour before sunrise was the best time to make a move," he'd said, "because the human mind and body are at their lowest ebb then."

"They are," Ryan had told him. "The light gets trickiest then, too, and it's hard to see right. But we're not trying a sneak attack. We're trying to sneak by. We want to be a mile or more south of the fleet when the sun comes up."

He turned his face to the side so he could roll one eye up to the sky. It was still black, although he could see some shadowy streaks where a few high lines of clouds were blotting the stars. Dawn looked as if it was still far away, even if it felt as if they'd been crawling along the water for roughly ever.

From somewhere ahead and to his left, a harsh voice barked, "Hey! Who goes there!"

"FIREBLAST," KRYSTY HEARD Ryan say under his breath.

Ahead to port a light suddenly glowed alive, not twenty yards away from them. It showed hints of fire-light-yellowed faces and a peculiar-looking superstructure.

Her heart sank. It could only be a New Vickville patrol boat. Somehow they'd almost run into it without even seeing it. It wasn't just the darkness, she realized. The craft's shadowed shape blended seamlessly against the larger shadow-masses of the fleet behind it.

"Speak the password," the angry-sounding male voice called out. "Or we'll open fire, you P'ville cock-suckers!"

From the right and almost abeam, a second light appeared, reaching out at them across the rolling Sippi waters. It was only a lantern, and its beam was feeble, but it was strong enough to shine upon them faintly. Mostly, it signified the presence of a second patrol boat.

"We're lost," Myron groaned, burying his face in his hands.

Krysty turned and put her arm around him to comfort him, but mostly in hopes of shutting him up. They didn't need to go out of their way to attract more attention. Although it was hard to see any way in which they weren't caught.

"Ryan," Abner said, "it's your call."

"Take her as fast as you can for the near boat," Ryan clipped out. "Pass close as you dare to port of her. On my word, cut power. Then when I tell you, accelerate, keep turning to port until you're near the bank and head back up Wolf Creek to the *Queen*."

Krysty saw the man's eyes widen, but he bobbed his head. The noise of the motor increased and the caravan slowly began to pick up speed.

Despite their initial threats, the crew of the first patrol craft didn't seem to know what to do. Krysty heard them shouting at each other about "raising a head of steam" and "orders." The chug of a much larger engine than the launch's came from the other boat, though.

A new voice bellowed from the near vessel. "Open fire, you stupes! Blow the P'ville taints out of the damn water!"

The deck cannon went off. It seemed to Krysty as if the muzzle-flare would envelop them. But although the noise of the cannon firing struck her in the face as if she'd been flung into a board fence, and seemed to deafen her, the shot flew high over their heads. High enough that she dared hope it missed their rafts and dinghy, as well.

Then she was choking on dense sulfurous smoke.

The bow of the patrol boat loomed like a peak over

them. "Cut the throttle!" Ryan commanded. With the powerful drag of the heavy-laden craft in tow, the launch rapidly lost way.

Ryan laid his longblaster on the plank seat between them. "Ryan, what are you doing?" she asked as he stood up into a pantherish crouch, steadying himself with hands on the gunwales.

"I'll be back, Krysty," he said. "Full power now, Abner!"

Then Ryan launched himself toward the enemy patrol boat.

Chapter Nine

I'm going to feel like the biggest stupe on Earth if I miss my handhold. The words flashed through Ryan's mind as he flew through the air above the darkened waters of the Sippi.

He barely had time to finish the thought before he struck the New Vick patrol boat's hull. His hands by sheer dumb luck found the scuppers. Behind him he heard the growl of a small motor rising as Abner, following Ryan's last commands, turned the launch and her tow-train and ran hard for the bank.

He hauled himself up, boot soles scrabbling against the wooden hull. He got enough of a purchase to push up and grab the rail. Then he got the toes of his boots into the drain holes at the base of the gunwale.

Holding on to the rail with his left hand, he drew the SIG from its holster with his right. A man with a billed cap and a beard stood to his right, not three feet away. He was already starting to turn.

Ryan shot him twice through the back. The shots were loud even over the ringing in his ears left by the deck cannon going off almost in his face. The sailor fell.

The one-eyed man vaulted the rail and landed in a

crouch on the deck. Somebody emerged from the cabin, to his left, and he sensed the man grabbing for him.

Ryan dealt him a sharp elbow strike. It struck hard against the man's chin, momentarily numbing Ryan's left hand. The sailor reeled back with a cry. The initial blow was followed by a side kick that slammed the man onto his butt on the deck. Ryan pivoted slightly and fired a single shot. Just as the sailor was starting to bound forward to his feet, he collapsed to the deck with a hole in his forehead.

Drawing the panga with his left hand, Ryan rushed forward and was among the still-confused crew like a tiger among sheep.

The man attending the surprisingly little deck cannon looked up in amazement as Ryan appeared around the corner of the mostly open cabin that lay in front of the vessel's exposed topside boiler. Ryan delivered two shots that drilled though the blasterman's throat. He emitted a sort of croaking sound and toppled backward over the rail, leaving his wet mop stuck down the fat smoothbore barrel.

A second man in a peaked cap stood behind the cannon in a spill of yellow shine from the lanterns mounted at the front of the wheelhouse, in front of Ryan and to his left. The Deathlands warrior chopped him at the base of the neck from behind with a backhand swipe. The officer went down.

That left two crewmen in sight, one to the right of the cannon, turning to face Ryan with a bag of what had to have been premeasured black powder in his hands, and the other on the cannon's far side, bending over a low crate that contained several softball-size iron balls. Ryan shot the nearer man, the one with the powder bag, twice through the chest. He collapsed in a heap beside the cannon.

Abruptly Ryan felt himself caught up from behind by a pair of arms snaking beneath his own. Then hands interlocked behind his head, pulling both his arms up while his neck was forced inexorably forward. His attacker, who had to have been bigger than he was, hoisted his boots off the deck.

Sparks began to pop like tiny muzzles-flashes behind Ryan's eye. He was in a beyond Code Red emergency. That full nelson neck lock could crank his spine far enough to put him out, cause permanent injury up to paralyzing him, or leave him staring up at the stars through the fleeting wisps of clouds above. All of which would mean he'd failed in his mission to cover his friends' slow-motion escape from the armored battle fleet.

The other gunner came at him, his bearded face a twist of rage. He held one of the cannonballs overhead in both hands, preparing to smash it down on Ryan's exposed and helpless head.

But while his skull was definitely exposed and vulnerable, Ryan was far from helpless. He'd been here before.

As the cannon-loader lunged at him, Ryan whipped up his lower body and pistoned both his boot heels into the man's gut—neither a solar plexus nor a nut shot, but between the hip bones, midway from navel to nut-sack. It was a blow meant to unbalance, not stun.

It did. The gunner was already leaning forward. As Ryan intended, the man's legs whipped out from under him. Though the motion almost made him black out, Ryan torqued his own hips rapidly counterclockwise, twisting his own legs out of the way.

By sheer luck the falling cannonball hit Ryan's captor somewhere between the same spot Ryan had kicked his pal and a thigh. Ryan had never counted on that— he had other means of getting his attacker to loosen his death grip—but he was certainly taking the gift that chance had given him. He got his right hand turned down and in far enough for his blaster muzzle to clear his own torso. And bear on his enemy's.

He fired a shot. He didn't care where it hit, only that it did. The burly crewman howled. The dreadful pressure on the back of Ryan's neck stopped as the sailor's interlaced fingers started to loosen their grip. Ryan managed to pull both arms far enough to get a boot down and turn his hips farther, enough to jab his left elbow into the man's ribs and gain even more slack.

He pressed the blaster under his left armpit, pressed it into flesh and triggered three more shots, fast as he could.

The New Vick sailor choked out a scream and fell to the deck, gagging on his own blood. He managed to take Ryan down with him, but was unable to keep any kind of hold on him. Ryan fell on his back across the man he'd double kicked, who was starting to push himself up, moaning from what was most likely a deck-smashed face. The man went down again with a fresh crack of face bone on wood.

Putting his left hand, still clutching the panga, on the prone man's neck to keep him down and help himself up, Ryan scrambled up to one knee. He raised the big blade, then slammed it into the cannon loader's neck. Blood gushed from the crewman's mouth and spurted from the wound. His neck broke with an audible crack.

The other patrol boat's engine was chugging rhythmically now. "*Yarville*, what's going on?" a voice bellowed. "Sandoz, Whateley—somebody answer me!"

Ryan saw the craft's prow swinging toward his boat. The lantern's beam swept a yellow path across the placid waters of the great river.

There was enough side-scatter light for Ryan to get both hands to brace his handblaster in a classic kneeling Weaver position. He got a hurried picture of the lantern's glow, then fired two shots. The light went out with a clatter and tinkle and a confused curse from the man who was holding it. It was rapidly drowned out by confused and panicky shouting as a spreading blue-and-yellow glare showed that oil spilled from the shattered reservoir had taken light.

Ryan caught a glimpse of somebody emptying a bucket of something other than water into the fire-pool. It made sense that a war craft would carry sand to use to fight a fire, especially when its main weapon or weapons were flame-belching monstrosities.

That didn't bother him. He had a new plan in mind. In a fight his mind was always working at high speed, even while his well-trained and experienced body did most of the work of minute-to-minute keeping him

alive. He was up on his feet at once, holstering his
9 mm blaster, and darting a few steps toward the bow.

He yanked the wet mop out of the wide, stubby cannon barrel and chucked it over the rail. He grabbed up
a bag of black powder from the little stack to the starboard of the cannon. It was surprisingly small—they
had to have access to good powder mills in New Vick.
A baron who had the means and mind to create a powerful war machine by the standards of the day would
make sure he or she had the best supply of powerful
and reliable black powder possible.

He cut the bag with his panga and dumped it willy-
nilly into the bore. Even though it was several inches
across, it looked almost small by comparison to the
thickness of the tube surrounding it. Not more than
three-quarters of the dark grains went down the black
hole, but neatness didn't count, nor did full power.

It wasn't *his* nuking boat. If he could use it to make
his own getaway, fine. If not, he didn't intend to leave
it in a condition to be used by anybody else.

He stuffed the empty hemp bag into the cannon to
serve as wadding. Then he sheathed the panga, ran to
the other side of the cannon and picked up a ball, which
he could tell by the heft was about four pounds. He
stuffed it into the barrel, where it fit just easily enough
to make a bit of rattling sound on the way down, until
the powder bag wadded enough to halt it.

Again, perfection was not an issue here. It so seldom was when the shit and lead began to fly. But while
Ryan didn't load and fire black powder cannon on a
regular basis, he'd seen the drill often enough to know

the salient points. And though optimum power didn't play into what he was fixing to do, the ramrod lay in carved-wood brackets on the same side of the weapon he was on, and Ryan grabbed it.

As he straightened, a blaster banged from the other patrol boat, a black powder longblaster from the sound. The ball didn't come close enough to hear, nor did it strike anything that made enough of a noise to be perceptible.

He ignored it. If they shot more small arms at him, they'd likely miss, too. If not—well, then he'd either deal with it, or he wouldn't be worrying about it anymore.

As he jammed the ball the rest of the way down the smoothbore, and tamped it once hard against the powder charge for good measure, he heard the steam engine of the boat he was on begin to chug. The boat slowly began to gather way up the river.

Ace on the line, he thought. They just keep making my job here easier.

Yellow flame flared from inside the cabin, right next to the spoked steering wheel. *That* shot zipped by the right side of his head.

"Fireblast!" he said, ducking. The best and closest available cover was the squat cannon itself. Unless the crew of this boat were more stupe and less trained than seemed likely, they would not have primed the initiator with powder, nor stuck a cap on the nipple before loading the cannon. But it still did not give him the best feeling to crouch in front of the bore of a loaded cannon.

Another shot blazed from inside the cabin. Time was

blood, and he was bleeding it out triple fast. He fired two quick shots toward where the flashes had come from. Both came from the same spot, so far as he could tell. He might have lowered his aim and punched the slugs through the thin wood of the wheelhouse, but he had no idea how the shooter's body was positioned, nor what ironmongery lay between the two of them. So if he couldn't chill the bastard, at least he'd make him keep his head down.

And in no way did Ryan intend to make himself an easy target. He moved from in front of the bow cannon in a forward roll, jettisoning the SIG's spent magazine as he did. He was likely going to lose that mag, and they were hard to replace, but it was small potatoes compared to catching the last train west.

Another shot rang out. This one went high. Ryan got back up to one knee, pulled a fresh magazine out of a belt pouch, jammed it up the waiting well and clicked the lever that let the locked-back steel slide slam home with a satisfying sound.

He lunged forward, catching himself on the jamb of the open portside hatch with his left hand, swinging around and leading with his blasterhand thrust into the cabin. He started firing as soon as he saw his target.

The muzzle-flashes illuminated a wide-eyed look of surprise in a blond-bearded face.

Terminal surprise. The man fell down away from Ryan, with the boneless rag doll flail of the well and truly chilled. His handblaster clattered to the deck right below the wheel.

Holstering his SIG, Ryan retrieved the blaster, a battered, remade Colt Navy revolver. That meant either two or three shots left, depending on whether the person who loaded it followed the common practice of leaving the hammer down on an empty cylinder for safety. He'd count on two and nuke it.

He stuffed the Colt down the front of his pants. That was definitely contrary to habit, and gave him a crawly feeling, even though the hammer was down. Since this was a single-action handblaster with a used chamber beneath it, it could only go off and blast his dick off if he snagged the hammer spur on his own clothes, and probably even then only if he had his finger on the trigger like a triple-stupe bastard. All the same it didn't feel good, even though he'd also slanted the long barrel away from his groin. Mostly to make it fit.

He grabbed the wheel and hauled on it. The vessel, moving slowly forward up the Sippi, began to turn to port. As it did, it crossed the bow of the other vessel, now about fifty feet away. That brought more exclamations. They might have been intending to fire on the boat he was on once their bow cannon came to bear, sister vessel or not. But even though it wasn't exactly moving fast, nobody was prepared for it to move at all.

Ryan guessed they were now frantically trying to reverse their turn, which was not a quick process, given the low relative speeds and the mass of their boat—and the water rolling against its hull. He stuck it out, only crouching when more longblasters boomed from the other craft. He kept the wheel cranked as his boat turned with gut-clenching deliberation.

He needed to do this to complete his plan to divert

the enemy from pursuing Krysty and the rest. Granted, he had already accomplished that, to a degree. But he wanted to give them the maximum time to get back to Wolf Creek. He doubted the New Vick blasterboats could even find it in the dark.

That meant he needed to stay and steer. The bow cannon had limited traverse, and as strong and adrenaline-hyped as he was, Ryan had no intention of trying to wrestle the fat bastard around on his own, so he had to aim the cannon by aiming the boat.

By the time he had the bow pointed at the other vessel he was almost due north of them, or so he reckoned. They were meanwhile still turning to their own starboard to line up their cannon again.

Letting the wheel go, he moved quickly back to the cannon. As expected, the primer flask and cap box were stored in a little open-topped wooden box, fastened to the deck just aft of the point at which the heavy-hawser arrestors would stop the big weapon from being blasted back through the front of the cabin by its recoil. He grabbed up both. Thumbing the cap off the flash, he slopped powder into the waiting primer pan. He covered it with the hinged, curved frizzen. Then he pulled back the hammer of the initiator and, standing as far to the side as he could just in case, stuck a cap on the steel nipple.

He picked up the lanyard. It was designed to allow him to step even farther to one side, which he did. Glancing up to make sure the other vessel was in front of his cannon, he turned his face away, stuck his left finger in his left ear, and hauled away on the lanyard.

The New Vick cannon-founders were belt-and-suspenders men. Cap-and-ball small arms didn't use a separate primer charge; the cap itself sent a spike of hot flame stabbing down into the propellant powder to set things moving. A lot of cannon did, too. But the smiths who made this piece wanted to make sure it went off when its crew wanted it to. So it used the cap to light a primer charge, to enhance the chances of getting the full charge in the barrel to go off.

It worked. The effect was as satisfying as Ryan could have hoped for: a world-shaking boom, a gush of flame the size of a derelict economy car, and the squatty little toad of a cannon jumping backward until its ropes caught it and brought it slamming to a halt in its track.

The shot struck the enemy wheelhouse between the midpoint and its starboard side. Planks splintered and chunks cartwheeled away into the night. Somebody screamed, maybe several somebodies. And even better, white steam suddenly enveloped the rear of the open-sided cabin and billowed up both sides of the roof, evoking a much shriller scream in a new voice. Briefly.

The round shot had either broken a fitting on the boiler, or cracked open the main tank itself. That was a better result than Ryan had even dared to hope for.

His triumph was short-lived. Inertia carried the prow of the oncoming boat around the last few degrees to point right at Ryan.

The fireball seemed to swallow up the world. He never even heard the sound of the actual cannon going off. Dazzled, he was aware of something long and dark and heavy—a chunk of something blasted off the rail—spinning toward his face.

It struck him full on, breaking his nose. Worse than the pain was the way the impact forced his head back almost hard enough to snap his neck. Not *quite*, though he felt the abused bones and cartilage creak.

It dropped him flat on his face on the deck. Stunned, his stomach surging with nausea, and completely unable to control his own body or even one of his limbs, Ryan was as helpless as a newborn babe—and barely aware enough to stay cognizant of the fact.

He lay there for what seemed like an eternity. He had no sense of time passing. It just felt *long.* Somehow.

The ache that filled his face and then his whole skull from front to rear told him he was starting to come back to himself from consciousness's Limbo.

And then rough hands were clamping on his still-jellylike arms, hauling him to his feet. Manacles closed on his wrists. He saw faces peering at him by lantern light at close range, some mottled and fisted with lethal rage, others somehow almost admiring.

And *then* the world got away from him, and the blackness took him.

Chapter Ten

With a sense as if her stomach was plummeting down a vast chasm and leaving the rest of her behind, Krysty watched Ryan fly through the air.

Helpless, and hating the fact, she held her breath as he struck the dark hull. A moment later had hauled himself up and over the rail.

She watched just long enough to see him explode into action, fast and lethal and thoroughly controlled. Then she turned her attention back to the power boat and the motley caravan of rafts and dinghy it towed. She had her own duties to perform. Failure to do so meant Ryan was sacrificing his—well, whatever this stunt would cost him—in vain.

"Cease-fire!" she yelled back to the trailing craft, which were now being drawn into a looping path away from the bigger vessel behind the launch. Abner was crowding his luck, pouring more power to the motor than was likely safe. But he knew his job the way Ryan knew his. He'd made that much clear. She trusted him because she had to.

"You might hit Ryan!"

Voices called back questions. One of them was Ricky's.

"Shut it down!" she snapped. "No more noise!"

She turned to Abner. "Once we're headed back south, cut back the power to keep down the noise. We won't outrun them."

"On it," he said.

Krysty looked back toward the enemy boats. The second one, off to the right, cast its wan spotlight beam onto the rafts of the little flotilla as they curved toward the eastern bank. She could see only the vaguest hints of light brush the gear and human bodies riding on them. She was concerned that the New Vick crew might open fire anyway, but for whatever reason they did not. They probably didn't want to risk a rocket from higher up the chain of command for wasting powder and shot on phantoms.

A flash snapped her gaze toward the first boat, the one Ryan was now aboard. A second followed almost at once. And then a third.

The sound of the first gunshot reached the launch, now nearing the shore and turning full north. Krysty relaxed. She was nowhere near the blaster expert Ryan and J.B. were. Nor even Mildred. But she *did* recognize the difference between the noise a smokeless blaster made and what a black powder one did.

And that meant it was almost surely Ryan doing the blasting.

The blasterfire continued at uneven intervals. Krysty sat tense, knuckles bloodless from her hands gripping the gunwales. She was unlikely to learn the outcome for sure until much later. But she couldn't tear her eyes away, even as Abner, who had as instructed backed off the throttle, proceeded north almost within touching distance of the weeds growing by the shore, at about the same pace they had traveled south.

The spotlight lantern, which no longer reached even as far as the dinghy following the launch and rafts last in line, winked out entirely. She saw fire flare aboard the second patrol boat, the one off to the right. Something was burning there, although the flames quickly diminished. Then more flashes from the first boat.

Then nothing.

Krysty waited, barely daring to breathe. It can't be over! she thought.

She refused to think further down that line. She always held that moral courage was more valuable by far than physical courage. To her surprise, Ryan seemed to agree—as, more surprisingly still, did J.B. Bravery was commonplace in Deathlands—and cowardice too, granted. In their own little group everybody was brave. But their real strength, so Krysty always thought, was the moral courage that kept them together, fighting for one another. And always fighting on, regardless of the odds.

But she didn't want to think what might have happened, that nothing more seemed to be.

And then two gigantic flashes went off, with barely the space of a heartbeat between. The glaze of the second overlapped the first's afterimage: they were that close to one another, or seemed to be at this distance.

The bass-drum booms of cannon going off, once, twice, reached her ears. And then a silence returned that seemed to stretch into eternity.

"He's gone!" Myron suddenly screamed. He cackled with a sort of insane, triumphant exultation. "Now you know what it's like to see your loved one die before your eyes! Now you know what my pain is like!"

She shifted her focus back inside the launch. She saw Abner's lips drawn back from his teeth, heard his dismayed and expectant hiss of indrawn breath. He clearly expected the redhead to unleash her full, righteous fury on the acting captain.

So, it seemed, did Myron Conoyer. No sooner had the words left his mouth than his eyes went wide, as if he had heard someone else say them, and his mouth dropped open in horrified anticipation.

But Krysty did not feel anger. Far less did she feel empty or numb. Instead a strange sense of peace filled her, a serene certainty that warmed her like fine brandy.

"He's not gone," she said calmly. "He said he would come back to me, and Ryan's a man who keeps his word."

She glanced back south. The only thing she could see above the blackness of the river was the glow of a now fully awakened New Vickville fleet.

"You'll see," she said. "You'll learn what so many people in the past have learned. *Never count Ryan Cawdor dead until you've seen his chill.*"

THE BLACK CLOTH bag that had covered Ryan's head since shortly after he had been seized aboard the patrol boat was whipped away. The shine of lanterns in the stateroom was almost blinding. He blinked his eye, trying to get it focused after having nothing but blackness to look at for hours of sitting in a chair. He was somewhere that smelled of wood, water, turpentine oil lamps burning and lavender.

He had come back into full possession of his faculties and strength quickly after he was hit in the face by what he could only surmise was a hunk knocked off the blasterboat's rail by the cannonball. But not quickly enough. He was already manacled and surrounded by angry men with black powder blasters aimed at his belly and face. He was somewhat amused to see one or two sailors with cutlasses.

Somebody spit in his face. He grinned. Voices snarled at one another that they should chill him then and there: shoot him, spit him, smash his head in with a mallet. Or just load his pants with cannonballs and chuck him over the side.

Ryan wasn't much concerned by that talk. Somebody had ordered him chained up proper. You didn't take that trouble with somebody you intended to murder out of hand. No matter how much hurt he'd laid on their comrades. And a pair of their armed patrol craft.

Granted, they might be saving him for some kind of excruciating torture later, but later was later. The key thing was that for now he was likely to be kept alive. The odds of his continued survival, minute to minute, were not much less than they had been every other moment of his long, eventful life. Even back in what he'd imagined to be the safe sanctuary of his father's baronial mansion back in Front Royal.

"Bring him aboard."

The cold, commanding voice came from the other boat.

As his awareness of his surroundings built back up, Ryan realized the vessel was now lying beam to beam with the one he'd 'jacked. He also realized with no little satisfaction that the return cannon shot that had taken him down had knocked the little cannon on the foredeck onto its side. It hadn't so much as dented it, that he could see. That didn't surprise him. Cannon had to be cast tough. And yet, for all the massive damage they could deal wood—or flimsy human flesh—they were fairly low-powered. It was why it only took a relatively light sheathing of scavvied plates to shrug off cannonballs.

He also realized, only a heartbeat tardy or two, that the voice was feminine.

A woman stood inside the rail of the other ship, trim and blaster-barrel rigid, though she looked no higher than Ryan's own shoulder. Her face was dark-skinned beneath her billed cap, which sported enough yellow bird-poop decoration to indicate rank, even if he couldn't read which one. He guessed it wasn't exalted, even if the black officer had command of the whole mess of little patrol boats.

But her expression, like her posture and her voice, left no doubt that she held the highest rank here.

"Get him aboard," she ordered. "And don't ding him. Not even a bruise or a scratch that he doesn't have already. His sorry ass is still more valuable to the fleet than yours is, for now."

"But why, Lieutenant?" one of the men holding Ryan's arms from behind whined.

"Because I said so."

Ryan felt his captor brace. "Sir, yes, sir!"

"When one man lays that much hurt on us," the lieutenant said, "intel is going to want a word with him. The baron might take an interest. Handle him accordingly."

The faces that had been turned toward Ryan were now all turned toward her. The anger and hate had all gone out of their postures.

"Shouldn't we hood him proper?" another one of Ryan's guards asked.

"Bring him aboard," the woman said. "Let him help get himself across. And *you*—"

She fixed the full force of her glare on Ryan. It was a pretty fair forceful glare, although it fell miles short of intimidating him. Then again, almost nothing on Earth ever did.

"If you act up or don't do your part, I give my crew permission to give you a couple of brisk butt strokes to your kidneys, so that you will be pissing blood up until the time it pleases the Baron Tanya Krakowitz of New Vickville you hang from the yardarm of the *Pearl*. Do I make myself clear?"

"Clear as glass," he said.

Ryan hadn't given his captors any trouble. He had stepped aboard the other ship as carefully as he could and submitted meekly when they stuffed a black cloth bag over his head and cinched it beneath his chin. It was coarse enough to let him breathe but not enough to let him see anything. There was plenty of play around his neck, as nobody cared to face the consequences of delivering a choked-out chill to his baron.

When the bag was finally removed, the person upon whom his eye finally focused was probably not Baron Tanya. Most likely she was another officer, this one as tall as Krysty, as trimly upright as the other, and her uniform as well turned out. Unlike the other, who had her hair hidden beneath her cap if she even had any, this woman left her severe blond bun uncovered. She was also young, fine-looking despite the professionally severe expression. Her posture, with her long, slender legs braced and her hands behind her back, was that of a person in charge *here*, not a person in charge overall. A baron's kid grew up knowing the difference almost by instinct.

"Who are you?" she asked. The footfall was cushioned by what seemed likely to be some kind of rug. The blonde officer clearly hadn't done it. And anyway a person in her position, whatever it precisely was, didn't pull the hoods off captives still reeking of gore and black powder—mostly other people's—herself.

"My name's Ryan Cawdor," he said. As a general rule he didn't like lying more than necessary. A person could easily be tripped up. And while he was reluctant to cede anything to an enemy, he also didn't see how knowing his name would help them. He cast his eye around the room. It was opulently furnished, with well-stuffed chairs and lanterns masquerading as fancy fixtures, and a series of paintings of various sizes adorned the walls. Most portrayed Greek gods, with very few goddesses among them, or clothes. The furniture, dark finished wood and dark green velvet upholstery, looked sturdy and well-made. Then again, it wasn't as if woodworking was some lost high-tech predark skill. The existence of this ship and her sisters, both large and small, gave testimony to that. Woodworking was a skill that survived the ages. When the world blew up, it became a very useful craft indeed, and as hardscrabble-poor as the world and its individual tribes and villes wound up, one that there was almost always a decent living to be had by following. So it survived, even where reading and other forms of conventional learning had not.

It was news he could use. Maybe.

The surroundings obviously belonged not just to somebody with the wealth and power to set them up and maintain them—or have those things done—but somebody who was squared away and cared about details. As opposed to a slovenly, drunk-ass brute of a baron—the far more commonplace kind. It was a stateroom belonging to the sort of baron it would take, say, to muster a battle fleet that was both massive and massively armed by Deathlands standards, and boss them in battle. Even if you fell backward into the job—inheriting from your dead baron husband.

"You have the advantage over me," he said to the officer.

She looked blank for a moment. Then she smiled, though not in any yielding way.

"I'm Flag Lieutenant Ellin Stone," she said.

"Why am I here?"

She didn't play any "I ask the questions here" games. She straightaway said, "You're awaiting the baron's pleasure. She wants to know how a single man could wreak so much havoc among her patrol personnel. And vessels."

That lack of overt bullying suggested she was comfortable in her, and her boss's, seemingly unassailable grasp on the upper hand. Her comfort was not unwarranted—right then. Ryan's wrists had been unchained when he was brought aboard the bigger ship. But his hands had been tied, as well as his ankles, once he was deposited in the chair. And a boat crew knew knots the way J. B. Dix knew blasters. He wasn't getting free on his own.

At least they were more comfortable than the shackles, although the ropes chafed his wrists some.

"Anybody can get lucky, once in a while," he said.

She scoffed. "I wouldn't try that line on the baron, Mr. Cawdor. She is no fool. Nor is she an empty-headed former gaudy slut who caught an older baron's eye, no matter what your employers may have told you."

"Why would my employers tell me something like that?"

She frowned. "Poteetville. You work for them, don't you?"

"You mean the bunch with the other fleet of nuking big ships with scrap iron bolted all over them?"

Her frown deepened at that description. He suspected her duties were more involved with waiting on the baron as an aide than nautical matters. But she still clearly felt pride in the New Vick fleet.

He shook his head. He had meant to dent her composure, and had.

"I don't work for them."

"Who does employ you, then? You're a mercie, right?"

Time to lie. He had already worked it out in advance. The lie was one the lieutenant and her baron would be predisposed to believe, so they weren't likely to question it.

Not that it was even that big a lie, much as he hated to admit it to himself.

He nodded. "Nobody you'd know. A trading ship down off the Yazoo, a tugboat hauling a big barge loaded with wood and cloth. Or were."

"Ah. The barge that burned between our fleets."

"That's the one."

"What were you doing out there tonight, then?"

"The tug got blown to nuke by cannon from both sides," he said. "We managed to get in close to shore before it sank and hid in the weeds along the Sippi while the two sides sorted things out between them."

He didn't know the details of how that worked out, of course. But he reckoned Stone did, and would feel no need to ask.

"We spent the next couple days salvaging what timber we could from the hulk, then cobbled it together into a few rafts and tried sneaking south past your fleet."

Stone cocked a finely arched brow at him. "Evidently you didn't expect our patrols to be so alert."

Evidently we didn't reckon our luck would go so far south so fast, he thought. If they were triple alert, they had a nuking peculiar way of showing it.

He shrugged. "Evidently."

"You seem...well-spoken for a man in your... profession."

Professional coldheart, you mean, Ryan thought.

"Let's say I didn't always do what I do now."

"So tell me, then, Ryan Cawdor," a husky female voice said from behind, "what possessed a mercie to single-handedly attack one of my blasterboats while your employers turned tail and scuttled for safety?"

Chapter Eleven

Ryan craned his head around as heavy heels tapped on the deck. The rugs beneath muffled the sound but didn't eliminate it.

"Baron Vickville, I presume," he said.

"The same."

When the same cloying floral essence he'd been breathing in through the bag over his head the past hour—which was admittedly an improvement over stale former-captive saliva—got abruptly much stronger, right before the hood came off, he hadn't needed more clues to follow the plot.

He also reckoned she hadn't pulled the bag off his head, any more than her high-assed assistant had. As she almost at once confirmed.

"You may leave us now, Dogbert," she said grandly.

"Yes, ma'am," a subservient male voice said. The heavy oak door to the stateroom opened and closed.

"You and the lieutenant aren't afraid of being alone with a dirty, desperate mercie?" he asked.

She laughed, a quick, deep sound.

"I find myself beset by enemies on every side," she said. "Not just that tin-sword Napoleon, Baron Harvey Poteet. But my own magnates who are supposed to be the staunch upholders of New Vickville. They claim I am nothing but a usurper, and seek every excuse and opportunity to pull me down. Do you think if I didn't trust myself, not to mention the exceedingly competent Lieutenant Stone and her sidearm, to keep me safe from a mercie, however desperate, however dirty, who also happens to be bound hand and foot, that I'd have kept the barony as long as I have?"

"Aren't you running a risk telling me that kind of thing?"

This time her laugh was full-throated.

"If I should decide such knowledge in your possession might pose a danger to me," she said, "it and you can go over the side, triple easy, with five hundred pounds of ballast tied to you."

She took her place across the room and a low table from him in what he suspected was the grandest chair, and crossed one plump leg over another.

"Now, Mr. Cawdor," she said, "perhaps you can enlighten me as to how a landless vagabond coldheart such as yourself happened to nearly write off two of my patrol boats and somewhere upward of a dozen of my officers and crew? We don't even know the total butcher's bill yet. And I shall reiterate my earlier question—once. Why?"

"It's my job. I get paid to do it. And I'm very good at what I do."

"That much seems obvious."

He was sizing her up, now that he could do more than infer her presence by smell. She was on the goodly side of medium height, a couple inches shorter than Krysty, allowing for the short, dark blond hair pomaded into sort of a low crest on top of her head. She wore a velvet jacket and pants that matched the upholstery, and may have been made of the same cloth, over a yellow blouse with a ruffled front and low-heeled black half boots. It struck him as being as practical as it was swank and comfy. She could move in it if she had to. She was definitely bigger around the middle than at the ends. But she was nowhere in the grossly obese category of other barons he had encountered—Jordan Teague came to mind. Nor did she appear to be the sadistic slob he had been. Still, he judged she had never been a lightweight, not even of the well-muscled kind Stone's well-tailored uniform revealed her to be. The late baron had to have favored a sturdy woman.

She did strike him, pampered baron or not, former gaudy slut or not, as a woman who packed a mean punch. And knew how to deliver one. If she did turn out to be sadistic, he reckoned she'd be anything but sloppy at it.

Some might consider her to be a handsome woman, if decidedly overly caked and rouged. Her eyes were probably large and green enough—darker than Krysty's—not to need the green paint she'd surrounded them with. Her painted lips seemed to settle into a smile that was neither cruel nor smirking, though he also would never mistake her for gentle. Or soft.

"So you did your job," she said. "And you do appear to be good at it indeed. But why in that way?"

"Your boats had us dead to rights. They could blow us all out of the water in half a second, with nothing we could do about it. And we already noticed how quick on the trigger your people were."

"Think of it as the predator's reflex," she said. "If the prey runs, they pounce."

"Yeah. Well. They struck me as already primed to pounce, with nothing else required. You know how they say to run away from a knife, but charge a blaster?"

She nodded. "Generally sound advice, I find, too," she murmured.

"Well, I calculated that a cannon is nothing but a big blaster. So I decided to charge."

"And after your employers ran off and left you to die?"

He uttered a wolf grunt of a laugh. "I didn't think your crew would be in any hurry to embrace me," he said, "seeing as I already chilled a couple of them to open our acquaintance. So I decided it was do-or-die."

"So you weren't trying to cover their escape?"

He laughed at that. "Theirs? I was trying to pull off my own."

She actually goggled at him. She looked to her aide, who stood not far from her right shoulder, just beyond a round table with a silver tray holding a cut-crystal decanter and several glasses. Stone shook her head.

"Are you suggesting, Mr. Cawdor," the baron said, looking back at him, "that you intended to hijack the *Yarville* and use it to make your getaway?"

"I *did* hijack it, Baron. It was the getting-away part where I ran into difficulty."

She stared at him. After an increasingly uncomfortable interval he began to wonder if he'd overplayed his hand. Then again, it wasn't as if he had much to lose, under the circumstances.

Then she started laughing.

He didn't join in. He didn't feel that faking his way along with her would help his cause. Baron Tanya was shaping up as a person who liked a man hard enough to maintain a cool attitude in his position—not defiant, necessarily, but the opposite of servile. And wherever his best shot at getting back to his friends and getting them out of this mess lay, aiming for Dogbert's job as butler was triple sure not it.

"I like you, Cawdor," she said. "You're my kind of asshole."

She uncrossed her legs and sat forward, putting her hands on her meaty, green-clad thighs.

"Come work for me."

"Why?" he asked warily.

"You're a mercie. I pay well for value."

"I mean, why would you offer me a job, instead of a bullet in the head? Or a quick trip to the bottom of the Sippi. I chilled a bunch of your people and messed up your boats."

Her dark green eyes met his steadily. "Their job is to die for New Vickville," she said. "If necessary. But their main job was to control the situation, not to get overrun by a one-man army. I don't feel good about the dead and wounded, but I don't blame you. You faced a threat, and you responded, which was better than two boatloads of my sailors did."

He sat back and looked at her. The persona he was choosing to present would be skeptical of the baron's apparent readiness to forgive, and would be shrewd enough to look over an offer to see if it sounded too good to be true—and if it did, to know that it *was*.

"You're dubious," she said.

"I'd be triple stupe not to be, wouldn't I, Baron?"

He glanced briefly at Stone. She stood by watching with a stern expression that he guessed amounted to neutral. Maybe she put it on and took it off with her snappy blue-green uniform. Maybe she didn't. But she wasn't giving away her own assessment of him or the situation for glowing nuke shit.

Fair enough. There was one boss in this room, and it wasn't her, as he had calculated all along. She might have influence over her baron, but Tanya Krakowitz was clearly headstrong, and inclined to make up her own mind.

The baron stood again.

"Here's how I see it," she said. "I think you laid your ass on the line for your former bosses. You could've started hollering surrender, or just dived in the river and swum for the shore."

Not with those bastard crocs in there, he thought. Although he didn't for a fact know if they inhabited this stretch of the big river, or merely stayed up Wolf Creek, for whatever obscure reason. He was too battered and wily to say anything that might expose his companions' hiding place. "So you went on the attack—" she was clearly warming to her narrative "—because, as you say, you thought it was the best way to do your job. Then your employers cut stick and ran off on you.

And you single-handedly set out to whip two blaster-boats full of crew and came close to doing it.

"If you were a Poteetville sailor who'd done that, you'd be treated as a prisoner of war. We're not stone-hearts. A lot of my people would admire you for your grit and skill, even if it was their comrades you chilled. You fought like a tiger, and there's too much eyewitness testimony to doubt the fact.

"If you were Baron Harvey's sworn man, stuck-up little prickamouse that he is, and you offered to turn your coat for money, I probably would send you to feed the channel catfish. But you're a professional. You have no reason to love your former employers, much less stay loyal to them. The way they ran out on you."

He tipped his head back to the plush back of the chair. "I have to tell you, I'm not exactly at my best right now," he said. "I had kind of a long day. I need time to think on it. And that's the only answer I can give you, even if it earns me a ticket to go meet the six-foot cats at the bottom of the Sippi."

She laughed. "They go bigger than that, hereabouts. I'm not offering to hire you on because you're a stupe or a simp. I admire your balls and your skill, but what I need is brains to go with."

She picked up the decanter and swirled the dark fluid that filled it just past halfway around its square, fac-eted sides.

"What do you say we have a drink and just chew the fat? You look like a man with a story to tell. Or even two."

Mutely Ryan held up his wrists.

"Oh," Baron Tanya said. "Right. Ellin, if you'll do the honors?"

Stone did not look thrilled to be setting free a captive who still had traces of the blood of so many of her comrades mostly dried on his face and clothes, but she also didn't raise any kind of objection. With the air of a person who knew how things would turn out if she did, she clicked open a lock-back folding knife and deftly severed the ropes binding Ryan's wrists. She didn't even nick his skin.

He suspected that had more to do with her own sense of professional pride than concern for him.

The baron poured them both drinks by hand. Stone freed his ankles with the same icy precision, so he got up, teetered briefly as full circulation came rushing back into his feet like a tide of pins and needles, and went and collected his goblet.

"Cognac," she said. "Made by some kind of sect of old-time hermits in the Zarks. Surly bastards, but everyone leaves them alone, because distilling this booze is their tight little secret." She shook her head. "It's triple smooth, and tastes just like angels' piss. Prosit!"

So he told her stories that had her eyes bugging out and her gut busting in equal measure. Sometimes at the same time. Some of them were true. Some had even happened to him.

Baron Tanya undertook to drink him under the table.

He let her think she had.

When he let his head loll back, and a well-practiced fake snore escape his slack and stubbled jaws, he heard her chortle softly to herself in triumph.

"So our new pet superman has his limits," she said, her speech showing little sign of the various forms of hard liquor—none on the remotest par with any so base a beverage as Towse Lightning—she'd been pouring for them. "Ace on the line, too. I was starting to feel it myself."

Stone said nothing. She had sat by the whole time, simply watching. And listening. Ryan doubted much got by her. The baron likely didn't employ her to be stupe, either. Nor a simp. And her thoughts and feelings were no more accessible to Ryan than if she'd been a weathered stone lion in front of some long-derelict city hall in some nuked-out megacity of old.

Putting her hands on her thighs, the baron hoisted her bulk aloft with a grunt.

"Get some sailors in here to drag the carcass out of here. Put him in the spare cabin a deck down and lock the hatch and door."

"Baron?"

"He hasn't said yea or nay yet, Lieutenant. And I'm nuked if I'm going to trust him until he does. He's too sly and too bold, all at once. It's a rare combination and a dangerous one."

There was a pause, during which Ryan's skin crawled as if he could feel her scrutiny. He put it down to a subconscious reaction to pretty near stone certainty she was doing exactly that.

"How I hope he does say yes, Elli," she said softly. "You know how badly we need a man like him on our side."

Chapter Twelve

The ride back to their campsite was one of the longest of Krysty's life, subjectively speaking, as the sky in the east had not yet begun to lighten as Abner steered them deftly toward the hand-expanded clearing.

The journey had been spent in almost total silence, after Myron's grief-maddened outburst, which allowed uncertainty to worm its way inside her mind. The peaceful conviction that nothing…irreversible… would happen to Ryan, because he wouldn't *let* it, had long since disappeared.

After a quick glance at the acting captain, who was curled into an almost fetal-tight ball of misery, Abner maneuvered past the grounded *Mississippi Queen*, whose stern was slanted downstream. That allowed him to clear the vessel and pull as far as possible into the shallows close to shore, in order to pause briefly to allow the occupants to debark one or two rafts at a time, and still let them ashore within the cleared space.

Krysty was not offended that Abner hadn't asked her for orders. She was relieved. *He* was the small-boat guru. She reckoned he'd know best, as he clearly did.

As he turned the launch to port, Jak suddenly said, "Wait!" from the second raft.

"Ma'am?" Abner asked softly. She held up a hand.

Myron raised his face from his palms. "What? What is it?"

She just shook her head, quickly, as if trying clear hair from her face. Jak jumped off the raft with a prodigious splash, and began wading in knee-deep water. Visions of gigantic crocodiles sliding eagerly and unseen toward a serendipitous midnight snack almost closed her throat. Then it registered how alarmed *he* had to be to raise a wave and a racket like that. He normally went into water with no noise and scarcely a ripple.

He had barely taken a step onto dry land when he froze. His head went left, then began to track slowly clockwise as he scanned the tall grass on the perimeter of the camp.

"Stickie sign," he said.

Suzan gasped. She might not have been the only one.

"We have to get out of here!" Sean yelped from the first raft.

"Where to?" J.B. asked almost conversationally from the tail-end boat, where he rode with Mildred, Nataly and the jovial giant, Santee.

"Anywhere!" the red-haired mechanic said. "I hate stickies. I can't stand those sucker-tip fingers they got. I can't let them get me, I can't!"

"Ma'am?" Abner said again. Since this was clearly a matter of security, he deferred to her, as she had deferred to him mere seconds before.

"Ease back off the trigger of the blaster there, Sean," Arliss said, patting his back in the way you might gentle a frightened horse. "They're not here now."

His head jerked up and around as a thought hit him. "Are they?"

"Gone now," Jak said firmly. "But—not far, mebbe."

Krysty drew her Glock 18 and thumbed the selector switch down to full-auto.

"I'm going to check things out," she said, climbing gingerly over the side of the small boat. "J.B., Mildred, cover us. Ricky, Doc—keep eyes skinned outward. We don't want to assume the only threats come from the land. Nataly and Arliss, would you come with me?"

"I've chilled stickies," Santee called from the dinghy, raising his hand.

"Come on, then. Hopefully though, you won't have to."

She walked up next to Jak, who was still standing where he'd stopped, legs slightly bent, taking in the scene as thoroughly as he could. Her skin crawled with every step she took that had *water* under it.

Attuned as she was to nature, Krysty was not the tracker Jak was. Nobody was. Not even in their tight-knit group. But she saw some of what had halted him, right off: weird, splayed impressions where the short grass was sparse, looking almost like handprints.

Stickies, all right. Not that Krysty had doubted Jak's assessment. Even in the darkness she could make out a number of the tracks, as far around the site as her eyes could see.

Nataly and Arliss joined Krysty, the first mate with her Ruger Old Army blaster in hand, the rigger with his lever-action Marlin carbine. Then Santee came up, swinging the ax he'd taken from the cargo raft up to his shoulder as if it were a willow switch.

"What did they do to the campfire?" he said.

They had buried the campfire, or its ashes, thoroughly and deep before departing. There was no compelling reason to. It wasn't as if potential hostile eyes could sweep the clearing without seeing a sure sign they'd been here, and frankly, it hadn't been worth their energy to make the effort to try. But that was just a habit people got into if they traveled around a lot, as everyone in the whole party surely did. You buried your ashes every time, if you liked the idea of not burning to death in your own accidental wildfire, even if fire wasn't a clear and present danger here in the middle of the swamp.

But the ashes weren't buried anymore. Dead and long-cold though they were, they had been scooped up and scattered across a ten-foot radius, leaving a funnel-shaped depression where the fire had been.

Krysty had Santee and Nataly go right a few paces, and she and Arliss went left, staying near the water, to take up positions there to cover Jak as he prowled around the site.

"Good thing we buried the heavy cargo, huh?" Avery called from his raft.

"You said it, man," Santee agreed.

There had been some controversy over that. Ryan had insisted that anything too heavy to travel easily on a small raft had to be left behind—Avery said that given the resources at hand, they were a lot better off making several small rafts than one big one. Arliss had objected to that. Some of that cargo, in particular the outsize Lahti antitank rifle in its casket-like box, was worth a fortune.

"I don't see that a fortune does a body much good," J.B. had observed in his usual laconic style, "if you get chilled trying to hang on to it."

Nataly and, after a little prodding, Myron, had backed Ryan. Arliss hadn't stuck on the point. He was neither greedy nor stupe. It was just his job to keep the balance sheet in mind, which was all the more necessary since his friends and bosses, the late Captain Trace and her husband, so often lost sight of it. He had acknowledged the truth of J.B.'s observation with a rueful grin.

Ricky, his young mind filled with fever visions of pirate treasure—granted, he came from a part of the world where pirate treasure was a real thing, as were pirates, for that matter—suggested burying it.

"Stickies don't dig," J.B. had said. So they loaded the rafts with their personal gear, or such of it as had survived—Krysty's and her friends' had all come through intact—along with necessities, and whatever cargo would fit. The rest they'd buried.

And there it remained. Or at least there was no sign that the ground had been disturbed since they tamped it down over the buried goods.

"But I thought J.B. said stickies didn't dig?" Arliss said in a bantering tone.

"They usually don't," Krysty stated.

"In all probability," Doc said from his raft, "they were expressing their rage at being denied a chance to play with fire. Frustration drives them to frenzy. They might have even expected to find coals still live."

"Be a good trick," Santee said, "staying on fire all buried like that."

"Who knows what goes on in a stickie's mind?" Abner asked.

Once Jak pronounced the area clear, the rest of the party came ashore. And no sooner had they done so than Krysty was stricken leaden-limbed by exhaustion.

Judging by the way the others' shoulders began to sag, when the immediate sense of danger had passed, she was far from the only one.

But not everybody accepted that the danger had passed. "We can't stay here," Sean muttered. "The bastards came here once. They'll come back, sure as glowing night shit."

"What would you have us do?" Arliss asked. He was starting to sound exasperated with his friend.

The mechanic just shook his head. "I don't know. I just want to get out of here."

"We need rest," Mildred said flatly. "When you get this tired, your judgment goes to pot. Tempers get thin. You spook easily. You don't want to be making decisions in that kind of condition, and you especially don't want to be around people waving blasters in that kind of state!"

"But how can we rest?" Sean demanded. His voice was shrill. It was almost as if he were compelled somehow to prove Mildred right. "If we sleep, the stickies will night creep us. And their sucker fingers will pull the skin right off our faces. From our faces!"

"Well, that is a thing that happens," J.B. said. "But if some of us keep good watch, we can discourage that sort of thing." He hefted his Uzi one-handed to show what he meant by discouragement.

"First watch," Jak said.

"Are you sure that's a good idea?" Nataly asked. "You always seem to have the watch. And while mebbe you don't need as much sleep as the rest of us, you need some."

"Once we got away from those New Vickville boats," Ricky called back over his shoulder from where he stood at the water's edge, keeping watch out over Wolf Creek, "he went right to sleep. Stayed that way the whole time."

"I thought he was always alert," Arliss said.

"As Nataly says, even Jak needs to sleep sometimes," Krysty added. "But floating back on the raft he didn't see much point in keeping watch. So he got some sleep."

"But I can't sleep here!"

"*Easy*, Sean," Arliss cautioned him.

"We don't have to."

The words, softly spoken, came from an unlikely source. Myron Conoyer stood hard by the waterline, as if daring his wife's killer to come take him to join her.

"What do you mean, Captain?" Nataly asked.

He waved at the grounded tug. "We can sleep aboard the *Queen*."

"You sure that's a good idea?" Mildred asked.

"Well, it is more defensible," J.B. told her.

"Yeah, but how do we know it's not crawling with stickies? Maybe they thought it was a nice place for a new nest."

"To say nothing of their habit of fouling human habitations when they intrude upon them," Doc added.

"Check out," Jak said. His manner made it clear even to the *Queen*'s crew that he meant he would do it.

"I'll go with you," J.B. said. "Everybody else, stick tight." After a moment's consideration he unslung his Smith & Wesson M-4000 riot shotgun, and slung the submachine gun.

"Just the two of you?" Jake asked. "Isn't that suicide, if there are stickies aboard?"

"Son," J.B. said, "the first sign of stickies, and I will be back here a lot faster than we left. No heroes in this bunch."

"No stupes," Jak agreed.

"But what if you have to go in the water and there are crocs?" Arliss asked.

"We'll use them for stepping stones," J.B. said.

But, miraculously, they soon reported to the group that there were no stickies aboard the partially burned-out boat, nor sign any had been aboard her. Krysty didn't believe in miracles, as such, but in her present frame of mind she was willing and ready to give heartfelt if silent thanks to Gaia for the gift.

They tethered the launch and the boats to the *Queen*'s stern in a cluster. Then leaving Jak and an uneasily wakeful Sean on watch, they found berths on deck or below.

Krysty laid out her bedroll by the stern rail. She couldn't remember when she felt so grateful for the relative softness and comfort of its embrace, with her rolled-up jacket for a pillow. This is probably the first time we've got a chance to rest after our last slow dance with death, she thought.

She felt herself plummeting toward sleep as though she'd stepped off a cliff, her last thoughts of Ryan.

"The Grand Fleet, Mr. Cawdor," Baron Tanya said, waving expansively to left and right. "The pride of New Vickville."

The sky was bright blue, with a wash of thin green and mauve chem clouds here and there. The morning air was still actually cool. The westerly breeze was stiff. It ruffled Ryan's hair as he stood by the rail on the flying bridge, atop and at the front of the flagship's multistory superstructure, and made the blue-and-white New Vickville flags flap loudly.

It also stank of carrion. The smell was stomach-wrenching even over the smell of the fires keeping the fleet's boilers warm for instant action. Something big, or a lot of something small, had to have died out there recently. Ryan had no idea what. The baron seemed not even to notice, which made him wonder if it was a regular occurrence here.

"Impressive," he said, because it was.

At least all that smell of dying gives me no cause to worry about Krysty and the others, he thought. They were to the north of here, and downwind to boot. Not that he worried much, anyway. His companions could take care of themselves with or without him, and the *Mississippi Queen*'s crew was keen on survival, unless grief drove Myron Conoyer over the edge and he did something stupe. Ryan didn't worry much. He'd learned early on it only ate up energy and brain-time that might have been better used thinking of a solution to whatever was causing the worry in the first place. Worrying never make things better.

"To our left," the baron said, "you see the *Clytemnestra*, an armored frigate with eight cannon. To our right, the proud *Medusa*, her sister ship."

Sister seemed a relative term. *Clytemnestra* had a markedly lower superstructure than *Medusa*. Both had been armored in whatever appropriate gauge iron and steel scrap happened to be available when they were being fitted, and appeared, more or less, in good shape. Still, they looked huge—and Ryan was looking down at both from his vantage point.

Of course, huge was relative, too. Any respectable predark tramp freighter was bigger than even the *Pearl*. To say nothing of the true monsters of the sea he'd encountered in his day, like derelict cruise ships or thousand-foot supertankers. But context mattered. On this stretch of the river, the baron's gaggle of slow, cobbled-together ironclads ruled unchallenged.

Except of course for the opposing fleet of armored war craft, lying plainly visible perhaps two miles south, just before the point where a bend in the big river began. The wind kept the smoke haze largely clear.

"Around us, you can see a few of our attendants— *Artemis*, *Hera*, *Revenge*, *Selene*, *Midori*. All six-cannon frigates, and all satellites to my beautiful flagship here, the *Pearl*."

The "frigates" were notably smaller than the so-called capital ships. But Ryan thought about how they'd have looked from the deck of the *Queen*—much less her bitty motor launch—and he got a queasy feeling in his stomach and a dryness in his throat.

"You seem to have a classical turn of mind," he said, "leaving aside a few fliers."

"Well, *Revenge* was a Poteetville ship. I took her myself as a prize from the Invincible Armada, back when my poor dear husband, Baron Si, was alive and ruling New Vickville. I was no mere trophy wife, you see."

She shrugged.

"Or not *just* a trophy wife."

"'Si.'"

"Short for Silas. We're less formal than those Poteetville snobs, with all their pretensions at aristocracy. A passel of phonies with sticks up their butts. And I notice that you recognize the classical allusions, Mr. Cawdor."

"I told you, I wasn't always a mercie."

"As for *Midori*, I like the name. I heard it means 'green' in Japanese."

"Yeah," Ryan said, rubbing his chin. His stubble was getting long enough the hairs were beginning to flop over and not even be prickly anymore. Much longer without a shave and he was going to start looking like a skunk-ape.

"What about *Pearl*?" he asked. "Shouldn't your flagship have a classical name, too?"

"Oh, but she does. She's named for the classical predark character Pearl Forrester. I saw her on a couple of old vids when I was a girl. She became quite the inspiration and role model for me."

Ryan had no idea who the character was, so he leaned

his arms on the rail and gazed out at the distant Poteet-ville fleet.

Invincible Armada, huh? he thought. I'm guessing Baron Harvey doesn't read history. Or doesn't read enough.

"I appreciate the guided tour, Baron," he said. "And I've got to admit that your fleet's an impressive enough sight that I'm glad I got my first real look at it from this side. But I do find myself wondering why the baron of New Vick and commander of that fleet is spending so much time on a dirty, desperate mercie like me."

"Not quite so dirty anymore, I'd say," she said with a grin.

They'd washed his clothes overnight, and let him bathe in the room devoted to the purpose on that deck, while a pair of armed sailors stood watch. But either the baron or whoever her sec boss was—Stone didn't seem the type—didn't trust him with a razor in his hand quite yet. So the stubble grew.

He turned and leaned his elbows back on the rail. That brought Stone into view, standing impassively behind them just beyond earshot, and also the pair of honest-to-nuke sec men who stood flanking her. They wore the same blue-green uniforms as the sailors, but they carried lever-action .44-40 carbines with matching 1873 Colt Peacemaker replicas in flapped holsters on their belts. They were black powder weapons, charcoal burner, but cartridge repeaters, not single-shot muzzle loaders or the single-shot Springfield 1873s with the trapdoor actions. They were serious blasters, even by modern standards, and not the sort of weapon that would be issued to random sailors told to watch the baron's pet coldheart captive.

"What did you bring me up here for?" he asked.

She nodded decisively. "You want turkey? We'll talk turkey."

She shooed her aide and the sec men farther back.

The baron went to lean on the rail beside him. At least her lavender body wash or whatever it was tended to cut the rotting-meat smell. "Like I said, there you see the Poteetville fleet. They outnumber us every which way, from Baron Harvey J. Poteet Junior's flagship, *Tyrant*, and her twin, *Glory*, and the lesser capital ships *Invincible* and *Conqueror*, down through frigates like the *Terror* and *Bocephus*, through a gaggle of unarmed patrol craft on down to the garbage scow, the *Baron Harvey J. Senior*."

"Garbage scow?"

She shrugged. "Harvey has daddy issues. Among others, given some of those ship names. I wonder if the Poteet males pass along under-endowment from one generation to the next. We have bigger cannon. We can put as much metal in the air at a time as they can, though they have four capital ships to our three, and ten frigates to our nine. Our weapons, ships and gunners are superior, however."

She paused to light a black cigarillo in an ebony cigarette holder from a spring-driven mechanical lighter.

"Of course, I'd naturally say that. My point is they are a formidable enemy, and their intent is to destroy New Vick as a sovereign riverine power. But they are not the only deadly enemy. There is another enemy who is intent upon destroying me in person. They're to be found on this side of the water, Mr. Cawdor."

"Why not take them down, then?"

"If only it were so simple. My enemies include some of New Vick's leading citizens, as well as the captains of some of my very fleet, and they're the snakes I know about. They are either too well hidden or too powerful to touch—unless I can catch them in the act, which in itself supposes that my best evidence is also the last, by seeing the faces of those who plant their daggers in my back."

Ryan wondered how a body could see the face of someone who was stabbing them in the back, but he caught her drift.

"You have a sec boss." It wasn't a question. She might not be a usual baron, but she was every inch one.

"Barleycorn," she said. "A good man, loyal and meticulous. He'd lay down his life for me. He is also unimaginative as an old oak stump."

"And?"

She sighed gustily, puffing out blue smoke like a restive dragon.

"I need a man of your talents on my team."

"You need a new sec man?" He carefully did not say "boss."

"I need a new *everything*. My enemies give me no peace, and they are not considerate enough to take turns. As soon as I turn to face the latest attack, the other is thrusting at me with their spears. Do you begin to see my situation, Mr. Cawdor?"

"Yeah. You want a problem solver."

Her face lit up. She was still handsome, that was sure, even if in an overstuffed, painted-up way.

"Exactly! And I am prepared to offer—whatever you want, within reason. And I have broad standards of reasonableness that include gold, property, women, even power. I can't offer you a title, not one that would mean anything. That's Poteetville's style, not ours. And our plutocrats would never accept you as an equal. Unless of course I was able to catch one of them at treason and squash him like the roach he is."

She brightened visibly at that.

"I believe I've about burned up my considering time," Ryan told her.

"You have."

"What if I don't want that kind of responsibility? Do you have any openings for a grunt?"

She laughed. "You're far too dangerous to be a common sailor, a soldier, or sec man. Strange as it sounds to say it, I can trust you completely, or not at all.

"Please understand my position with regards to you, Mr. Cawdor. I find myself in the position of the lady riding the tiger. I dare not dismount."

She suddenly grinned. "Don't look at me like that with that dangerous blue eye. You are a magnificent hunk of masculine lethality, and not at all my type. I prefer my men younger, tenderer and blond. Your duties to me would be strictly professional."

The grin faded. "But from where I stand, I can either bind you to me with whatever appeals to you—or bind you to ballast stones headed for the bottom of the Sippi. Do you honestly see a third way?"

"Not offhand."

"So there you have it. The carrot and the stick, as it were."

"Put that way," he said, "I'll take the carrot."

He reckoned he had played hard to get long enough. She had reminded him of just how baronial she could be, with all that ballast-in-a-bag talk, and getting to know the legendary channel cats. And how ruthless she'd had to be to hold on to her position, once her husband died and the sharks began to circle.

She turned and stuck out her hand. "I knew you were a smart man. The lieutenant will return your weapons."

He shook. Her grip was strong. He expected no less.

Smart enough to try to see all the angles, he was thinking. While going over the rail into a stolen rowboat some night was still the likeliest option for getting out of there and back to his friends—or just getting sent on some mission ashore and slipping away, leaving any comrades who thought to bar his way behind with extra smiles—he was beginning to glimpse a new, if distant possibility: that he might distinguish himself enough that, as a reward, he could negotiate safe passage out for him and his friends. And even the *Queen*'s old crew, since there'd be no point in cutting one loose but not the other.

That was a tall order, given how little time he had before his friends found their own way out—or the rads got them. Or the stickies. But Ryan could distinguish himself a triple load, triple fast.

"Does this mean I get a room that doesn't lock from the outside?"

"Not yet."

"But you said you'd either trust me all the way, or no way."

"There's trust," she said, "and then there's trust. You still have to earn the full consignment. Lieutenant Stone, please show our new, ah—special consultant—around."

"Yes, Baron."

She seemed neither pleased nor displeased. That high-cheekboned, broad-jawed face might as well have been the beautiful sculpture it resembled.

But what was the light he glimpsed behind those dark brown eyes?

Chapter Thirteen

"But what can we *do*?"

The words—almost a wail of despair—penetrated the fog inside Doc Tanner's tormented mind, but only barely.

He was walking through Hyde Park arm in arm with his beloved Emily, while their children, Rachel and Jolyon, trailed behind, his daughter excitedly pointing out features of the great glass-and-iron Crystal Palace, that wonder of the world and jewel in Great Britain's imperial diadem.

"If you both quiet down and behave," their mother told them, "we shall take you to see the dinosaurs!"

"Dinosaurs!" Rachel shouted.

Emily sighed. "At least the spectacle—and the prospect of dinosaurs—is distracting them from all the bearded, smelly anarchists squawking from their soapboxes for the workers of the world to unite. Isn't that a boon, dear?"

"Pardon? Why, yes, my darling. Of course." He himself was barely paying attention to his surroundings or even his adored family. He was engrossed in an article in The Times of London, concerning a private prosecution for libel the day's most famous Irish poet had

brought against the Marquess of Queensberry, for leaving at his club a calling card on which he had scrawled "For Oscar Wilde, posing somdomite."

He stirred himself from his daydream, back to the here and now. It would be less unpalatable than continuing where his thoughts had taken him. Yes, as horrible as his current reality was…

"We have to do something!"

Doc recognized the near-panicked voice of Sean O'Reilly. He fears stickies to the verge of outright phobia, Doc remembered. Not that there's anything inherently irrational in that.

"We all realize that, Sean," Nataly replied calmly.

Doc focused his gaze on her tall, slim, upright figure. She was the functional acting captain much of the time, when that poor wretch Myron was sunk in the twin miseries of losing his ship and his wife on the same dire day.

"And it leaves the question of *what*," Arliss said.

"Get out!" Sean yelled.

"We know," Mildred said patiently. "If the stickies don't kill us, the radiation and heavy-metal poisoning will."

"And that's if the swampers don't get us!" Ricky added.

"I keep telling you," Myron muttered. "We have to repair and refloat the *Queen*. She'll take us out of here!"

"Myron," Arliss said gently, "we tried that. That's what put us here."

"Sneaking out on rafts didn't play out so ace, either," Jake stated. Whereas Nataly often struck Doc as fatalistic, the cadaverous navigator seemed to revel in wallowing in gloom.

"It's all Ryan's fault," Sean said. "It was his idea. It was triple crazy, all along! We're lucky it didn't get us all chilled."

Doc looked to Krysty, but the statuesque redhead merely sat on her backpack on the short grass with the others, a battered boonie hat sheltering her pale, perfect features from the hot midmorning sun. She showed no sign of the brutal day and night preceding, nor the too-short sleep that had followed. She seemed crisp and alert.

Doc had entered back into the present world fully enough that he did not fail to notice it was *Ryan's* backpack. Like his prized longblaster, he had left it behind when he made his mad, brave and inspired leap to single-handedly attack the New Vickville blasterboat.

She also seemed just as unaffected by the criticism of her lover, now presumably captive—Doc could not bring himself to believe that Ryan Cawdor was dead, not that he really thought he was. Her expression remained calm. Serene, almost. Like a childless Madonna from a Renaissance painting.

"Ryan's the only reason any of us are here!" Mildred snapped. "Several times over!"

"The whole idea was triple stupe!" Sean screamed.

"She's right," Nataly said quietly. "Anyway, pointing fingers is one thing we know won't get us clear of this mess."

Sean dropped to the ground in a heap of misery as complete as the one constituted by Myron Conoyer, who was sitting with his back to the hull of his beloved wreck, as though deriving strength from it.

"I keep telling you," Myron told the bare patch of ground between his listless, outspread legs. "The *Queen* is our only hope of getting out alive."

"You know, I think he's right."

The words, delivered softly, seemed to hit the group sitting or standing around on the beach like a charge of electricity. Everybody looked to the eastern end of the cleared shoreline. J.B. stood there, his fedora tipped back on his head, gazing, or so it seemed, toward the rusty remnants of a derelict railroad bridge, a quarter mile or so upstream.

Doc found it hard to repress a shudder. If he had ever laid eyes on a more certain nesting place for a colony of stickies, he could not summon it to mind.

"Who's right, John?" Mildred asked. "Don't keep us in suspense."

The Armorer turned. "Why, Captain Conoyer, of course."

Myron jerked at that. The memory it evoked of the former Captain Conoyer—his wife, Trace—clearly hit him like a spear. But then it seemingly registered that J.B. meant him, not his beloved partner who had been torn limb from limb before his eyes.

It was Myron who asked, "What do you mean?" incredulously.

J.B. took off his wire-rimmed spectacles and began to polish them with a handkerchief.

"We need a way out," he said, "and fast. And the *Mississippi Queen* will give us just that."

"Against a whole ironclad battle fleet?" Arliss scoffed. "Have you lost your mind, J.B.? I thought you were the most sensible of the bunch. But if one thing in this world is triple sure, it's that if we get near those ships—either set, take your pick—they'll finish the job they started a few days back. How do you propose to get around that? Make the poor *Queen* fly?"

"Oh, no." J.B. replaced his glasses and smiled. "The opposite. Have any of you ever heard tell of the ship called the CSS *Arkansas*?"

R YAN OPENED HIS EYE.

The nighttime blackness inside his modest cabin was broken only by a few wisps of starlight shining in through the porthole above him. It was little more than a horizontal slit with a shutter on the inside, currently raised to allow a little muggy air in.

A cat might have gotten through it, but not Ryan Cawdor, nor any human he knew, including Jak.

He frowned. He had come all the way awake and alert at once. There was nothing unusual about that. What was unusual was that he had awakened with a sense of alarm thrilling through his body.

What troubled him was, he didn't know why.

He lay perfectly still on his left side, facing the hatch to the passageway outside. He could feel the slight but complex movements of the ship at anchor as the current shifted its enormous mass. He could hear the water slogging against the hull; the chugging of a distant patrol boat's engine, steadily receding; the faint strains if a harmonica.

And then he heard *whispering*, and knew what had awakened him.

A moment later he heard a faint scrape, little more than a whisper itself, as of wood on steel.

"Fireblasted amateurs," he muttered to himself.

He whipped the cotton sheet off his body and sat up. He was naked. It was a luxury to be able to strip down completely for sleep. Most nights he was lucky if he felt confident enough to take his boots off when he bedded down.

He dressed in the dark, purposefully but without haste. He knew what had to be happening. It was why he and J.B. schooled their friends to a strict discipline of speaking only in undertones when trying to be covert. Whispers carried, and part of the reason they did was that they were unnatural—out of place. That was why he awakened.

He only wondered how the raiders had evaded the New Vick guard boats when he and his friends could not.

As he pulled up his pants and did up the fly, the answer came to him: however low an opinion Baron Tanya had of Baron Harvey, or how justified it may be, he had to have people under him who were anything but stupe. They were smart enough to infiltrate observers in small boats, probably by skulking in the shadows near the shore, close enough to observe the New Vick patrols without being observed in turn. The steam-powered blasterboats probably followed set patterns and a set schedule. Given long enough, the Poteetville spies had charted them out.

He heard the sounds they made: small, furtive sounds, but detectable simply because they were not the sounds of the ship's routines, even in their endless minor variations: more whispers, more scrapes, a clink of improperly secured gear.

Despite himself, Ryan wondered why the sentries on board the *Pearl* didn't hear those sounds as plain as blaster shots. He slipped on his holster belt and secured his weapons, then drew the SIG Sauer and, folding down the small writing desk from one bulkhead, dropped the mag from the well and laid it on the table. Next he worked the slide deliberately, ejecting the chambered round into his palm. He dropped it into a pocket; there was no way to ensure it wouldn't roll off the table from the boat's slow and not entirely predictable pitching.

He pulled the slide all the way back, and locked it open with the slide-catch lever. His experienced fingers found the takedown lever, on the blaster's left side above the trigger, then turned it down. It was a simple matter of pulling back on the slide to disengage the catch, then easing the slide forward off the frame.

He turned the slide upside down in his palm and carefully removed the recoil-guide rod, to avoid shooting its spring across the dark cabin and losing the nuking thing. He laid the slide on the table, then pulled the spring off the rod and set it down propped at an angle inside the trigger guard, to keep it from rolling off the table.

The hatch had a lock of simple, ancient design—the sort that had a keyhole. J.B. would have opened the door with barely more delay than if it wasn't locked to begin with. Lacking his friend's prodigious level of skill, or his communion with mechanism, it took Ryan what felt like a fumbling, clattering eternity to pick the simple lock with the guide rod.

At last he was done. The latch turned and the hatch was unlocked.

Closing it again for the moment—and trying the latch again to make sure it wouldn't lock itself—he went back to the table and reassembled the SIG the way he'd stripped it: by feel. Urgency sang in his veins, and gave him a prickly sensation between the shoulder blades.

He reloaded the blaster and eased the slide back and forth to chamber a round. Babying it that way was a good way to get it to jam, but right now he reckoned stealth was worth the risk.

Ryan had been able to perform the actions without haste because he knew that it would take time for a raiding party to work its way out of their boat—*boats*, almost certainly—and up and into the big ironclad warship. They had to be careful lest they do something obvious enough to raise the alarm. In which case they'd be blasted off the hull by the *Pearl*'s crew.

But he didn't have forever, and he sensed somehow that what time he had was rapidly running out.

He padded barefoot to the hatch and opened it cautiously. He knew from listening the first night when they locked him in, imagining him to be passed-out drunk, that his captors didn't post sentries by the hatch. But it wouldn't do to just walk blithely out into the corridor and straight into the arms of a passel of sec men.

Nor, he realized, would it have done to walk blithely out into the corridor and straight into the arms of a Poteetville raiding party with blacked-out faces and weapons in their hands.

KEYED-UP AS the raiders doubtlessly were, they weren't expecting to encounter anybody *else* sneaking around the *Pearl*'s superstructure. They were on guard for somebody obliviously emerging from a cabin, and were no doubt prepared to neutralize anyone who did so before they gave the alarm. Probably permanently.

Nonetheless Ryan pulled his face back and eased the door closed. Only when he was sure they'd moved past did he open it again. He poked enough of his face out to get a quick glance at them—and had to pull back fast to avoid being spotted. The invaders, five of them that he could see, were wary enough to check *behind* them periodically.

Ryan risked another quick look to make sure no other groups were following the first one. The first he'd spotted, he reminded himself. Then a final check showed them moving stealthily up the ladder to the cabin's second and top story.

Where the bridge lay, and aft, the way they were going, the baron's chambers.

He went after them as fast as he could without making noise. The fact he'd forgone pulling on his boots helped.

Had he been a loyal sailor of New Vickville, he'd have raised the alarm straightaway. But as always his interests were his own—and his friends'. He could alert the *Pearl* and the fleet at any time. For now, he wouldn't.

After all, if this nighttime raid managed to win the war for Poteetville, that might just open up an escape route for him and his companions.

The baron's stateroom, actually two rooms plus a tiny bath, was on the starboard side—the east, away from the heat of the afternoon sun. As he suspected, he found the raiders arranging themselves for surprise entry: one against the bulkhead on each side flanking the door, the other three in a semicircle with blasters ready. Two of them carried remade double-barreled, sawed-off shotguns. The others held revolvers. Just as they were cocking themselves back to pounce, the door opened. Lieutenant Stone strode purposefully out—and almost into the barrels of blasters. In the spill of lantern light from within, appearing a lot brighter than it was to his dark-accustomed eye, Ryan saw her eyes grow huge.

He also saw the intruders tense to blast her down.

Crouched in the stairwell, he already had his SIG leveled in a two-handed Weaver stance, his right arm almost at lockout, his left elbow down and crooked, that hand applying steadying pressure on the one wrapped around the grip. He had already aimed at the head of the raider closest to him, a guy in a black knit watch cap carrying a replica Remington Army wheelgun, seemingly propped like an apple on the front sight post. Ryan squeezed off a round.

The blaster barked and blazed. The head jerked before the raider fell to the deck. There was naturally a chance the loud noise from behind would cause the hyped-up raiders to blast the winsome lieutenant from pure reflex. In which case, that sucked for her, but didn't bother Ryan. Instead the shot caused an instant moment of confusion.

Ryan was already doing his best to increase that confusion—and better his own odds—by pumping a shot into the small of the back nearest the hatch. The man yelled and discharged his Peacemaker into the ceiling.

The raider crouched on the far side of the door yanked both triggers of his scattergun. Stone had leaped back. Ryan ducked as the doubled charge smashed full into one of the shotgunner's teammates.

The man Ryan had back-shot spun to the left as if some of the shot had hit his left arm. He dropped his weapon and went down howling in pain.

Two shots roaring from inside the open hatchway dropped one of them. Stone kept presence of mind in a fight, apparently. Mebbe this wasn't her first rodeo. The last raider snapped a shot toward Ryan, which thunked into the hardwood over his head. He double-tapped the man through the sternum and down he went.

"Clear out here!" he shouted, so Stone wouldn't try to blast *him* when she emerged, as she did an instant later. Ryan was already kicking a blaster away from the moaning, writhing man he'd shot from behind. From a glance he'd taken at least one .33 caliber double-ought ball to the elbow, which meant he'd likely lose the arm. If he lived.

Ellin Stone stepped out—behind the squared-off muzzle of an extended Colt Model 1911. Her face was white, her dark eyes still saucer huge, but her somewhat square jaw was firmly set.

A bank of greenish-white smoke hung from waist height up in the corridor. Any more black powder shots and everybody would have been blind. It stank of burned powder, caps and voided bowels.

Other doors were opening. A couple of sec men appeared from the direction of the bridge. Seeing Ryan standing up by the ladder through the stinking smoke, they raised their handblasters at him.

"Stand down!" Stone snapped. "The intruders are all down. Secure them."

She looked at Ryan. "Thank you."

He was about to say something self-effacing. Instead he snapped, "Fireblast!"

Chapter Fourteen

"What?" the confused-looking lieutenant said.

"Something I should have thought of first. Come with me!"

Hand-cranked sirens began to grind and wail all over the big ironclad. "Up!" he said.

"But the baron—"

Ryan heard the unmistakable sound of a shotgun action being pumped. He decided to waste the second it took to peek in through the open door.

Clad in a luxurious green nightgown over something white and lacy, Baron Tanya sat in her big chair. She held a 12-gauge Mossberg 590 marine shotgun with matte-silver metal and synthetic furniture with her two strong, square hands, and the air of a person who knew exactly how to use it. Clearly there was no screwing around with black powder smoke poles for the baron, just like with her assistant.

"I've got this," she said, with what Ryan took for relish. "You go!"

He left, running for the stairs. Stone followed. There was no dither in the woman, he had to give her that.

As soon as he burst out into the open air of the un-armored top deck, his growing suspicions were con-

firmed. A low fog overlaid the great, black river. It
wasn't thick. He could plainly see the looming, shadowed bulks of the *Clytemnestra* and the *Medusa* to either side. He could even see a handful of patrol boats,
off upstream. But beyond a hundred and fifty, two hundred yards, the Sippi and what was on it might have
been on the other side of a big wall.

"Fire all the cannon you can upstream," he told Stone.
"Whole fleet. High as they can."

"But—"

"Now!"

He didn't even see resentment flash in her eyes—
and by the light of the lantern hung at the aft end of
the top deck, he would have. Instead she sprinted to a
speaking tube by the aft rail and began barking orders.

In a surprisingly brief amount of time, a flash from
the *Pearl*'s bow lit up the river clear to where the sight
line got swallowed in the mist, throwing a pair of steam
blasterboats into garish relief before winking out. Baron
Tanya ran a taut ship; Ryan had seen that much during the tour of the iron-sheathed giant Stone had given
him that afternoon. From the noise and the concussion
that shivered up through the deck and his bare soles,
Ryan could tell it was a *much* bigger cannon than the
patrol craft carried.

A flicker of yellow light came from the flying bridge
of the *Medusa*. Turning his head the other way, he saw
a similar signal from *Clytemnestra*. Then her bow cannon belched vast yellow fire. The report of the *Medusa*'s
bow cannon hit the other side of him a heartbeat later.

As he suspected, Stone spoke with the baron's own voice when need be.

He felt a change in the vibrations from beneath. He guessed that meant the steam engines that drove the *Pearl*'s colossal bulk were firing up, but it was not the kind of mass you got moving in any kind of a hurry. The ironclad war craft were built for power, not for speed.

Cannon were booming from the rest of the New Vick fleet. He couldn't see where the shots hit. The splashes were lost in the fog. But just as he began to wonder if he'd crowned his coup at saving the baron— and her chief aide—from the raiding party with a giant economy-size fuckup, wasting his new employers a ton or so of powder and ball, he saw a diffuse yellow flare blossom inside the fog. More followed.

A waterspout rocked a blasterboat back and sent a wave of river water crashing over its deck. A lucky shot: lucky for the patrol craft that it was a near miss, lucky for the Poteetville gunners to have come that close, shooting stone-blind as they were for the very fog that hid their approach.

"The Invincible Armada!" Stone shouted at Ryan over the din of cannon. Some of the patrol boats were getting into the act now, banging away with their own bow cannon. "How did you know?"

It amused Ryan how much different *perspective* made. When he'd been staring up the business ends of the cannon, they'd seemed as huge as the mouth of a predark railroad tunnel. But from up here, on top of what was almost certainly the biggest, baddest warship on the entire Sippi River, they seemed pathetic little popguns.

"Heard noises," he said, "where noises didn't belong. So I decided to investigate."

"And you released yourself on your own recognizance."

He just grinned. It wasn't a question. The facts spoke as loud as an eight-pounder cannon.

"So you could have left at any time?"

"I told you and I told the baron. I get paid, I do the job." Which was even true—so far as it went.

She shook her head. While she had been able to get the party started on her own hook, she was clearly leaving the conduct of the naval battle in other hands. Ryan didn't know whose. Probably Captain Delgado, on the *Pearl*'s bridge.

Stone turned back to the speaking tube. She listened a moment with a hand covering the ear not pressed to the polished brass funnel. Ryan was amazed she could hear much for the racket of cannon banging off. It took time to get one swabbed out and reloaded after a shot, but as he knew firsthand, it wasn't hard, since the cannon were smoothbores. And with as many cannon as the three big boomers, the frigates and the swarm of blasterboats boasted, there were shots cracking off pretty much all the time.

The *Pearl* was beginning to lumber ahead. Ryan was no naval tactician, but it was plain to him that the New Vick ironclads wanted to bring the full force of their broadsides against the attacking fleet.

"But how did you know Poteetville's whole fleet was coming behind the cutting-out parties?"

"That's what I should've checked right off," he said. He didn't miss that she'd said *parties*, not party. He guessed she'd got reports of other groups of raiders. "The bastard weather. That's why they happened to come tonight instead of some other. The fog."

"Right."

She turned back to the speaking horn and listened for what seemed like a whole minute.

Ryan stood and watched the fireworks. The two main fleets were plainly out of range of each other. He'd wanted the big cannon to start blasting in hopes of keeping things that way. Once the element of surprise was lost, Baron Harvey Junior would decide to withdraw and try his luck again some other time. It had to be clear to the enemy commanders by now that their ballsy little commando decapitation strike had gone bust, too.

So I might as well enjoy the show, Ryan thought.

Stone nodded briskly and straightened. "The bridge is secured—that raiding party's down and the main decks are secured, but there's still fighting outside the engine room and the powder magazine."

Ryan rammed home a full magazine into the well of his handblaster. He grinned at her. "What're we standing here for, then? Time's blood!"

"You saved the Grand Fleet, Mr. Cawdor," the baron said over a steaming cup of coffee in her stateroom. "Meaning you saved New Vickville, and you also saved me, which I appreciate. Thank you."

"And you saved me," Stone added. She was looking at Ryan with an unusually doe-like look in her big, dark eyes.

He had long since learned that all those stories of his childhood about the damsel in distress falling for the big strong hero who rescued her were a steaming load of glowing nuke shit. In the case of his own crew, honors were about even where it came to Mildred and Krysty saving one or more of the males as opposed to being saved by them. They'd certainly hauled his chestnuts out of the fire on many more occasions than one. And if he tended to hold the greater number of successful rescues, that applied to the whole group, not just the two women.

But—sometimes it happened. Even from a woman clearly as capable of handling herself in a fight as Ellin Stone. She'd gotten more blood on her than Ryan had in the brief but vicious mopping-up actions, having picked up a cutlass on her way down with him. Both of them sat on tarps to save the baron's fine upholstery, the way Ryan had his first night.

He sipped his black coffee. It was real coffee, too. The baron didn't believe in stinting herself. Not that that wasn't obvious from looking at her surroundings. And her. Then again, squatting astride the lower portion of the biggest trade route remaining across the Deathlands had its privileges. It made sense she'd have access to the real thing, not the awful chicory coffee-sub drek they liked to pretend was coffee in most of Deathlands.

"Yes," Baron Tanya said with a nod. "Thank you for saving my aide, as well. I find her services invaluable. And Elli has known enough tragedy in her life, poor girl."

Ryan saw a flicker cross Stone's face. He could not interpret it.

Outside it was still dark, or maybe false dawn was beginning to gray out the skies to the east. He couldn't see anything through the slit-like open port. No more cannon blasts came from outside. As he'd anticipated, Baron Harvey had opted to cut his losses and try his luck another time. Though shots had continued to bang back and forth for half an hour while Ryan and Ellin jumped raiders from behind and butchered them handily, the battle had ended as soon as the enemy ironclads could steam back out of range upriver.

"So," Baron Tanya said, draining her cup with a slurp, "you picked the lock on your cabin. Care to tell me how you managed that, Mr. Cawdor?"

"No."

She set the cup in the saucer with a slight clatter, and put both down on the round teak table beside her.

"Ace," she said. "That just goes to prove you're resourceful as well as bold. And decisive.

"We got off double lightly, thanks to you. No more than a score of casualties. And only two of those weren't from fighting off the boarding parties. When the Armada swung closest to us as they were trying to turn tail, a shell came down on top of *Hera*'s cabin and chilled her second lieutenant and a steward. Though I suppose casualties are never *light* to the poor bastards who have lost their limbs. Or their lives."

"No," Ryan said. "They're not."

She shrugged and made a face. "Well, it's war. That doesn't mean I have to like it."

"In my experience, my druthers don't seem to matter one way or another, as to how war is."

"Truth."

She smiled.

"So, I suppose there's no locking you in your cabin anymore, is there? It's not as if there's any point, obviously."

He grinned. "No, ma'am."

"I think you've passed your probation with flying colors, Junior Lieutenant Cawdor. So haul your newly promoted ass back to your quarters and get all the sleep you need. I want you nice and rested when I get you started *really* earning your pay!"

Chapter Fifteen

"I see stickies!" Mildred heard Ricky shout from the roof of the *Mississippi Queen*'s half burned-out cabin. He lay up there on his belly behind Ryan's prized Steyr Scout, with the bipod down, watching the action through the Leupold scope.

A quarter mile away, the launch was just approaching the ruined bridge, towing the dinghy behind it.

"Pipe down, kid," she snarled. She sat watching the scene from the shore through Ryan's navy longeyes, trying to keep her heart out of her throat.

There was a curious contrast in the hair of the occupants of the towed craft: flame red, snow white. Krysty and Jak rode in it, along with a mounded mass of what looked like wadded-up bedding, which was in fact a heap of clothing ruined by fire or flooding. J.B. rode in the launch with Arliss and Abner at the tiller. All were dwarfed by Santee.

"But I wish I could warn them!"

Mildred saw stickies now, too. They were appearing from the deep shadows of the far end of the bridge, under which the launch and dinghy were set to pass.

"They know," she gritted. "Jak's with them. Mind you don't warn the muties."

That wasn't really rational, of course. The stickies were too far away to hear anything shy of a gunshot, just as their friends were.

"What's happening?" Suzan asked excitedly from behind Mildred.

She, Jake, Avery and Nataly were clustered by Mildred upstream of the prow of the grounded *Queen*, as close to the waterline as they dared for fear of crocs. They had started seeing their log-like shapes, or just their lumpy heads, in the couple of days since they'd run back to the wreck site with their tails between their legs. The creatures had shown no sign of interest in the refugees, nor ventured too close to the shoreline clearing. Doc stood behind the others, LeMat and sword in his hands, just in case.

Myron and his assistant, Sean, were back in the bowels of the tugboat, doing something mysterious to the Diesels. It might soon make sense for them to bother, if J.B.'s crazy scheme worked. Or even if this first phase worked.

How strange is it, she thought, that sailing right into the middle of a stickie nest in the least whacked-out part of the plan?

"They're going under the bridge now," Ricky called out. "Here come the stickies. Should I open up?"

"Wait for them to start blasting," Mildred replied. She was in charge of this group in J.B.'s and Krysty's absence. The others were deferring to her too, at least for now. "Stick to the plan."

Water splashed as stickies dropped abruptly out of the rusty girders near the launch. Those passengers of both craft unfamiliar with fighting stickies reacted with every sign of unbridled terror, whipping their heads this way and that and gesticulating. J.B. shouldered his S&W M-4000 12-gauge and fired at the closest stickie. It fell back in the water, trailing ropy yellow tendrils of ichor. Arliss blasted another on the far side of the launch, as it capered toward them through the weeds by the bank with comical high steps of its splay-toed feet kicking up sheets of water.

"Now, Ricky!" Mildred cried, as the sound of J.B.'s booming M-4000 reached her ears.

The Steyr cracked. Two stickies were almost on the launch, one on either side. The one on the right, away from the near bank, threw up its sucker-fingered hands as the 7.62 mm bullet burst its head like a balloon filled with yellow paint.

"Show-off!" Mildred said. Santee split the second stickie's head with a full-sized ax, swung across his body one-handed as if it were a hatchet.

Abner panicked. His usually firm hand faltered. As he steered the motorboat, it swerved in toward the north bank, instead of away for open water. And in that brief misstep, disaster struck. The dinghy it towed nosed into a tangle of fallen steel truss-work that had rusted almost the color of blood. It stuck fast.

Stickies swarmed toward it. Krysty's Glock ripped them with a burst of 9 mm bullets. Mildred couldn't see the flashes at that range, nor the shock waves rippling the air, and the sound wouldn't reach her ears for just over a second. But she knew by their effects: three stickies went down flailing.

Abner had turned the launch's nose toward the middle of Wolf Creek, trying to dislodge the dinghy from the snag with no success.

Krysty stopped shooting and put her hands on the sides of the boat, rocking left and right in hopes of working the craft free. Jak fired his Colt Python and blasted a stickie that was about to leap aboard.

Mildred, watching the drama aboard the dinghy in mounting fear, saw its right shoulder practically explode. Its arm fell into the water.

Traumatic amputation or not, the stickie kept coming. Jak met it with an overhand left to the face with the steel-studded brass knuckle guard of his trench knife. Stickie blood showered him as the mutie fell backward into the creek.

Tethered to the trapped dinghy by the towline, the power launch had turned completely and swung back almost side to side with it, though only the sterns overlapped. Santee reached out for Krysty, and she grabbed his tree-limb arm. He swung her into the boat, well clear of the submerged propeller of the outboard motor, as if she were a doll.

Arliss and J.B. were gesturing and obviously shouting for Jak to abandon the dinghy and join the redhead in safety. But Jak did a curious thing.

Shooting down the nearest stickie, the albino bent over in the dinghy. He was clearly doing something that required attention. A stickie clambered up onto the steel snag and sprang at his unprotected back.

J.B. shot it in midair as if it were a grouse starting up from a bush. The charge of Number 4 shot caught the mutie midtorso and ripped blue organs clean out of its body. It fell into the water between the unpowered boat and the bank. Usually only a head shot or a shot to the heart chilled a stickie, but there was no coming back from such a devastating hit.

It was a triple-risky shot, so close to the albino, but not even Ryan had a surer hand with a blaster. J.B. was as precise as a machine in combat.

Ricky blasted a mutie as it reached to grab for the boat's stern. Jak came up to a crouch. He had holstered his Magnum revolver. He slashed through the towrope with a stroke of his trench knife, then without apparent hurry he sheathed the blade. As the launch pulled away, he dived into the water and swam for it.

Santee fished him out in the same manner as he had hoisted Krysty. The albino weighed less than she did, even with all the weapons on his body.

Abner opened the throttle all the way. The launch's prow lifted on a pale bow wave as it sprinted away. Stickies ran after it waving their hands in futile pursuit.

J.B. had switched out his shotgun for his stutter-gun. He bowled over a couple of the nearest with two quick bursts. A couple stickies had climbed into the abandoned dinghy. They flung themselves overboard in alarm as flames abruptly blazed up, a shockingly bright orange in the gloom beneath the bridge. Stickies loved fire, but they didn't love getting burned.

"They all got away," Mildred reported as Ricky's borrowed longblaster banged again. Those around her whooped and danced. "Everybody seems to be in one piece. You can stop wasting rounds up there, Ricky. Look for danger to the launch."

The junk cloth heaped in the dinghy had been soaked with pine oil. The pile blazed up brightly in the gloom just beyond the reach of the morning sun, quickly involving the wood of the small boat in the fire. Stickies began to dance and shriek, bending back and forth as if genuflecting to the fire. Others began to caper around it. They reminded Mildred of apes from the Tarzan books she'd read as a preteen.

"That was a good job," Nataly pronounced somberly.

"The fire looks ace," Avery said.

Mildred shifted her vision field from the fire to the returning boat. As she focused, she saw Krysty waving toward them, Santee brandishing his ax over his head, Arliss pumping his rifle in the air, and J.B. sitting with his hat tipped back on his head examining his weapons. Typical, she thought, as was Jak's demeanor, crouching in the stern just ahead of Abner, staring moodily astern along their wake as if regretting the lost opportunity to chill more stickies.

"Here come more of them!" Jake exclaimed. He sounded not just animated but excited. "Man, look at all those bastard devils!"

Mildred raised the navy longeyes back to the bridge. The muties were swarming from the south side of the dilapidated bridge, clambering along the truss-work beneath the track bed in the dozens, their pale bodies gleaming in the sun. When they hit the gap they simply dropped to the creek below. Some climbed up the juts and snags of fallen steel beams, springing from one to the next as much as they could. Others simply paddled across, as did their comrades capering on the steel when the gaps became too far to jump.

"They're swarming to the fire like flies to a fresh cow flop," Avery said in satisfaction, although for once the always optimistic carpenter was more subdued than the normally glum and few-spoken navigator.

"Don't worry, Jak," Mildred said. She stood up and lowered the longeyes. "You get your part in plenty of stickie-chilling soon."

"It's actually gonna work," Suzan breathed reverently. She smoothed back her graying hair. It sprang immediately out again, as wild as ever.

"Don't count any plan a success until you see how it actually turns out," Nataly advised. Mildred wasn't sure if that was the tall woman's fatalism speaking, or practicality. Sometimes the one could be hard to tell from the other. Especially these days.

"The ancient Norse had a saying," Doc said. "'Never count a man happy until the day he dies.'"

"Rad waste, old man," Avery said. "Have you been taking Gloomy Gus lessons from Jake?"

Doc shook his white head and smiled thinly.

"Ah, no. I learned from a far longer course of study, in a far harsher school."

"Let's keep the negative waves down," Mildred said, "just in case." That was a reference to a movie she'd seen as a little girl, she realized. But she couldn't place it. She remembered it had a railway bridge in it. And tanks. They could use a few of those right now.

Then she smiled to herself. No, they couldn't. Tanks

would bog right down in the swamps surrounding them. But what J.B. had in mind was along those lines.

"I never thought this part would work," Nataly admitted, despite her admonition of a second ago about premature celebration. "But if this part comes off…"

"That leaves a lot of work to do," Jake said, starting to sound like his normal dour self again.

The first mate blew out a long breath. "It'll feel good to be able to do *something*," she said. "Half-baked and hard as it may be, anything is better than scurrying helplessly back and forth like a mouse between cats. Or between battleships and muties."

"You got that right," Suzan said.

Coming from anybody else, Mildred reflected, as the launch putted back toward the shore where they all now stood except for those on the *Queen*, just upstream of the tug's bow, she would have taken the scheme as more hopeless than half-baked or even crazy. But J. B. Dix remained the most practical man on Earth. Or at least the most practical she'd ever met walking to and fro on it. In her own day or this one.

If he set out to do a thing, it was because he was certain he could do it, and had at least the glimmering of a plan as to how. And then, more often than not, he went and did it. Whatever it took.

She looked on the returning group with love, and not just for her lover. She was proud of them all. Even their temporary allies.

And she knew she could never get across to John her private reservations about his grand scheme for them and *Queen*. Though he knew a fair amount about it,

J.B. was no profound scholar of military history. Not the way Ryan was. His was interested primarily in all the weapons, neat toys and gadgets warriors had used over the ages.

And even Ryan cared little for the political and cultural context of the wars he'd studied and thought about. He was interested in the lessons he could derive from them to help him fight his own better.

Abner cut back the outboard motor at just the precise instant to allow the launch's pointy prow to slide up smoothly on a low patch of shore with short, dew-damp grass to lubricate its way. The barrier to J.B.'s understanding her misgivings about his plans was simply the times they had grown up in. Slavery was very real, and accepted as a thing that happened. Almost universally, in fact, or at least it wasn't uncommon and tended to crop up anywhere. Her friends all hated it. They'd fought a loose network of slavers whose reach encompassed the whole Deathlands and beyond. And Ricky had sworn eternal vengeance on them after they butchered his village, murdered his parents before his eyes and carried off his adored older sister, Yamile, into bondage. He was still obsessed with searching for her, and one of his main reasons for remaining with Ryan's group was to keep looking for her against all hope.

But to them slavery was just another thing coldhearts did. It didn't hold the horror for them it did for her. Because the idea that it would focus its evil on one group of people because of the different color of their skins was as alien to them as universally available electricity and running water. People hated and discriminated,

as they always had and always seemed to—whoever
and wherever they were. But modern prejudices were
directed against muties and their "taint" of not-quite-
humanity. Normal humans—norms—of all descrip-
tions were "us" against the mutie "them," even if the
muties were otherwise norm or even exemplary people,
like Krysty, say. They were despised and even feared
scarcely less than the vaguely humanoid and outright
monstrous stickies, or the barely better scalies.

Arliss and Santee scrambled from the boat to help
pull it farther onto the grass. Krysty, J.B. and Jak
alighted. Abner shut down the motor and followed. Mildred grabbed J.B. and hugged him until he winced.
Then with her arm around his waist he turned to share
quick, warm cheek pecks with Krysty.

"I'm so proud of you all," she said. "You played it
perfectly."

"Ace job of acting scared out there," Avery said, slap-
ping Abner on the shoulder.

"*Acting* scared?" Santee asked. He rumbled a distant-
thunder laugh.

"Not a lot of acting required," J.B. said, "when there's
stickies so close you can smell them."

"You handled the boat perfectly, Abner," Nataly said
to the cox'n and bosun's mate. "You would have fooled
me that you stuck the dinghy on that wreckage by accident because you flipped out."

Abner just bobbed his head and mumbled, "Thanks."
He seemed embarrassed at the attention.

"I thought our performance was mebbe a little broad,
myself," Arliss said, though he was smiling. "Like

something you'd see in a traveling show, overacting being scared all over the place."

"I doubt stickies have refined critical senses," Doc said drily. "Nor do they pay overmuch attention to the nuances of human emotion and behavior."

"Unless they're torturing some poor bastard," Jake said. "Then they pay plenty attention."

"Stickies triple deadly," Jak said, "but triple stupe."

"And there you have it," Avery said.

J.B. made a show of checking his chron, even though Mildred could tell he barely glanced at it.

J.B., you total bullshitter, she thought. *You know to the second how much time has elapsed.*

For a man who seldom had much to say, at times he sure showed a flare for the dramatic.

"Big surprise coming up for the stickies," he announced, turning his gaze upstream toward the bridge. "In three, two, one—"

A fireball engulfed a horde of hooting, celebrating stickies. It in turn was instantly swallowed up by an expanding cloud of white smoke with a yellow sun at its heart.

"Now, that's something you don't see every day," Santee said.

What the onlookers could not see from a quarter mile away was the twenty-pound black powder bursting charge going off. The blast sent a hundred pounds of rusted nails, sharp pebbles and broken crockery that had been packed around the powder keg in a larger barrel and covered with oil-soaked cloth sleeting through the bodies of scores of muties.

"They love fire and fireworks so much," J.B. said, "let's see how they like being *part* of them."

The smoke rolled upward in a ball to split and flow around the stump of the railway bridge. The bonfire had been blown out, but smoldering fragments lay everywhere. As did stickie bodies. And body parts.

The murderous show had been set off by a fuse that had been inserted in one end of a precious cheroot. Jak had lit it along with the oil-soaked cloth when he bent down. Because the cheroot would burn at a consistent rate, J.B. had calculated it should give him and his friends plenty time to get to safety and plenty time for stickies to join the fun.

J.B. disentangled himself from Mildred. "Right. It's time to go back to the scene of the crime for the mop-up. Make sure the nest is cleared out."

"Want me and Santee with you again?" Arliss asked. He was feeding fresh black powder cartridges into the side-gate in the receiver of his carbine.

"Yeah," J.B. said. "Mildred, Krysty and Doc, you come along, too. There's just room in the launch for you."

"If everybody's friendly," Abner said, "since Santee's double large. We can make it for this short jaunt, though. No problem."

"I've got to warn you, ladies and gentlemen," J.B. said, "after we get the nest cleaned out, break time's over. The real work starts, and the last easy day was yesterday."

And I'll save the breath it would cost me telling you I don't like your plan, Mildred thought, just because it was something the slave-owning Confederates did two hundred years ago. Neither you nor anyone else but Doc would even understand.

Chapter Sixteen

"Nope," Manda Kwon said, holding up the rad detector with her floppy hat over it to shield its vanes from the light of the scorching noonday sun. "Not detecting any rads yet."

"What we want to be concerned with," Ryan said, "is the crocs that infest these bayous. They'll chill us quicker than the hot spots. Or any but the hottest, anyway."

His skin crawled at the fact that he like the rest was wading hip deep through one of the myriad little channels twisting their way through the bogs inland east of the Grand Fleet's anchorage.

Still, he missed his lapel rad counter, which presumably—hopefully—was with Krysty and the others back at the *Mississippi Queen* right now. Because it was attached to his coat.

He was leading a party of seven New Vick sailors—or rather, six sailors and one sec man—down a nuke-forsaken bayou in the ostensible hope of finding a way to outflank the Poteetville fleet.

Despite the offer of the choicest available blasters from the armory, including black powder lever-action repeaters like the ones Baron Tanya's sec men carried,

Ryan had picked a double-barreled, sawed-off 12-gauge shotgun to augment his SIG. The Baroness, in her real if carefully doled-out gratitude, had provided him smokeless ammo and even a 15-round magazine. But as a primary weapon, he thought the sawed-off gave him the best option for surprises of the up-close-and-personal kind.

Shaking her head, Manda put her hat back on and stowed the glass globe with its miniature four-blade-weather-vane assembly back in its padded box. She didn't put it away in the light pack she carried, same as all the rest of them. She didn't seem willing to let go of her treasure.

"Does that thing even work?" Mohoric asked. Like most of the unit he carried a Springfield trapdoor blaster with a carbine-length barrel. It wouldn't have been Ryan's choice even among breech-loading smoke-poles, but it seemed to be the basic weapon issued to Grand Fleet landing parties.

Ryan led them slowly forward as Manda tucked the box back under her shoulder. Almost at once a flock of cattle egrets took startled flight from off to their right, squawking and flapping almost over their heads as they ducked fast and cursed.

"It works," Manda insisted. She carried her M1873 slung.

"How do you know?" Chief Petty Officer Jarvis Jones asked from the rear of the file. The young and handsome black man was one of Baron Tanya's sec men, not a common sailor. His manner was flippant and often abrasive, although he seemed competent enough to back his brash self-assurance.

Ryan was at least sure he was assigned to be his babysitter. The baron of New Vick was not a trusting person. Whether that was paranoia, justified or unjustified, Ryan as yet had no objective evidence.

"It works," Ryan said. "I've seen them before. What I wonder is where you get one of those things in this day and age?"

"They're not that hard," Manda said defensively. "Blow a glass, suck the air out, stick one of these little propeller doohickeys with the panels black on one side, white on the other. Seal it back up airtight. No great shake."

"If you say so," Pottz said.

"Lotsa craftsmen in the ville could do it. My family could, if you gave us the right equipment."

"How far are we supposed to go, anyway?" Mohoric asked.

"Two miles inland, is what I was told," Ryan said.

He glanced up at the sky. Chem clouds seemed to be approaching out of the west.

"How far have we gone, then, sir?" Jones asked.

"Beats the glowing nuke shit out of me," Ryan replied. "There's no way to tell. Unless one of you has got some way of measuring distance that I don't know about."

That brought a chorus of nos, as expected. "If anybody does, it's Manda," Jones said. "How about it, Mandy?"

She shook her head. She looked more than a little miffed. "You been keeping your sketch map up, Atcheson?"

"Yeah," the weedy blond man said in his nasal voice. "What I can't understand is, why me?"

"Because the new junior loot told you to, Earl," Jones said.

"I got told somebody had to do it," Ryan said. He could have chosen to get pissed at the chief's manner, skirting insubordination pretty closely as it did.

Instead he grinned. "And it wasn't going to be me. Shit rolls downhill."

"Welcome to the Grand Fleet," Pottz said.

"What I don't get," said Boggert, another black guy who came from small-boat river people south of New Vickville proper, "is what we're supposed to accomplish."

"We got ordered to look for a way to go sneaking up on the P'ville pukes," Pottz said.

"But what's the point of carrying on past the point we could even bring the rowboats? If they won't make it this far, and we all know they won't, a patrol steamer sure as nuke won't. Much less the *Pearl*."

"Orders," Ryan said. "They said two miles. If we find a likely route, then mebbe the baron will look into dredging out a channel to get boats to it."

"The *Pearl*? She draws so much she has to keep a leadsman working constantly in the bow to keep from getting grounded on a sandbar, and that's in the big river!"

"The details are far above my pay grade," Ryan said. "Feel free to ask Baron Krakowitz when we get back."

Boggert hastily shook his head. "You mean she didn't tell you that, Lieutenant Cawdor?" Jones asked. "Thought you were the Hero of the Fleet, after that little fandango last week."

"Yeah, well, this is what that gets you. In turns out. You might keep that in mind."

He wasn't happy to be reminded how long he'd been held in the Grand Fleet. He may not be a prisoner, as such, but until he had a way to spring his friends from the rad- and stickie-infested trap they were stuck in, he stubbornly refused to leave.

Fact was, he was more than a little disappointed. He thought that maybe his feat in foiling the Poteetville sneak attack might've been enough to buy them all a ticket out. Instead he was tramping pointlessly around the same swamp complex. Even if it was less radioactive—if Manda's glass gadget worked.

"I still don't see the point to sloshing half a mile or more in this slop," Boggert said. "Any channel we find's liable to move next time it rains. And then Earl's map won't be worth runny dog crap. And it's fixing to rain, in two hours, max."

"Reckon you're right, Boggert," Ryan said. "All right, everybody. Time to head back."

"Have we really come two miles, sir?" Manda asked.

"Atcheson, you got our progress all caught up and everything?"

"If by 'caught up' you mean I got a sort of squiggly line meandering across a sheet of otherwise blank paper like an earthworm that got dropped in a mug of Towse Lightning, sir, yes, sir."

"Ace on the line. Then write 'two miles' at the point you're at."

"Yessir! Done, sir."

"See how simple it was?" Ryan cast another uneasy look at the clouds. They were starting to pile up along the horizon and the sun was already closer to them than he cared for. "Time to get back to the blasterboat."

"ALMOST GOT IT," Myron called up from the beach.

Santee looked at Ricky down the four-foot length of truss and grinned. The youth wasn't sure how one of his group's smaller members had gotten paired with the biggest of the whole contingent. Not to mention the strongest.

But when it came to implementing J.B.'s scheme of turning the wrecked *Queen* into a makeshift ironclad herself, before the rads and heavy metal poisoning— and the crocs, and the stickies—chilled them all, everybody found him- or herself doing everything. Whatever happened to be needed while you were around, you did.

And that's leaving out the swampers, Ricky thought. We haven't seen any sign of them yet, *muchas gracias a Nuestra Señora*!

They'd been stuck there over two weeks now. Ricky was feeling a constant turmoil in his guts. He didn't care to mention it to anyone. He didn't know what was causing it—whether it was the effects of prolonged rad exposure, or the grinding tension of being slowly roasted by nukes while awaiting death at the suckered fingertips of the Deathlands' most feared muties, there wasn't a nuking thing anyone could do about it. Except get their posteriors out of there.

"Right," Myron said. "Ease her down." He was acting mostly normal and not at all depressed these days. Apparently having hard and serious work—work that carried with it even the smallest glimmering of hope, which was about what this had—agreed with the bearded acting captain. Anyway, this was his idea— or obsession—fixing up his beloved boat and using it to get them out of there. What J.B. contributed was a sliver of a chance it might actually *work*.

"One," the big Indian counted, nodding. "Two. Three." And he and Ricky eased the truss down onto the railing.

Ricky cussed under his breath. He knew Our Lady could hear his unseemly language. That didn't mean his friends had to. He had gotten the rag he was using to protect his left hand from the rusty, cut-steel edge stuck between it and the wood. Now he had to winkle it out somehow. They didn't have any infinite supply of rags. Nor anything else—which was going to become a serious concern in not too many more days.

If we live that long, he thought. There were times Ricky felt almost tempted to hope something happened to get it all over with. Almost.

They had caught a true bit of luck in the form of the damage the mega-quakes had done the old-style railroad bridge. It had broken a lot of the structural steel—and some which struck Ricky as mostly orna- mental, if not totally so—all to hell. So it was possi- ble to look for sections that mostly fit the spots on the *Queen*'s hull and superstructure that Myron, working heads-together with Avery, J.B. and his assistant, Sean, picked for them.

But they did not miraculously all just fit exactly, which meant brutal work cutting and trimming. That meant using a hammer, a cold chisel and a file. It was possible, but it was slow, and it sucked the life out of a person like a bleeding wound.

They did their best to knock off the worst jagged-ness on cut or broken edges with a file. But the constraints of their own endurance, and the fact that here and now time was almost literally blood and it was steadily draining out, imposed limits on how good a job they could do. Even Santee, whose palms and finger pads just seemed to be giant predark baseball gloves of calluses, had to use bits of folded-up cloth to protect himself.

Of course, they got cut anyway. Ricky's hands hurt all the time, both from the gashes and the exertion. He knew everybody else's did, too. And he had determined from the first moment fate had thrown him in with Ryan Cawdor and the rest that he would do what the others did, and never falter, never complain.

If it didn't work out quite that way for him…well, truthfully it didn't for anyone else, either. Even Ryan, even the stolid J.B., had been known to piss and moan every once in a while. A *great* while, granted.

He leaned on the rail for a moment to get after his breath. It had gotten away from him again. He suspected somebody would yell at him pretty directly about his bad habit of forgetting to breathe during intense moments of concentration combined with effort. He had blacked out and keeled over more than once during the week they'd been at work repairing the *Queen*'s breached hull, shoring up the half-gutted cabin, gathering and shaping bridge and railway iron, hauling it downstream and hefting it into place.

Behind him he heard Krysty muttering something under her breath as she and Doc lowered another, similar U-section length of red steel onto the analogous segment of the port bow, the one toward the center of the stream. There had been some spirited debate among the *Queen*'s crew as to whether to try refloating her before adding a few tons more weight. Myron had decided it was better to leave her partially beached. That meant they wouldn't have to mess with trying to haul the improvised armor chunks onboard off a boat. Or a raft, really—the motor launch was occupied pretty much full-time hauling crews upstream to gather scrap, and then towing the loaded rafts back. They had cobbled their small flotilla of five rafts into two bigger, stouter ones.

"By the Three Kennedys!" Doc exclaimed. "All this and now it starts to rain."

As if to confirm the old man's words, a drop struck the back of Ricky's right hand. He looked up. The clouds, which had been colluding in a threatening way overhead as the afternoon grew on, were now a solid dark mass overhead. And delivering on their earlier threat, as more drops struck his head.

Santee grinned.

"It rains on the just and the unjust alike," he said.

"So somewhere, there are just people getting wet, too. They're the poor bastards we should be pitying."

Everybody laughed. Ricky wasn't sure if it was even funny, but he laughed, too. Anything to ease the burden of the day.

Arliss had been dubious about leaving the tug grounded to armor her up. The weight of all that steel would make it harder to dig her out and refloat her. He wanted to do it once Avery had overseen the hull patch, which had taken no more than a day, since the *Queen* carried stores designed for just that purpose. But Myron held firm, and Nataly backed him. They didn't have a dry dock in which to armor his vessel, so he'd let the shore do the job.

Krysty, J.B. and the rest of the companions mostly stayed out of it. These were the people who knew boats and the river. The job was going to be tough whichever way they did it. Ricky was glad that he didn't have to help manhandle multiple hundred-pound lengths of rusty metal off a raft in the middle of Wolf Creek. The crocs had started coming around more often. The group had taken to occasionally throwing a shot their way, just to remind them what blasters were, which seemed to be working.

So far.

Nataly knelt over the piece of truss Ricky and Santee had just placed with a spool of 16-gauge fence wire and a pair of wire cutters. Just as they didn't have cutting torches to ease the work of shaping the scrap to fit, they lacked welding heads to fasten them together once they were in place. J.B. remembered, and Doc confirmed from his own firsthand observation, that back in the nineteenth century the armor for the first ironclads, and the later hulls of full-metal ships, were bolted together. The *Queen* didn't carry in her stores or in her cargo bolts that were big enough to do the job.

But she did carry a few hundred-pound spools of that fencing wire, enough, or so they reckoned, to secure the pieces, using the bolt-holes in scavvied rails and the trusses that had them. Or they could simply wrap them in place when they lacked holes, as this chunk did.

They weren't building for the ages, J.B. pointed out. And as his apprentice in fact if not in name, Ricky knew what that cost him. The Armorer was a perfectionist. But, like all things, only when he could afford to be. In this case, he observed, all the so-called armor needed to do was hold together long enough to let them run a fleet of hostile big-blaster ships. Specifically, to run the New Vickville fleet, since the run would be significantly faster downstream, and that was the one which lay that way.

It would be good enough, or it wouldn't, which described the way Ricky Morales had led his whole life after the coldheart raiders came and destroyed his village, his family and the life he had known for all his sixteen years.

"The launch is coming back," Santee remarked, glancing upstream. It was raining briskly now. "Last run of the day, I reckon."

"By the Three Kennedys!" Doc exclaimed again, this time much louder and with considerably more emphasis. Ricky turned to look at him. It was his favorite exclamation, but usually he didn't give vent to it more than once a day if that.

But the old man was standing upright, pointing a long arm.

"Stickies!" Doc hollered. "A veritable horde of them!"

Chapter Seventeen

To Mildred's horror the cleared space of shoreline around the *Queen*'s bow was instantly thronged with stickies. The rain wasn't coming down hard enough to shield the awful scene from view.

"Cut the towline!" J.B. immediately snapped to Arliss, who was steering the motor launch. Abner was on the scavvy party, too. But as with every job they'd been doing since they got started on this insane project, that was rotated as much as possible. They didn't want anyone getting burned-out. Or no quicker than utterly necessary.

"But the crap—" Arliss began.

"Gotta move," J.B. declared. "The raft will float downstream."

"What if it hits the boat?" Jake asked.

"You want there to be a boat to get to? No time!"

The navigator looked ready to argue more, but Arliss drew a sheath knife and slashed the towline with no further argument.

It wasn't hard to see why. Myron and Sean were already almost surrounded by loathsome, pale rubbery bodies.

The outboard motor's grinding churn rose to a snarl.

The bow lifted up on a V-shaped wave the craft leaped forward at the best speed it could muster with eight bodies on board.

But will it be in time? Mildred thought, drawing her ZKR 551 blaster. Will anyone be left?

Aiming with both hands she began to fire. At this range and speed, in a bucking boat, she had no chance of nailing a specific target. But she was aiming inshore of where the acting captain and his assistant mechanic were fighting for their lives. She had a reasonable chance of missing them—and an equally reasonable chance of one of her soft lead 158-grain slugs finding a home in stickie flesh.

And if she accidentally hit and chilled one of the two men—would that be a bad thing? Or an act of mercy?

KRYSTY DREW HER Glock handblaster. Inconvenient as it could be, with holsters and protruding butts wanting to snag the heavy pieces of scrap metal, all of the companions had their weapons near to hand at all times.

Of the *Queen*'s complement only Nataly wore a sidearm, but the others made sure to keep a weapon nearby.

On board the ship, Myron and Sean had been caught unarmed onshore.

Krysty thumbed the Glock to full-auto fire. Now was not the time for concerns about safety. She aimed it down into the mass of bodies converging on Myron from her left and fired a quick burst.

The blaster climbed, but her 9 mm copper-jacketed slugs sent a couple of stickies sprawling onto the ground.

Others tripped and fell across them, their hoots rising to a crescendo of frustrated fury.

She heard Ricky's Webley handblaster cut loose to her right. From the corner of her eye she saw Santee swing a big leg over the rail, looking to climb down to rescue his friends.

"Stay back, you big stupe!" Myron cried, his face red behind his beard. A stickie grabbed him from behind. It missed its grip, but its suckered fingers yanked the man's gray plaid shirt back. It pulled itself against him, groping for his face with its free hand. He jabbed an elbow back into its face, and the mutie fell back.

Krysty fired again, staring at a point just over Myron's right shoulder. When recoil made her blaster rise slightly, bullets continued to rake the stickies thronging behind the ones closing in to swarm the captain. Yellow blood flew up in horrific counterpoint to the rain.

Myron flung himself forward desperately. Krysty flicked the selector switch to single shot, leaned over the rail, reaching out with her left arm while she continued to snap single head shots into the mutie mob. With a roar and a gout of flame from her blaster, Nataly pushed up beside her, likewise stretching a hand toward the captain.

Myron flung his hands out and took immediate hold of both. The two women began to haul him upward with all their strength, as he scrabbled with his boots against the hull to get purchase.

Krysty was almost yanked over the rail when a stickie, scrambling up the backs of its mates, landed on Myron's back. Then a slim length of steel punctured the creature's eye. The blade was withdrawn with a revolting sucking sound. The mutie's corpse fell back.

Stickies came in a bewildering variety of appearances. Some lacked any trace of a mouth. This breed had them, filled with curving black needle teeth.

Another pair of stickies hurled themselves toward the rail, using their comrades as combination ramps and ladders. As they sprang, the shotgun barrel of Doc's LeMat roared. The charge of shot clawed the face off one creature, the blast of pellets smashing into the side of the other's round, hairless, earless head. They struck the steel-truss section, squirting yellow gore and blue-green clots of something across Myron and the two women as they got him safely aboard. "Oh, no! Somebody help me! Please help me!"

A terrified scream brought Krysty's head up. Sean was struggling with a mob of stickies who practically engulfed him. His arms thrashed frantically, but his movements were mindless panic and too random and undirected to do him any good. Not that anything likely could.

Santee was whaling on muties trying to scramble over the rail on the starboard bow. Ricky had his top-break Webley cracked open and was fumbling in his pocket for a full-moon clip with six fat, fresh .45 ACP cartridges to feed it with.

"No! Don't leave me! Don't let the stickies kill me!"

The assistant mechanic's screaming plea turned to shrill inchoate shrieking as stickie finger suckers tore away a palm-size chunk of his right cheek.

Myron held a clawed right hand out to Nataly. "Your blaster. Give it to me!"

He was screaming, too. Wordlessly Nataly slapped her Ruger Old Army revolver into his upturned palm.

"Just one bullet left," she said.

He transferred the grip to his right palm. Then, using his left hand to support the other, he poked the blaster down over the rail, took aim and fired a single shot.

Sean's rolling blue eye and surrounding flesh erupted in a red explosion. His wordless pleas ceased. His body dropped down limply beneath a vile seething sea of stickies.

There was no respite for those on board the grounded boat. The stickies hit the hull with a spatter of heavy impacts as the rain began to pour from above. They clambered up one another to get at the railing.

Myron handed the blaster back to Nataly. There was no refilling its chambers with loose black powder in this rain. It would all be soaked and ruined unless she retreated back onto the bridge. Instead she reversed her grip, seized it by the barrel and swung it overhand into the face of a stickie that came lunging up over the rail, crushing its skull.

Myron turned away briefly, bending down. He seized a one-piece steel hammer from an open toolbox with one hand and a foot-long adjustable wrench with the other. Conscientious workman to the core, he flicked the lid shut with his fingertips as he stood up from it.

Krysty put the sole of her right boot against the chest of a stickie that reared up over the side of the boat right in front of her. She pushed hard. It fell over backward, squealing. She doubted she had done it any actual harm. Their bodies were springy and resilient.

Reloading her handblaster with a fresh magazine, she cast desperately about for some hand-to-hand-combat weapon. There were more stickies than she had bullets. More than *all* of them had bullets, she feared.

A two-foot wrecking bar was propped against the gunwale nearby. She picked it up in her left hand. Then swung it backhand into the face of a stickie that had plopped on the deck and was running for her on its short, bowed legs. Slim, curving teeth shattered.

The muties had begun to splash into the water beside the boat. It was only a matter of time before they rolled over the handful of defenders in a revolting rubbery-fleshed wave.

She heard a snarl of full-automatic fire. Shrill sounds of agony came from beyond the port bow.

"It's the launch!" Ricky shouted. He had found a push broom and knocked the head off. He held the staff like a lance. "It's J.B. and the rest!"

COOLLY AND METHODICALLY, J.B. reloaded his Uzi with a full mag as Arliss nosed the motor launch against what the boat crew called the *Queen*'s port quarter. Haste made waste, he always said. And never was calm efficiency more needed than at a time like this.

Of course, there were no guarantees that it would do a speck of good. He'd dumped most of a mag into the stickies making themselves into a living ramp onto the boat. He had to have chilled at least six of them with head shots. But they never slowed down, climbing right over their wounded and dying fellows with no more concern than if they were fallen leaves. And more just seemed to be pouring out of the weeds all around the clearing.

Well, there were no guarantees in this life, other than one day you'd be leaving it. J.B. wasn't ready to board the last train to the coast this day. A ladder was hooked over the rail, just in front of the stern. Avery, standing cautiously in the launch's prow, tied a rope to it.

Meanwhile Jak simply sprang to the ladder and swarmed up it like a monkey. Arliss and Jake cursed as the boat rocked.

As the shipfitter made the rope fast, J.B. leaped to the ladder and followed the white-haired young man. He had both his Uzi and his shotgun slung over the back of his brown leather bomber jacket.

"Grab yourself a hand-to-hand weapon," he called back, as Jak disappeared over the rear end of the superficially restored cabin. "Something to put some distance between you and the stickies."

Unslinging the M-4000 and making sure his hat was settled upright on his head, the Armorer made his way quickly along the port side of the boat. Ahead of them he saw Krysty decapitate a stickie with a baseball-style swing.

That was well done, he reckoned, but it was not good that the muties were aboard.

As he advanced, one got up on the rail and gathered itself to jump at Krysty. J.B. was carrying the shotgun with its butt plate just in front of his shoulder and the muzzle angled down. Now he shouldered the piece fully, snugged it in tight and got a flash picture. He blasted just as the mutie launched off. The buckshot ripped out what passed as the creature's guts. It dropped to the deck and began rolling around, squalling and licking at its innards.

J.B. charged onto the foredeck, keeping his head turning left and right to keep any of the ugly bastards from blindsiding him. He found Nataly lying with her head against the front wall of the bridge with an angry red sucker mark in the middle of her left cheek. It looked to him as if she'd jumped back to get loose from a stickie finger stuck to her face and cracked her head. Her eyes were open but not staring with the fixedness of death.

Ricky crouched to one side of her, blasting a charging stickie in the head as he held a broomstick jutting from under his arm to ward off the creatures. Myron stood on his fallen officer's other side, windmilling a pair of hand tools into onrushing muties. By the starboard bow Santee stood swinging at a stickie with his ax. Its head was throwing up strips and drops of yellow blood into the now-pouring rain at every stroke. He now and then let go with one hand or the other to peel off muties that were trying to scale his enormous body. Or just punch their round heads concave.

A stickie hopped onto the rail to J.B.'s left. He was carrying the big shotgun across his body, as ready to use it to push, poke, or smash as to blast. Now he twitched the front end slightly up and back and pulled the trigger. The recoil hurt his left elbow and right wrist, but he didn't feel half so bad, he reckoned, as the stickie.

The shot simply obliterated the chinless lower quarter of its face and its skinny neck. What was left of its head fell back over the rail to its right. The decapitated body, hands patting wildly at the air, toppled straight back.

Things looked bad. They looked worse when a fresh wave of stickies broke over the bow to descend on the supine Nataly and press Krysty and Myron back to the bulkhead.

A white figure with a black torso dropped from above on the back of the stickie that was crawling up the first mate's belly and reaching for her face. He squashed it onto her, eliciting a squawk from both of them. It turned to a whistling scream as the stickie's spine broke beneath the combat boots Jak wore. He smashed in a second stickie's face with a backhand blow from his trench knife's brass pommel. He had one of his butterfly knives in his left hand. It slashed at a stickie that was reaching for him. Sucker-tipped fingers flew, and three streams of yellow blood fountained.

Another stickie landed on the albino's back, wrapping him with its arms. It instantly whipped its arms open wide and fell backward off him, keening in pain— a horrible broken, gurgling sound. Its front and the insides of its arms were gashed and running yellow from the bits of broken glass and sharp metal Jak kept sewed to the shoulders and collar of his jacket, to discourage just that sort of unwanted intimacy.

Arliss came around the other corner, levering shots from his Marlin as fast as he could jack the action. Then the rest of the scavvy party rushed forward around him and J.B., smiting or shooting.

They quickly cleared the foredeck of muties, then they crowded to the rail. In response to an almost-screamed order from Myron, Nataly retreated to the shelter of the bridge to reload her handblaster and re-assemble the wits scattered by the crack to her pony-tailed head. J.B. could see how the captain might have made an impression. Aside from the fact he was her shipmate, her employer and her commanding officer, he was a terrifying sight himself, with stickie blood and bits of flesh strung all through his curly beard and hair, his eyes wild.

The rest of the crew rushed to the rail. They fired into the horde of stickies with all the bullets they could put in the air. J.B. had swapped his scattergun for his Uzi once again and burned through a pair of mags before he had to ease off to let the blaster cool.

The muties dropped in waves. The attack faltered. Even insensate muties had their limits. So many were thrashing underfoot, or lying inert and in the way, it was hard for their hideous kindred to advance. The nearer half of the open air was cleared of stickies that were still capable of keeping on their feet.

But others continued to stream from the woods. The horrors had to be converging from miles around. Now the new arrivals crowded forward so powerfully that the shrinking muties in the front ranks were driven toward the blasters that had been chilling them by the dozen.

And the fire was slackening as first one and then another defender had to stop to reload. Those who lacked cartridge weapons had to withdraw to the wheelhouse to reload. Even Arliss had to thumb one cartridge after another into the side of his repeater's breech.

The muties advanced deliberately. And then Suzan, her voice cracking in terror, yelled out, "They're coming over the stern! The bastards are behind us!"

Chapter Eighteen

As fast as he could draw them—an eye blinked more slowly—Jak put his knives away. He was already in the act of sprinting a few steps back across the deck. He jumped, caught the forward edge of the wheelhouse roof with his hands and hauled himself onto it.

They had all been warned not to trust their weight to the roof. Although the walls and interior upright of the burned-out parts of the cabin had been shored up, and the roof patched, it was nowhere near sound. But Jak already knew where the roof was strong enough for his slight weight or not. He didn't have to look where he put his feet. He just charged.

A mutie was already standing up on the rear of the roof, suckered hands held high. It rushed to meet him as Jak drew his knives. He kicked it in the belly and it sailed back off the cabin.

A trio of others scrambled up. Jak grinned. To die chilling stickies was beneath a hunter's dignity, but it beat the glowing nuke shit out of dying while *not* chilling them.

The albino charged straight at the mutie on his right. He gave it a flying punch in the face with his trench knife's studded hand-guard, smashing in its skull.

The middle stickie turned toward him. He slashed

its palms with a figure-eight cut of his blade. It pulled its hands over its head, looking hilariously as if it was surrendering.

If it had, that would have made no difference to Jak. He rammed the tip of his knife into the creature's eye, killing it. It collapsed to the deck as the remaining one charged Jak with its head down.

He stepped to his left and engaged the stickie by ramming the blade of the trench knife to the hilt in its gut. He twisted the blade, feeling the tip grate against the monster's spine. Then he yanked it out right to left, spilling ropes of blue intestine. A mutie popped its head up to his right. He guessed they were pulling their usual mutie-pyramid trick: not boosting one another, but simply one scaling another like a ladder whether the first one agreed to it or not. He'd seen them stack so high making a ramp against a tall wall that it squished the ones on the bottom, and the blood ran in yellow streams from its base.

He spun his hips clockwise, bringing his right foot up in a scything kick. It caught the side of the stickie's face and snapped its head right around. He heard the thin neck break like an oversize stalk of celery.

Then through the sheets of rain he saw something that made even his blood run cold. The hot joy of battle drained from him in an instant.

"Boats!" he called out to his comrades, who were now battling the stickies face-to-face on the decks to either side of the cabin. "Plenty boats—all around!"

"SWAMPERS!" RICKY HEARD Suzan scream. She fell back a step from the mass of stickies, letting her guard down, lowering the stray chunk of lumber she'd been using to batter them to the deck. With a grunt, Santee pitched a section of bridge truss that had to have weighed one hundred pounds or more over her head to pulp a quartet of stickies against the decking. Aiming over her shoulder one-handed, the youth saw Mildred deftly shoot the eye out of the mutie that was trying to take advantage of the woman's vulnerability to suck her face off with its fingers.

"Let that be a lesson to you, son," J.B. said to Ricky, smashing a stickie's head in with a piston stroke of his shotgun's buttstock. "No matter how bad things seem, they can always get a lot worse."

"They'll eat us!" Suzan shrieked. However, the fresh dose of adrenaline this new fear gave her seemed to energize the woman. She raised her plank and jabbed a stickie in the throat with its jagged end. The mutie went down holding its neck with both hands and making unmistakable choking sounds. The injury would slow it for a while, but not chill it.

"I heard they roast people slowly over fires," Santee said, sounding as if he thought that was the best joke ever. He grabbed one of Suzan's shoulders and pulled her away from the muties who were picking their way over the rubble the defenders had made of the latest batch of attackers and stepped up to take her place. "Quit hogging all the fun for a while, will you?"

Ricky had put away his handblaster to use his broomstick as a lightweight quarterstaff. It wasn't a very good weapon, but these stickies, resilient though they were, were markedly on the lightly constructed side. It didn't take that hard a crack to shatter a mutie's skull like an egg, with yellow ooze for a white and clumpy blue stuff for a yolk.

"Well, the swampers got a job of work ahead to kill us harder than the stickies would," J.B. said.

"Not boarding!" Ricky heard Jak shout from on top of the cabin.

Blasterfire ripped out to left and right of the beached craft, which given its angle meant just as close to fore and aft of her. He saw yellow flames stabbing through the rain, then blurred shapes of canoes and other small boats pushing ashore.

"Let them fight it out!" Krysty's voice rang like a trumpet over the din. "Let's clear the decks of these monsters, then deal with the swampers!"

Since between them Suzan, Mildred and the giant Indian pretty much seemed to have the starboard side handled, not to say blocked, Ricky followed Krysty around the port side of the cabin. He took the opportunity to tuck his stick under his arm and clumsily reload his Webley.

Doc and Avery, who also had axes, had been holding off the muties trying to attack that way. Even though Doc had emptied his LeMat revolver and discharged the stub shotgun, he kept it in his hand and used it to bludgeon stickies. From the way the weapon was coated in stickie gore and brains despite the now-torrential rain, Ricky feared for Doc's safety if he tried to shoot the thing again before giving it a thorough cleaning.

He heard hoarse shouts from the shore behind him, some masculine, some feminine. There was less blasting going on now, but he heard the unmistakable sound of hard wood and steel meeting stickie flesh with bad intent.

He heard J.B. milking short bursts from his Uzi and took a look over his shoulder. The Armorer was shooting at the swampers who had now formed a line in a rough semicircle inland of the *Queen*'s bow, and were smashing the stickies back toward the tall grass step by gore-slippery step.

Then Ricky realized that wasn't the case at all. J.B. was firing over the heads of the swampers into the mass of the stickies beyond.

Well, that makes sense, he thought. I'd rather die at the hand of a human than a stickie any day.

Then he blundered into the rail, knocking all the breath out of him and bruising a rib. He turned and hurried after his friends, who had already reached the afterdeck, leaving busted-to-nuke stickies lying in their wake. He wasn't moving top speed, either. He had given himself a definite hitch in the side.

Ricky reached the end of the cabin in time to see Doc driving his sword into the open mouth of a stickie. He realized there were no other muties vertical, anywhere he could see.

Jak was at the taffrail, leaning over. "All gone," he said. He sounded at once triumphant and disappointed.

The other survivors had crowded onto the aft deck now, except for J.B., who was still banging away in the stern.

Krysty slammed a magazine home into the butt of her Glock, then she wiped yellow ooze off her face and whipped her hand to the side to clear as much of it off as she could.

"This stuff is *never* coming out of my hair," she said. "The rain's not even helping anymore. Ace. We got the ship. Let's take a deep breath and go help the swampers."

"Help the swampers?" Jake demanded. "Have you slipped your mooring, woman?"

A whole flap of skin had been torn free and hung loosely from his right cheek, and it was oozing blood. He seemed unaware of it, though Ricky was sure it had to sting like all get-out.

"They're human," she said, "and they're fighting stickies. That's enough for me. They want to chill us later, they can take their best shot."

Myron and Nataly stared at her. They were shipboard, of course, but neither seemed inclined to force the issue with the tall redhead. The fact was, Ricky thought, they looked relieved to be following her lead.

"I'm in," Arliss said. "They had plenty chance to jump us when we were sorely pressed. Or merely sit on their boats and laugh as the stickies tore us to pieces."

He looked around. "Everybody fit to fight?"

Miraculously, everybody was. Except for the unfortunate Sean, who had died the death he most dreaded in all the world. The memory made Ricky shiver.

"Okay," Krysty said. "Ricky, nip inside and get your longblaster. Yours, not Ryan's Scout."

It made sense. They had a lot more .45 ACP rounds than 7.62 mm NATO. And at the ranges he'd be shooting, he could hit a stickie as well over open sights with the homemade carbine as the fancy Steyr. And chill them just as dead with .45-caliber rounds.

"Then you and Mildred climb up on the cabin and snipe. As for me, I'm going on the beach. The rest of you can go or stay as you please!"

"Yes, *ma'am*!" Ricky replied eagerly. Then he was filled with the embarrassed fear that his eager assent would be construed as betraying that he was secretly relieved at not having to get close to any more stickies, at least for a spell.

Especially since that was exactly what he felt.

He did notice, as he headed for the hatch inside, that everybody except Mildred followed Krysty forward to join the swampers in battle.

Chapter Nineteen

I can't remember when I've ever been this tired, Krysty thought.

But humans—if swampers were truly human, as they looked to be at close range—were the only things left alive in the clearing now. Or would be after the work of finishing off the wounded muties and prodding every one of the more than a hundred stickie bodies strewed across the clearing was done.

She sat down where she was. The rain drenched her. She raised her face to it, grateful for its caress as she was for the solidity of the ground on her tired rump.

She had long since holstered her Glock. She didn't have any more magazines with her, anyway. But the last of it had been melee, smashing the stickies with the steel wrecking bar until the last remnants turned and vanished into grass that was far taller than the muties were. She let the gory bar fall to the grass and practiced trying to open her hand.

"You all right, sister?" a female voice asked.

Krysty looked up. She hadn't even been aware her head was drooping between her spread-apart knees.

"I'm not hurting, thanks," she said. "At least, nothing major. Yet."

She smiled, and then realized she had never in her life seen the woman she was talking to.

It shouldn't surprise me this much, she thought. I've been standing between a pair of swamper men, with none of us showing sign of anything on our minds but chilling stickies. Whatever they really are, they're sure not acting hostile.

She renewed the smile, with full intention this time, not mere easygoing habit.

"I'm pleased to meet you," she said. "I'm Krysty Wroth."

"Ermintrude Strank," the woman said. "No thanks to my paw and maw."

She was of medium height and wide, pretty much all the way from shoulders to thighs, but she didn't seem fat. Not at all—she looked sunken-in, somehow, as if her bones were a rack her black skin had been spread on to dry.

"You saved us when the stickies almost had us," Krysty said. "I reckon we owe you a lot of thanks."

"We did."

Krysty turned her head to look toward the voice. A tall, rangy, knobby-jointed man strode toward them, grinning. He had a pair of machetes with sturdy bow hand-guards, not unlike Jak's except for lacking studs, tipped back, one over each shoulder. The big, broad blades were so encrusted in stickie blood and brains and other tissue that it had started congealing into an ugly blue-and-green-shot mass of yellow despite the rain that continued unabated.

"And you do," the tall man continued as he ap-

proached. "I'm Joe Trombone, and I mean to have a
little talk with you about that."

"You don't seem to be doing too good of a job of living up to your reputation as cannie murderers," Mildred said.

The rain pattered again on the makeshift lean-tos
they'd assembled with tarps from the *Mississippi Queen*
and swamper oars. It kept coming and going. A few little fires burned among the circle of shelters, just enough
under the canopies to keep from getting doused while
still allowing the smoke to escape. Or that was the the-
ory, anyway. Krysty's eyes and throat stung.

Krysty looked at her friend. She knew that Mildred's
bluntness would have won an eye roll from Ryan, if
not a bark of reproof, and sometimes her sharp tongue
had been known to cause trouble. And not just for her.

But the swampers seemed amused if anything by her.

"Sadly, no," Joe Trombone said in his dry way. "You
might call it advertising."

"Why would anybody advertise being cannie murderers?" Santee asked.

"Keep people out," J.B. said, poking the fire in front
of him with a stick. Sparks flew up as one burned-
through driftwood chunk collapsed into the red em-
bers. "Right?"

"Why would you need to keep people *out* of a strontium swamp?" Arliss asked. He was managing to keep
up a pretty brave front, although Krysty knew his
friend's horrible death was hitting him hard. "That's
not what I'd call a big attraction, right there."

"Sadly, it doesn't keep out as well as you'd expect," Ermintrude said. She sat next to Joe. She didn't seem to be his wife. Or if she was that didn't seem to be why she was sitting there; she seemed to be a co-leader of the group with him. Or possibly the leader of a component band. Krysty wasn't sure.

Only a dozen or so of the swamp folk remained in the clearing. The others had pulled their boats into the water and headed back up Wolf Creek not long after the battle ended.

"Who would come in here after you?" Krysty asked. "We know the rad count's high in here, and we know the stories are true about killer crocs and the stickies."

"Our charming neighbors," Joe said, biting off a chunk of crocodile jerky they'd given him and chewing vigorously. "Huh. Bit bland—could use a touch of ghost pepper—but you don't do a half-bad job for outlanders. Anyway, you already met 'em, our biggest problems. People from New Vickville and Poteetville hunt us for sport. Sometimes it even seems like they think if they somehow wipe us out, it'll take care of the rads and the death-metal and the stickies and all."

"So on the rare time when one or two of us go out on the river and to a ville," Ermintrude said, "they make sure to talk the place up as Hell on Earth. Ain't far wrong, of course."

"And we're not saying we don't ambush them when they come in looking for us," Joe said. "Helps to keep up appearances. And also keeps us from winding up slaves on some New Vick plantation."

"So how come you can survive in here?" Ricky asked. "Are you muties?"

That brought a suddenly intent stillness to every swamper in earshot. Ricky shrank from the look Joe gave him, even though there was no overt hostility in the anthracite eyes.

"Since you're young 'n' ignorant," the swamper boss said, "I'll just go along pretending like I never heard that. We're not muties. What we are is *survivors*. Our ancestors got chased here, generations back, by some triple-bad people. They weren't even all people, mebbe."

He shook his head. "Anyway, it's all just stories now. Point is, the rads and the fallout poisoning sickened and chilled us, just the same as everybody else.

"But not *all* of us. Some of us proved to just be naturally resistant to all that. Only stumbling into the midst of the nastiest nuke hot spot would have any effect on us. That a person could see, anyway.

"And after a spell, we started building our numbers back. There's bands of us scattered all through the strontium swamps."

"So why'd you help us?" Nataly asked. She sat cross-legged under a lean-to next to the one Krysty sheltered under, gazing somberly into the fire. She was the ranking member of the *Queen*'s crew present. Myron had retired to the ship for the night.

"We aimed to put you in our debt," Ermintrude said.

"Well, that's candid," Arliss replied. "Why?"

"We want out," Joe said.

"Say what?" the master rigger said, blinking in surprise.

"We're sick of living stuck in this radioactive asshole," Ermintrude said. "When Joe says we're survivors and all, you've got to understand what that means. And that is—the rads and the heavy metal poisoning just chills us slower than it's chilling you."

For a fact, though they seemed healthy and vigorous, the swamper faces around the little fires didn't look quite right to Krysty. They were gaunt and hollow-eyed, and like Ermintrude's, their bodies mostly looked sort of shrunk.

And of course Krysty wasn't feeling altogether healthy these days. She doubted anybody else from her group was, either.

"Why haven't you left before?" Avery asked.

"Same reason you're still here," Joe said. "Got no good way to get past our friends out there on the Sippi."

"But surely they have not maintained their current deployment blocking the river for generations."

"If you mean, have they had their big old fleets toe-to-toe the whole time, no. But they had patrol boats ready to troll us in, and either enslave us or just massacre us outright. So once we came here, we found ourselves stuck."

"We've only been thinking of it, making a break for it, for a couple years now," Ermintrude said. "Joe and me."

"But why us?" Avery asked.

"Well," Joe said, "to start with, you didn't come in here acting all hostile, like outlander folk usually do."

"Except to stickies," Ermintrude added. "But that's ace with us. We hate stickies."

Mildred waved at the rest of the clearing. "We kind of got the idea."

For her part, Krysty just hoped the rain would wash the stickie blood far enough away that the place wouldn't reek for days of rotting stickie. The bodies they'd just tossed into Wolf Creek. The crocodiles were welcome to them, if they wanted them.

"Also you have that big old ship," Joe said. "And you seem to have a double-clever idea of how to pull off getting out of here, too. Making your own ironclad and everything. Where'd you get an idea like that?"

"It's all J.B.'s notion," Nataly said. "I'll let him explain."

"Years ago," the Armorer replied, "a trader I ran with had a history book that said how way back predark in the Civil War, these Confederates armored up an ironclad of their own, to run the Union fleet that was blockading the river and bust out. Dark night, I think it was even on the Yazoo, that we come down.

"Supposedly they did it all out just setting in a cornfield, using old railroad iron. I also recall reading somewhere else as to how it didn't rightly go down that way. But that doesn't matter here. What does is that it set me to thinking."

"Well," Joe said, "I like the way you think. And that brings me to the business proposition we had in mind afore we decided to come lend you a hand today."

"What's that?" Arliss asked, his brow narrowing in reflex concern. Krysty thought that was tipping your hand a bit much for a man who was supposed to be a master negotiator. Then again, they'd all had a hard day, and nobody harder than him. Well, except for his friend Sean.

"We help you finish getting your ship ready to go," the swamper leader said, "and you take us with you."

"How many people have you got?" Avery asked.

"Two hundred fifty souls, give or take. Ermintrude's and my bands."

The boatswain shook his head. "No way. Sorry. We can cram a dozen or two inside the cabin or belowdecks."

"Nobody's riding *outside* the armor," Abner said from another lean-to, "unless they don't mind winding up a red smear on the ironmongery."

"We've got plenty of boats," the swamper woman said. "And you've got plenty power to tow them, I bet. Even with all that excess scrap iron onboard. You were a river tug, weren't you?"

"We have the power to tow almost any number of light craft," Nataly replied. "Especially downstream, which is the way we're going. But how will you survive, without armor to protect you from the New Vickville cannon? Not to mention possible small-arms fire."

"You think they'll waste time on us, not to mention powder and ball, when there's another big old ironclad driving right through them thumbing her nose?" Joe asked. "They'll be too busy shooting at you."

"There's a reassuring thought," Mildred said.

"What are your thoughts, J.B., Krysty?" Nataly asked. The formality meant she was asking, What do you think of it as people who, though you don't like to call yourselves professional trigger-pullers, most certainly find yourselves pulling triggers a great deal more than we do?

"Sounds ace to me," J.B. said, after Krysty looked pointedly his way. "Don't see how it's going to worsen our chances any."

Krysty nodded. "I certainly have no objection."

"I trust you will pardon me for asking," Doc said, "but what if our gratitude at being rescued by you failed to overcome your fearful reputation—or our own debased natures, should we turn out to possess such?"

Joe grinned. "We'd just wipe you out, feed what's left of you to the crocs."

"Why not do that anyway and take our boat?" Jake asked.

"We're not coldhearts," Ermintrude said. "We're mean because we have to be, when we have to be. And then, of course, we're powerful mean. But we don't cotton to chilling them as doesn't harm us."

"Besides," Joe added, with a grin even more lopsided than his oddly uneven features could account for on their own, "should you turn out to be snakes after all, we can always wipe you out and feed you to the crocs then."

Nataly cocked a brow at Doc. "Does that reassure you?" she asked.

Doc grinned and shot his cuffs. He had his long black coat on.

"Speaking just for me," Abner said, "I wasn't looking forward to digging enough of a hole to float the poor old *Queen* out with just the hands we had. Goes triple with all that pig iron piled on top of her."

None of the other crew objected. Nataly nodded in her ultra-precise way.

"Very well. Captain Conoyer has authorized me to make all such decisions, including agreements, in his absence. And I am pleased to accept your kind offer, Mr. Trombone, Miss Strank. As well as to thank you again for saving us today."

She reached out and shook hands with the two chieftains.

"It's not like Myron's gonna object," Moriarty said, rallying somewhat, "at the prospect of anything that'll help him get the *Queen* underway again."

Joe and Ermintrude rose together, then the other swampers stood.

"We'll be heading back, then," the tall man said. "Long row back upriver."

Ricky scrambled to his feet. "Mr. Trombone?"

The swamper looked at him.

"Do you play?"

Joe laughed.

"Kid," he said, "I play chess and mumblety-peg, but I don't play a note of music. My name's Trombino, actually, but nobody ever bothers calling me that."

Chapter Twenty

Another sunset over the Sippi. Another little steamblasterboat was making its way toward the flagship of the Grand Fleet, carrying Ryan and his squad of the day. The sky had mostly gone indigo, with streaks of blue-gray emanating from a yellow glow where the sun had just rolled down beyond the western weeds.

Ryan didn't remember the blasterboat's name. He barely even recalled the name of the squaddie who'd been bitten by a water moccasin, bringing an end to their day's patrol down another dead-end bayou. The man looked to Ryan as if he'd make it, even if they had to tie him down to a makeshift stretcher to haul him back. Water moc bites were painful. He'd quieted down now, since the blasterboat crew had poured half a bottle of local rotgut down his throat to shut him up.

It was uncharacteristic of Ryan to have trouble keeping track of details like that. It didn't help that his personnel changed day to day. The only constant was Chief Jones and his sarcastic manner, always just nosing almost up to the point of challenge or insubordination. Ryan took for granted he was a spy for the baron now, not just a sec man along to give some seasoned backup as the new officer got some experience, although he was also good at his job, and handy in a fight, as he had shown in a couple brushes with crocs and stickies.

They were working their way closer to Wolf Creek with every new reconnaissance patrol. That concerned Ryan, though not as much as the fact that two weeks had gone by since he'd been hauled aboard the *Pearl* with a bag over his head and deposited in Baron Tanya's stateroom.

His plan to do something fancy enough she'd be willing to let him and his friends just steam out of this place was starting to seem mighty threadbare. Between the slowly accumulating rad count his friends were experiencing, and the risk they'd be discovered, he was going to need to make something happen, sooner rather than later.

"Hail the blasterboat!" a voice called through a bullhorn. "Stand by while we pull alongside."

"Fancy buggers," remarked a crew-woman of the patrol boat Ryan and his troops were riding. She spit over the rail. "Think their drek don't stink."

Ryan eyed the approaching steam launch. It was narrower than the blasterboat, if not much shorter. Instead of a permanent wooden structure that covered the helm and the boiler, if it didn't quite enclose them, the launch had a canopy of fancy-looking cloth set up on the forward half of it. The boiler was exposed to the elements in the stern.

The officer commanding the blasterboat ordered the helm and engineer to comply. He was a young man and seemed cowed.

"What's going on?" Ryan asked. "Who are these people?" They did fly the colors of the Grand Fleet from their stern. Then again it wasn't as if a Poteetville craft would steam brazenly in here, in blaster range of some of the capital ships' screening frigates.

"Captain's launch from the *Revenge*," the black-haired woman said.

A young officer stuck his head out of the canopy. "Is Junior Lieutenant Ryan Cawdor on board?"

Ryan stepped forward. "Yeah. That's me."

"Compliments of Senior Lieutenant Danville of Danville, and he wishes to speak to you on board *Revenge* at your earliest convenience."

"MR. CAWDOR," THE TALL, thin young man said as an orderly ushered Ryan in. "What a pleasure to make your acquaintance. I am Senior Lieutenant Dober Danville of Danville, First Officer of the *Revenge*, at your service."

He stepped up and shook Ryan's hand. His hand was very slender, but his grip was firm enough. He was a few inches shorter than Ryan, and slim, with impossibly sleek brown hair. His uniform had been fussily tailored.

The stateroom was far less spacious than Baron Tanya's. It wasn't much bigger than Ryan's cabin aboard the *Pearl*, but it was decorated enough for two of the baron's rooms, with lots of bric-a-brac and a big painting of what looked like Lieutenant Dober standing with an older, heavier version of himself.

"My dear old da," Danville said, following Ryan's eye. He released his hand. "I'm not *the* Danville yet, of course. Not while the old dragon breathes. Ha, ha."

That didn't seem to call for any response, so Ryan made none. "Please, be seated. Brandy?"

"No, thanks," Ryan said, as he parked his weary behind in a red velvet chair. "So, what do you want from me, Lieutenant?"

"Ah, direct, as befits a man of action such as yourself."

Ryan couldn't help noticing the young man wore a sidearm in a flapped holster. He hadn't gotten enough of a look at it to identify it.

The lieutenant leaned forward. "Tell me what you think of the baron," he said.

That set warning bells to ringing loud enough in Ryan's head that by rights they should make his forehead bulge. So that's how it goes, he thought.

"She's the boss," he said. "I do what she says."

"Oh, of course. Of course." The man sat up again. "You're a man who does his duty."

"I do my job."

"Yes, yes. Precisely. And since you put it in those terms—would you consider a change of employers?"

"Baron Tanya seems to like my work," Ryan said. "I don't reckon she'd exactly release me from my contract."

"Ah, but the baron doesn't need to know! Not until it's too— That is, there would be no reason to consult her preferences in the matter."

"What's your proposition, exactly?"

"The baron is a usurper," Danville said. "She's leading New Vickville to disaster."

Why are you telling me this? Ryan wondered. He already knew the surface reason. It was the reason for

them making the offer to him, now, in this way. There
had to be more.

Arrogance was clearly part of the equation. Ryan
knew the signs double well.

He leaned back in the chair, scooted his butt forward, crossed his legs and settled into a relaxed sprawl.
"That's pretty blunt," he said.

Danville smiled. "You are a realist, Mr. Cawdor, and
you are a man whose loyalties are for sale. The baron
seems to value your services highly. Understandable,
based on your recent actions during the nighttime sneak
attack by Poteetville, and the way you came to be in the
Grand Fleet in the first place."

Got it now, Ryan thought. The conspirators Baron
Tanya had said were out to get her? They were. It didn't
mean there was no such thing as paranoia. But in the
world Ryan had grown up in if you thought somebody
was plotting against you, he or she probably was.

And likewise if you didn't. "I represent a cadre of
leading citizens of New Vickville, which you must understand is by way of a federation of villes, joined into
a more powerful whole for mutual benefit and defense.
As such, we have banded together in recognition of the
benefits of a strong guiding hand on the tiller of state.

"But when that hand is itself guided by the mind and
morals of a gaudy slut, well…"

You've decided I'm dangerous, Ryan was thinking.
So you're thinking you'll either turn me, or burn me.

He remembered an expression he'd heard somewhere: You're so sly—but so am I.

"And?" he said.

For a moment Danville blinked, seemingly nonplussed. Then he recovered and plastered his smarmy smile back across his face.

"And so I want to hire you on behalf of my associates, Mr. Cawdor. To the extent you may care about such things, the future welfare of New Vickville lies at stake here. But you're an outlander as well as a mercie. What do you care for that sort of thing, right? We can pay. And offer what this Baron Tanya would not—true status among the landholders of the barony. A barony of your own, I mean."

"You have a few lying around spare."

This time Danville's smile had fangs. "Some are likely to become available in the not-so-distant future, let us say."

Ryan rubbed his chin. "Very generous," he said. "And mighty appealing. But again, why would you make an offer like this to a scabby mercie who got fished out of the river?"

"Because unlike the usurping bitch, Mr. Cawdor, we recognize the true value of a man like you. We won't pass you off with promises of reward. We'll deliver the real thing!"

Now, how would you know a thing like that, Junior? Ryan wondered. He filed the question away in his mind.

Revenge had a rep among all the crews for having the shiniest brass and the most atrocious gunnery skills in the Grand Fleet. Her captain, Edmund Geislinger, was a weakling who was easily influenced and manipulated by his underlings. Not a plotter, but a weakling. If this well-turned-out young traitor depended on his crew for his sec, Ryan should have no trouble turning down the offer—and making his way out alive.

But if not-yet-Baron Danville had his own sec men along, things might get dicey. Ryan was good, but he had too many holes in his hide to pretend to himself he was bulletproof.

I got to get back to Krysty and the others, he thought. That's my only job here. Help get them out. Even the rest of the crew, if they don't slow us down too much. I can't risk throwing my life away here. I have to think of them.

He stood up, grinned and stuck out his hand.

"Looks like you hired yourself a blaster, Baron Danville."

"Ah, if only." The young man's smile was the most generous Ryan had seen on his face. Apparently Ryan's rare attempt at flattery had worked. Not that this case had been much of a challenge.

The lieutenant rose and extended his hand.

"Welcome to the right side of history, Mr. Cawdor," he said. "It gratifies me that my estimate of you has proved correct. You have made a wise choice."

Ryan gritted his teeth behind something he figured would pass for a smile, nodded and focused hard on not crushing that hand to pulp.

Triple hard.

"AND YOU TOLD them you were in?" Baron Tanya Krakowitz of New Vickville asked. It was just the two of them by lamplight in her stateroom.

"I did."

"And then you came right back here to me as fast as those long, lean legs would carry you to rat out your new employers?"

Ryan just spread his hand and tipped his head, in such a way as to point out, I'm here.

She tipped *her* head to one side, almost matching his gesture, and studied him frowningly from behind a rope of gray smoke from her cigarette.

"If you'd go back on your word to them, can I trust you?"

"I came here," he said. "Like you said. You got to make your own mind up what that means to you."

"Are you here looking for me to outbid them?"

"I would've said that straight, if that was my plan. Your move."

She laughed. "Good man! I'd have thought you'd turned stupe on me if you hadn't lied to them. Not that I ever would have seen you again."

"That was how I sized up the situation, Baron," he said, although he still would not have bet against his chances of making it out still breathing.

But he had also seen yet another chance to maybe buy safe passage clear for his friends before they all died convulsing in their own runny shit. Or wound up looking at the lining of a stickie's bellies.

"Now that the hydra has exposed a head," the baron said thoughtfully, "I intend to stamp on it hard with my heel. To encourage the others, you know."

"Remember what else there was about the hydra that made it special."

She laughed. "So erudite for a mercie! And yes. I recall quite clearly that along with having an overabundance of heads, they grew back when you cut one off. That's why I would prefer it if you return this treasonous little shit to me alive. If that proves impossible, well—message sent."

"If *I* return him?"

"Who better to arrest him? By coming here like this you've cemented your place as one of the few people in this fleet I know I can trust."

Her brow wrinkled in thought. "Let's see…you'll need a squad to back you up. At the least. Sec men or naval infantry? I leave it up to you."

"Just a boat with a pilot to get me back there and bring back a prisoner."

Her thoughtful look got squashed together in the middle in a look of puzzlement—and fresh skepticism.

"Mebbe you *are* crazy. You're talking about going in and arresting him on your lonesome? Even if you can deal with his daddy's hired bullyboys— Never mind. I'm sure you can. But Eddie, wimp that he is, will still get flash-heated past nuke red if you lay the hard arm on his current pet executive officer."

"Then if I need troops along, a squad's too little," he said. "What I do need is for you to be prepared to back my play."

"How far?"

"All the way."

A smile slowly grew across her broad face. She leaned forward. "Come closer and tell your auntie Tanya what's on your devious mind."

He did.

RYAN RODE ACROSS the nighttime water in a vessel known as a packet boat. Its function was to deliver messages—or messengers, as it was doing now. Ryan carried an arrest warrant in a pouch on his holster belt next to his panga sheath.

The *Revenge* was lit up, at least as brightly as dozens of turpentine lamps could make her. It did make her bulk seem even more looming and gigantic, even though she was far smaller than the *Pearl*. An unusual number of lights were lit because the frigate had reversed orders to take its place screening the flagship, replacing the *Hera*, which had been slotted there. Such shakeups were not uncommon, to keep captains of the lesser ironclads from getting complacent. The new placement also accounted for the trip to the vessel being so short.

Likely Captain Geislinger was cussing up a storm on his bridge right now. He took such unexpected changes in routine personally. A man who was serious about his complacency, by all accounts.

They dropped a wooden ramp with side railings as the packet approached the frigate's starboard quarter. Such comings and goings were routine, at any time of the day or night.

"Junior Lieutenant Cawdor," Ryan said to the single sailor standing stiffly at the top of the ramp. "Carrying a personal message to First Officer Danville from Baron Tanya." He waved a piece of lumpy paper that had been folded and stamped with the baron's seal in red wax.

The sentry ran a contemptuous eye over Ryan. The sailor had a shiny chin strap fixing his pillbox hat to his head, and a full-size Springfield 1873 replica with a fixed bayonet slung over his back. If the blade had ever nicked an edge scraping human bone, or had its shiny finish sullied by blood, there was no evidence Ryan could see.

The kid nodded wordlessly. Courier from the baron or not, Ryan was clearly not important enough to be worth actual *words*.

The one-eyed man walked on his way, purposefully, but without hurry.

RYAN TURNED THE latch and pushed open the door on the upper deck of the *Revenge*'s cabin.

Senior Lieutenant Dober Danville sat at a fold-down desk, writing. He had little pince-nez specs perched on the end of his long nose. He looked up.

His expression of rising rage turned to blank befuddlement. "Cawdor. What are you doing here?"

Ryan held up the paper with his left hand. "Senior Lieutenant Danville, I'm placing you under arrest by the baron's personal orders. Stand up and turn around."

He had a pair of predark handcuffs jingling from his belt. They were easy to pick, if you could get hold of a little piece of metal and bend it a little. He did not make Danville for a man who knew that.

Danville leaped to his feet. "What's the meaning of this? Why, you traitor!"

His handsome and insipid face had turned purple. Now it flashed to a pale white.

With a commendable turn of speed, the senior lieutenant undid the flap of his holster and began to haul out his sidearm.

Before the handblaster cleared leather, Ryan had drawn his SIG, dropped into a crouch and fired two quick rounds.

Danville jerked as the 9 mm slugs punched through his sternum to pierce the left atrium and aorta of his heart, respectively, like little blood-pumping balloons. His right arm dropped, returning the handblaster to its carrier.

Ryan fired a third shot on top of the classic double tap, right through the middle of his forehead. Danville's eyes rolled up, his lower jaw dropped, and his tongue flopped from his mouth. Then he folded to the deck like an empty suit of clothes.

Ryan shoved the door closed behind him with his boot heel. He holstered the SIG and drew a stubby handblaster from behind his back. He cracked it open from the top. In his pouch he carried two flares for the device. He slid the red one into the single chamber and locked up the piece. Then he stepped to the port.

Less than two hundred yards away the *Pearl* rose like a shadow iceberg. Ryan aimed the blaster high over the flagship's top deck.

The flare that blossomed against the night sky burned red.

Not a minute later the door, which he had pushed closed with his heel after chilling Danville, was kicked open by a heavy boot. A *Revenge* sec man appeared in the doorway, pointing a longblaster into the room.

He looked confused. There was no one in front of him. Unlike Baron Tanya's sec men, with their longblaster repeaters, he had to make do with a single-shot

Springfield 1873 carbine. It did have a bayonet fixed, though. "Over here," Ryan said, from the wall to his right of the door, where the late lieutenant's fold-down bunk was folded up behind walnut paneling. "Twitch that blaster even a hair this way and you're a dead man."

Ryan was holding both his SIG and Danville's weapon at arm's length in front of him. He mostly did it to intimidate: if you actually tried to shoot two hand-blasters at once, you could wind up missing with both. It did make for a mighty fast reload, though. You just switched hands when your first blaster ran dry.

A man bustled into the cabin. His short, wide shape was wrapped in a purple dressing gown over pale blue pajamas. Ryan thought they might be real silk. He had a shock of white hair and a face that likely wasn't always that red.

"I'm Captain Geislinger," he said, not altogether nec-essarily. For one thing, Ryan knew his cabin was across the corridor. "What is— Oh, great flame-puking death angels, Dobie!"

He looked at the chill, lying on its back staring up at the ceiling, with arms outflung.

"What have you done to him?" The captain gobbled like a tom turkey in his rage. Ryan would barely have understood the words, if hadn't already had a general idea what they were going to be.

"Placed him under arrest for treason," Ryan said. He kept both blasters trained on the captain, who to his credit didn't flinch—although Ryan suspected that might either be sheer obliviousness, or the belief that a low-life coldheart like Ryan would never pull the trigger on such an important man as himself.

Ryan hoped he wouldn't have to disabuse the captain of that notion. Thing could get triple sticky, triple fast.

"He resisted arrest," Ryan said. "Saved the baron the cost of a court-martial, anyway."

"Court-martial? Court-martial!" The stocky captain actually barked a mad-sounding laugh. "I'll convene my own captain's mast right here and now, convict you of murder, and have you dangling and strangling to greet the morning sun!"

"Hail, the *Revenge*!" a male voice bellowed though the slitted port. "This is Captain Garza of the *Pearl*. If I do not see Lieutenant Ryan Cawdor, unharmed and unimpeded, making his way back to my ship on his launch within two minutes, I am ordered to open fire on you. Count begins—now!"

"Or mebbe not," Ryan said.

Chapter Twenty-One

The sound at his door brought Ryan instantly awake. He sat up with his SIG in his hand without awareness of having drawn it.

He thought about firing up the lantern hung from the bulkhead, but decided against it. If this was more plotters come to avenge their fallen lieutenant, he didn't want to simplify their targeting solution by lighting up his own stupe ass for them.

But he frowned for more than the thought of danger. That he could deal with, especially if all the conspirators were cast in the same pot metal as Danville. Though as a matter of survival, he knew not to take such a thing for granted.

It was that he hadn't quite made out what the sound was. He only knew that it didn't belong and issued from the door.

It came again: a thumping sound, not loud but somehow insistent, followed by a whisper like something sliding down the wood on the other side.

Ryan got up and went to the near side of the door—the hinge side. Reaching out carefully, he took the hold of the latch, then turned it and hauled the door wide-open, fast.

When no blaster shot exploded into the cabin, he risked a look around the open door.

The tall, nicely built Lieutenant Ellin Stone fell into his arms.

The instant he caught her he knew this was not some romantic ploy. Never mind the way she'd been looking at him since the night he saved her from getting blasted by P'ville raiders.

From the blood trailing from one side of her mouth and coming in pink froth from her fine nostrils, and the feel of warm, sticky wetness on the palm supporting her beneath her back, he knew he wouldn't be saving her this time.

"Must...talk," she said. She coughed blood all over his face and bare shoulder. He was still sleeping in his skivvies, enjoying that luxury while he could.

He half carried her to his bunk and laid her down on it. "Let me call you a medico," he said.

She shook her head. She saw that was a waste of time, too.

"They—will chill you," she said as he lit the lantern. Her teeth were a ghastly red by its light.

"The plotters."

She nodded slightly. Her breath was coming in progressively more rapid wheezes as her lung filled with blood.

She was drowning from the inside out, and there was not one nuking thing Ryan could do about it. He sat beside her. She gripped his hand in both of hers. Her grip was still strong. "Was—one. Told me Tanya...had my brother chilled. Found out...it was a lie. By then, I was with them..."

"So you were the one who told Danville that Tanya was slow in coming across with the promised rewards."

She nodded again. It visibly pained her, but clearly less than speaking would.

He'd known, almost at once. Or *suspected*, but right to the edge of conviction. He hadn't outed her to her boss, and not just because it was still suspicion, however strong. He had wanted to see how things would play out.

He hadn't expect them to play this way.

"Tanya—treated me well. I learned my brother died…mysteriously on patrol. He wouldn't join—"

Her brown eyes, which had been all but closed, snapped open. "They're going to do that to you too, Ryan!"

She tried to say more, but a coughing fit hit her. She rolled onto her side, gagging on her own blood. For a moment Ryan thought he'd lost her.

"There was. A meeting. Aboard *Pearl*. Heard talking. Storeroom. Listened outside. They spotted. Me. Tried. To run. Back-shot me."

"Are they still aboard?"

She shook her head, then winced. "Ran. Came here. Had. To warn. You. Don't go. Out again. Chill. You. My. Luhhh—"

Her head dropped loosely to the side. The gurgling, rattling wheeze stopped.

Ryan shifted her onto her back and laid her hands across her chest.

He knew now what he had to do.

And part of it involved doing the very thing Ellin had died to tell him would get him chilled.

"GOT SOME MIGHTY strange things going on down here," Ensign Paxton shouted, trying to make himself heard over the chug of the blasterboat's steam engine. He was a man not too many years younger than Ryan, a little shorter, lean, with an oily manner and a head that put the one-eyed man in mind of a kidney bean. He stood directly behind Ryan, leaning with arms folded against a brass upright, just in front of the boiler tank.

This engine was the loudest Ryan had encountered. He wondered if there was something wrong with the mechanics, or if it was just an unusual design.

The sun, not long risen, was still warm slanting in from the right. Its beams glinted off the river's slow roll like a thousand tiny mirrors afloat on the brown water. The day was cloudless except for a low shelf of slate-colored clouds to the east. Ryan stood at the front of the wheelhouse next to the helmswoman, a random rating whose name he didn't remember. He had his right hand up against the brass pole that formed the starboard-front corner of the patrol boat's open-sided cabin. It held the pocket chron he'd drawn from stores after having been given his latest assignment by the baron herself. It was an ancient one, but accurate, its steel case kept polished shiny by diligent New Vick quartermasters.

As Ryan had suspected she would, Tanya once again failed to come through with any kind of significant assignment for him. Not even one as obvious as putting him in charge of purging the highly placed plotters in the Grand Fleet. The conspirators who had murdered Tanya's beloved aide had not only escaped clean, but her sec men couldn't even ID them. Ryan reckoned he could track them down quickly, and that should have put him over the top in looking for some achievement stellar enough to swap for safe passage for himself and his friends.

But no. It was straight back on patrol for Ryan. Tanya's rationale this time was that she wanted to get him away from the fleet and out of sight until things calmed down.

"Last week one of our recon boats sneaking home from scoping out the P'ville fleet got caught in that big old cloudburst we had," Paxton hollered, "just about midway between our big ships and theirs. And floating out of some weeds on the east side they saw what they said looked like a raft with a bunch of old scrap iron piled on it. Crazy, huh?"

Ryan turned north, the way they were still headed. He didn't trust his face not to show some reaction. He had no idea why, but he felt gut-sure he knew where the scrap had come from.

What the rad-blast are they up to down there on Wolf Creek? he wondered.

"Raft was already foundering in the storm," Paxton shouted. "Comin' apart. Sank before it even got all the way out in the main channel. Left not a trace. Recon crew weren't able to get an exact fix on where."

Tanya shipping Ryan right back out on recon patrol made at least a degree of sense, until she stopped and realized that this wasn't something that was going to just blow over. Even if all the other plutocrat plotters and bad-apple officers had hated Danville Junior, they would never forgive Ryan for "betraying" one of their own.

He flicked open the watch's highly polished cover: 8:15. Not that he cared.

"Intel bastards took until a couple days ago to even notice. Then some bright boy figured out a hidden tributary might mean a way to get around on Baron Harvey. So they decided to send us down to check it out."

The good news was the area on the map where they'd been ordered to start the search lay south of Wolf Creek. The less good news was that the patrol was supposed to stay out looking for several days.

That was Tanya's way of keeping Ryan out of sight until her enemies' vengeful hate blew over.

"Found some stickie bodies caught on anchor chains from *Medusa* and *Harpy* a couple days later," the blond and ponytailed enlisted woman at the wheel said. "They'd been clubbed, cut, or shot."

She shrugged dismissively. "Probably just swampers, all of it. They're triple crazy on the rads. I hear they're cannies who eat their own babies."

"True fact," Paxton yelled. "All them rads make 'em stone crazy. Them and the stickies deserve each other, if you ask me."

"You fixing to order helm to make the turn soon, *Captain*?" Chief Petty Officer Jones, walking up from the stern, called sarcastically.

Of course that was the only way he ever talked to Ryan. But he put some extra emphasis on the "Captain," which itself was an ironic term, since in Grand Fleet regs the *Doria* was too small to rate the title even as courtesy to its commander.

"Chart says yes," Ryan said. He had never yet risen to the chief's bait, nor would he. "So yes."

That was a big difference on this assignment: in the past, Ryan had commanded a squad on patrol, but the boat they rode in on was commanded by an actual Grand Fleet warrant. Today, by personal order of the baron of New Vickville, Ryan was the full-on commander of the steam blasterboat *Doria* and her crew of four, as well as the actual six-person recon team Jones was attached to. Of them all, Ryan only knew one—the black chief petty officer, whose presence on this mission he had expected. The other five members of Ryan's squad were sitting on the afterdeck, no doubt pissing and moaning because they had to sit in the sun while the two *Doria* crew members got to work in the shade. Of course, they didn't take into account that the crewmen had to work up close to the boiler and the firebox that heated it.

Eleven people were on board the little boat. With odds of ten-to-one, Ryan was confident. Tough odds even for him—and tough even when some of those who were almost certainly in on the plot to chill him were probably not much use in a fight. Unlike Wolf Creek, the mouth of Dead Man's Creek was plainly visible from several hundred yards south. "Commence your turn to starboard as you come to bear, helm," Ryan directed. He wasn't sure that was proper navy lingo, but he also reckoned it would get his point across.

They could have passive-aggressively made him look like a simp by following his command in a way that would run the blasterboat straight aground. But if Ellin

Stone had been right, the plan was to chill him on this trip. Since she'd died to bring him that warning, he was inclined to take it seriously.

However, the *Doria* was still in line of sight of the Grand Fleet, and with no haze on the river, might be under observation through powerful field glasses or even telescopes. It was too risky to try an assassination until the blasterboat left the Sippi.

Sure enough, the rating waited a handful of seconds before commencing to turn the wheel. Marinelli—Ryan recalled her name now—seemed to know her job, anyway. The little craft heeled slightly as it turned up the side-stream.

This one wasn't as wide as Wolf Creek. In fact the banks made solid walls of six-foot-high weeds that seemed claustrophobically close to the *Doria*, even though the deck was high enough that Ryan could see over their tips.

"Slow her down," Ryan commanded the helm. "Better get a leadsman out sounding the channel, just in case." The plan was to take the *Doria* upstream as far as she could safely go, then continue the reconnaissance using the rowboat towed behind the patrol craft's propeller.

Marinelli cast a nervous side-flick glance at him. "Channel looks ace ahead, sir."

"Do it," Ryan said. "You want to ground her in the middle of a stickie-infested strontium swamp?"

Paxton guffawed. "Nuke, no! Vasquez, get your ass in the bow and start dropping the lead."

Another of the *Doria*'s four-man crew left the boiler

and scuttled forward from under the curved wood canopy as the craft slowed. He knelt beside the swivel blaster and began tossing out his knotted rope with the weight on the end.

The vessel that was Ryan's first command didn't even rate a proper cannon. The swivel blaster was just an outsize cap-lock shotgun with a two-inch bore. Ryan had personally overseen its loading that morning. It was a basically an outsize version of the "buck and ball" load, universally popular with those who fired smooth-bore black powder weapons, including the shotguns kept for boarding actions by crews in both ironclad fleets: a one-pound lead ball with a dozen .33-caliber double-ought buckshot pellets. Behind that two pounds of lead he'd poured a full pound of New Vick's best cannon-grade gunpowder.

It was a lot for the blaster to handle, but the fleet armorer he'd talked to assured him the piece could take the pressure. It was designed to do maximum damage to anything unarmored past the muzzle, out to a hundred yards and beyond. It could drop a dozen stickies charging on dry land—or swampers, whatever they were, and if they even existed—and also knock a hole in a *Doria*-size boat that could sink her.

"Uh-oh," Marinelli said. "Crocs."

"Yeah," Paxton agreed. "A mess of the bastards. Ugly as P'ville gaudy sluts, ain't they?"

Ryan saw a few of the characteristic log-with-eyes shapes lying in the water ahead. Looking left and right, he saw more come slithering out of the grass of the banks to slide into the creek, and swim curiously toward the intruding vessel with undulations of their broad, powerful tails.

"Good thing we're in the boat, ain't it?" Paxton yelled. Even with the engine throttled down enough to let Vasquez cast the lead, the engine was still loud enough to overwhelm normal conversation at greater than arm's length.

"Can't get cocky," Ryan called in reply, without looking back over his shoulder. "I've seen the bastards come flying out of the water like they got rockets up their scaly asses. Best stay back from the rails, just in case."

"Encountered these monsters before, have you?" Jones asked from behind Ryan's left shoulder. He was close enough to pitch his voice conversationally and be heard. "Say, whereabouts were you and the employers you ran out on camped, when you built those rafts?"

"Like I told the baron, I don't know. I'm not a navigator. All these creeks and streams and runlets of piss dribbling out of these stinking swamps look the nuking same to me. Anyway, it was my employers ran out on *me*, if I remember right."

"Look there," Jones said, thrusting his left hand past Ryan's face to point through the open front of the cabin, above the waist-height front bulkhead. "Here comes a double-large one. Better take a look.

"A nice, long look."

Chapter Twenty-Two

The words and tone of voice should have been enough to warn Ryan what was coming.

Jones had a tendency to run his mouth. Ryan guessed the man had been put on him as a spy because he had proved himself as an elite fighter. But while he was an ace soldier, he wasn't much of a spy. A more skilled spy would have avoided the near-insubordinate banter in which Jones constantly engaged Ryan. He would have tried to befriend his mark—although Ryan might have seen through that almost as quickly. Or better still, maintained an air of neutral competence and ready compliance with Ryan's commands. In other words, not made a point of calling attention to himself.

But Jones clearly had an ego, and it had to have rubbed his ass raw that some random mercie fished out of the Sippi was getting so much fuss made over him, when a seasoned New Vick warrior like him labored in obscurity. So he ran his mouth.

It should have been enough.

But Ryan didn't have to rely on the chancy interpretation of his tone of voice, nor his take on what *might* have been a man with a habit of talking too much. Because he was watching from the corner of his single eye in the mirror-polished cover of his pocket chron as Jones quietly undid his holster flap and began to ease his handblaster free.

He turned slightly clockwise and back-kicked Jones in the upper-left thigh as the man began to bring his revolver up to put a bullet in the back of Ryan's head. Taken utterly by surprise, the chief was flung back against the brass pole to portside. He fell to the deck behind Marinelli.

Ryan was already in furious motion. Using the impetus imparted by his powerful kick meeting the meaty part of Jones's leg, the one-eyed man threw himself forward over the front bulkhead, right out of the cabin. Tucking his head and shoulder, he hit the foredeck, rolled and came up in a crouch, still moving forward fast.

Vasquez was on his knees in the bow, reeling in the knotted rope with the lead weight with the scooped-out nose full of wax at the end, after taking another sounding of the Dead Man's Creek bottom. He turned to look back at the onrushing one-eyed man in surprise.

Without a word, Ryan kicked him right over the prow into the water.

He grabbed the grip-shaped handle cast into the breech of the swivel blaster and, using the last of his forward momentum, swung it 180 degrees right around. His own grip on the handle prevented him from pitching overboard to join the unfortunate leadsman and the somewhat more fortunate crocodiles.

Paxton, slow on the uptake, was only now clawing for his own sidearm, but Marinelli had let go of the wheel and was bringing up the sawed-off 12-gauge shotgun that was kept in a holster by the helm to discourage boarders.

"Mine's bigger," Ryan said, as he yanked the swivel blaster's lanyard. The hammer dropped on the percussion cap.

The weapon roared and belched a cloud of smoke. The slowly expanding column of double-ought buckshot smashed through the cabin's front bulkhead, clawing Marinelli from behind it and throwing her out of sight. The two-inch cannonball behind punched a neat hole through the already perforated panel to strike the boiler with a clang so resounding Ryan heard it over the ringing in his ears from the swivel blaster's shot.

The effect was even better than he'd expected. The fast-moving one-pound ball ruptured the boiler. A giant cloud of steam suddenly billowed out both sides of the cabin and filled the little pilothouse. Scalded sailors shrieked in agony.

It was also worse than intended. Ryan had hoped to jack the boat himself and take it back to his friends. In a pinch, he thought there was at least a gambler's chance he could sneak them past the Grand Fleet in her, given that *Doria* was one of theirs. Now that prospect didn't look possible. With her boiler busted, and with the spoked steering wheel no longer visible and likely knocked to nuke and gone by the ball, the patrol boat was just another floater, stuck in the midst of a strontium swamp and a passel of hungry crocodiles.

A figure staggered forward out of the steam. It had its arms extended toward Ryan. He couldn't tell whether it carried a weapon or not. He let go of the lanyard to whip out his SIG Sauer P226 and aim it at the apparition.

It was Paxton, or so Ryan guessed from the general size and shape. It was an unrecognizable red mass with the skin of its face and arms hanging down in flaps that swayed with its tottering steps.

Ryan fired once. The head snapped back. The flayed and parboiled body slumped to the deck. Ryan was ruthless to his enemies, but he wasn't a sadist. The scalded ensign's suffering wouldn't buy him any advantage, and thanks to Tanya's generosity Ryan had plenty of 9 mm ammo. Apparently the barony stockpiled it even though few blasters in the fleet could fire it.

Orange lights flashed through the thinning white steam. A bullet punched through the bow to Ryan's left, outbound. Some of his former squaddies were firing at him from the afterdeck. They were firing blindly, but it wouldn't last. A lucky shot could find him at any time.

Ryan swung the swivel blaster sideways and hunkered between it and the prow, using its hard metal mass and that of its brass column upright for cover. He also now had the steam, the bulky boiler, and what remained of the scorched and battered forward bulkhead for concealment. He kept his weapon held in front of him in both hands and waited.

He kept his head swiveling left and right, so that he didn't get caught out, when two more figures came charging through the steam on either side of the cabin. The man on the left was firing shots from a longblaster, meaning that whether or not that bastard Jones was well-done from the boiler blast, one of his five-man, handpicked hit squad had the sense to make use of his weapon. At least two of the coldhearts survived and were still determined to carry out their real mission on behalf of Baron Tanya's enemies.

Ryan double-tapped the man to his left—the one with the Winchester—before he'd gotten clear of the steam still pouring from the ruptured boiler. He fell on his face and slid forward along the deck. The carbine left his hands and skittered toward Ryan, slowly turning.

Even better. But the second chiller took the warning and hunkered down behind the portside brass pole by the helm and fired a handblaster at Ryan. The bullet struck the black iron barrel just to the side of its mounting hinge and screamed off at random across Dead Man's Creek, leaving a streak of lead on the harder metal, surprisingly bright.

From somewhere off the starboard bow—currently Ryan's left—came frenzied splashing and a series of agonized shrieks. Somebody, possibly the hapless leadsman Vasquez, had found a new life partner in the form of a Nile croc. In that, they were destined to spend the rest of *his* life together.

The second gunman popped out and fired another shot at Ryan. This one punched through the decking by his right boot. He fired a return shot through the thin wooden front panel just inboard of the upright, hoping to hit his hidden opponent. Or just give him something to think about.

Ryan fired another shot, this one aimed to whang

off the brass pole just above the bulkhead level. Then he threw himself into a forward roll that ended next to the fallen repeater. Holstering his SIG, he scooped up the longblaster and worked the lever.

A fat .45 Colt cartridge promptly flipped out of the receiver, its brass casing glittering in the sun. It was a round wasted, but Ryan would rather that than pull the trigger to save his life and have the hammer click down on a spent round.

Of course, now he had to wonder how many cartridges were left. He took for granted it was fully loaded. Whatever he had been—or still was—CPO Jones was too seasoned to keep his mag anything but topped off. The man Ryan had shot had fired several rounds—three, Ryan recollected. Maybe four. And he'd just jacked one onto the deck and had it roll promptly out the scuppers, as the boat, having lost way, began to turn in the current carrying it back toward the Sippi. So count on the worst: six done, which left nine in the tubular magazine.

Ryan fired two quick shots through the front bulkhead, just to starboard of the main cannonball hole, and angled tight enough they *should* have intersected the assassin. But "should" and a half a bottle of Towse Lightning would get you a blowjob from the ugliest toothless slut in the Deathlands' lowest gaudy.

He pulled yet another forward roll. This one brought him up to a crouch just aft of the starboard front brass upright with his hip pressed against the gunwale and his head in a swirl of steam that was too hot for comfort. He had the blaster to his shoulder as he came up.

Across the brass bead front sight he saw his assailant, standing up, with his right hand stuck out over the bulkhead pointing a Navy Colt, and his left wrapped around his midriff. Likely one or even more of Ryan's guess-shots had found a home in his entrails. But he was hard-core and dedicated. Ryan fired his first shot as his blaster came to bear on the stooped form. The target was just under the exposed right armpit and designed to smash through lungs and heart. Rather than waiting to admire his perfectly placed shot he fired again.

The round hit the man in the neck on his way down.

Ryan turned to face aft and backed out of the steam. The day was getting hot and humid enough without needing the extra steam treatment. As he did so, he saw an orange glow come to sudden life through the steam that was still just thick enough to screen the aft half of the craft.

Flames began to dance eagerly up from somewhere. Despite the fact the boiler break had splashed the deck with water, they acted healthy and happy—and hungry. That suggested the firebox had been breached and spilled white-hot coals onto mostly dry wood belowdecks. For the boat, which was already a write-off from Ryan's point of view, being on fire didn't mean much. To Ryan it meant plenty. Because stashed down there in what passed for the boat's hold were the powder stores for the swivel blaster and ammo for the occupants' blasters. While the *Doria* didn't carry enough black powder to cause a true detonation—that required several hundred pounds going off at once—she did have enough to break her in two and chill everybody aboard.

At least, everybody *lucky* aboard. The unlucky ones would be dumped in the water, maimed and half-cooked morsels for the crocs.

And speaking of the crocodiles, Ryan reckoned it was time to make their acquaintance. Keeping hold of the longblaster, whose length could come in handy fending off a welcoming committee in the form of carrion-infested teeth set in giant reptilian jaws, he dived over the rail.

Ryan plunged deep enough that his boots touched the soft mud bottom. Keeping his eye open, though there was enough silt in the water to make it murky, he pushed off. A moment later his head broke the surface. Still holding the longblaster in his left hand, he began swimming toward the stern where the rowboat lay. He was a strong swimmer, and even with his boots on kicked hard enough to drive himself despite the impediment the Winchester caused with his arm strokes. Because he wasn't likely to outswim a crocodile that had targeted him, he focused on splashing as little as possible.

With his head above the water, he heard at least two more splashes. Two of whomever remained on board had decided to take their chances with water rather than face the certainty of fire.

Immediately ahead of Ryan a head bobbed above the waves. Its face was turned away and with its short hair slicked down to the skull he had no hope of guessing who it was. All he could tell was that it was somebody lighter-skinned than Jones. The person seemed to be thrashing, either because he couldn't swim, or because panic had set in. Ryan didn't especially care about identities, since his only concern now was whether anyone would still be fanatical enough to still try to chill him. He was focused on his survival and returning to his Krysty and his companions, and he was ready to chill anyone who looked like they were getting in his way.

All of those thoughts dissipated when the surface seethed, just beyond the bobbing head, and then the sideways-turned snout of a huge croc burst out in a geyser of spray. Long, strong jaws opened wide—and clamped down on the head. Ryan saw blood spurt, and then with another splash both the crocodile and its next meal disappeared.

Ryan looked uneasily around. No other crocs appeared nearby. Although as he'd just been uncomfortably reminded, they could swim underwater just fine. But the hints of lumpy brown hide seemed to be keeping their distance, after the one had decided to take easy prey. It was readily apparent that the crocs didn't care to get too close to the boat, which was now burning briskly.

Encouraged by both the crocs' standing off and the blaze aboard the boat, Ryan redoubled his efforts. He did not want to be in the creek when the powder magazine blew. Water transmitted shock waves way too efficiently, never mind the very real threat of getting smashed to bits by flying debris.

By chance the *Doria* had already rotated almost ninety degrees clockwise, and the boat was naturally lagging behind on its towline. That conveniently reduced the distance Ryan had to swim.

He grasped the gunwale of the boat with his right

hand and deposited the Winchester inside with his left. The black powder casings inside were probably waterlogged and useless, but he could always whack the longblaster over some overly aggressive croc's head or snout without too much regret. He began to haul himself in, deliberately despite the adrenaline singing in his veins that he had to get out of the crocodile-infested water *now*. He didn't want to overturn his ride out of here.

The boat, built broad enough to confer some lateral stability, heeled toward him, then it settled abruptly back toward an even keel.

And Ryan found himself staring into the murder-filled eyes of Chief Petty Officer Jarvis Jones.

Chapter Twenty-Three

A clang like a giant bell resounded when the sledge-hammer's ten-pound head hit the railroad rail angled up along the portside front of the *Mississippi Queen*'s cabin. A shock ran through Krysty's palms, up her bare arms and into her already aching shoulders.

"Right," J.B. said from the top of the cabin. "Looks good now."

"Yeah," Nataly agreed from behind her. "Looks fine from this angle."

Easing the business end of the sledgehammer back to the deck, Krysty took a moment to wipe sweat from her brow with the back of one hand. The blue hand-kerchief she'd tied around her hair was already soaked through from hard exertion in the humid morning heat.

As the biggest person on the job—the swampers, though willing and able workers, were not healthy—Santee would have seemed the logical choice for such power work. But he had a tendency to overswing, and knock the misaligned workpiece out of true the other way.

For some reason Krysty proved to be the best for this task. She was tall and strong for a woman, if a child next to the happy Indian in both departments. She had a pot of stamina, and she was frankly more coordinated than Santee at a task like this. "There's not much to do," Ermintrude observed. She had just hauled on board a four-foot section of bridge truss that would fill in some of the gaps between the rails armoring the cabin.

"Which is ace," Arliss called from somewhere aft where he was helping fit another rail into place. "We're down to the dregs of our wire."

"Will it hold?" Ermintrude asked.

"For a spell," J.B. said. "Bounce enough cannon-balls off any piece, the wire'll shear. That's just a fact."

"How long will it last?" Arliss called.

"Till it doesn't anymore. That's the best answer I can give."

"Look north!" Suzan shouted from atop the cabin roof, seeing a white puff of steam from the north.

Working or not, J.B. made sure somebody kept watch at all times. With even Jak lending a hand with the work of armoring up the Diesel tug, sentry duty went to whoever currently needed a breather the worst.

Krysty looked. White smoke was billowing up from somewhere beyond the tall grass wall rising on the far bank. Not far away, either.

A bang reached her ears. It sounded like a cannon's report, but it had a ringing undertone to it, too, that put her in mind of the sound she'd been making altogether too much of, whanging on rails this past hour.

"Oh, thank Gaia!" she exclaimed. "It's Ryan!"

"What on Earth makes you jump to that conclusion, Krysty?" Mildred demanded from the shore, where she was tending to a teenage swamper who'd gotten his hand mashed by a rail. No bones broken, though. "That's not your—uh—intuition kicking up, is it?"

Krysty laughed and shook her head. She felt her living strands of hair twining in among each other like happy snakes. If such a thing existed.

"Who else could cause that much mayhem?" she asked.

The smoke changed color, or rather was joined by dirtier-looking smoke.

"Wood fire, looks like," J.B. observed.

Despite the press of work, everybody stood and watched. There wasn't much to see, but almost at once came a flurry of blasterfire.

"What do you think it is?" a swamper woman asked.

"If I had to," J.B. said, "I'd say somebody sent a patrol boat up a creek mebbe a quarter mile north of this one, and that it's come to no good end."

The blasterfire ceased. The gray-tinged smoke increased as the whiter stuff diminished. "Bet that was steam from a ruptured boiler," J.B. said.

Mildred finished wrapping the kid's wounded hand in a bandage of clean cloth she'd retrieved from her med kit. "Try not to mess it up any more, is the best advice I can give," she told him. He thanked her and headed left to join his kin.

Krysty sighed and hefted the sledgehammer. She felt a constant stirring in her guts now that was either the effects of rads and heavy metal accumulation, or was her imagination letting her know what it thought those poisons were doing to her body. She felt fatigued all the time, too. Whatever was happening to the north was happening without her or any of her friends being able to do a single thing to affect it. But the work here had to get done, fast.

"Do you really think Ryan's involved with that mess up there?" Mildred called to her.

A bright flash lit the sky beyond the tall grass. Another, bigger ball of smoke shot skyward. The tops of the grass actually bowed toward them with a shock wave, although it passed over the *Queen*. Or at least Krysty didn't feel it from the deck. They heard the boom of a major explosion.

Brown eyes wide, Mildred stood watching the latest ball of smoke rise into the clear blue sky.

"Right," she said. "Totally Ryan."

THE SECOND THING Ryan noticed was that Jones had a knife in his teeth. The right side of his face was a raw, bloody mess. Apparently he'd gotten over the side without being chilled by the live steam leak, but he had not done so without cost.

Taking out the knife with his right hand, he put his left down in the bilges and catapulted himself right at Ryan.

Ryan simply let go of the side of the boat and slid back into the water.

His side of the vessel promptly whipped up, without his weight to counterbalance all of Jones's being put on the other side at once. Ryan heard a satisfying thwack, as of a side-to-side bench hitting the enraged and heat-flayed face of the other man. Then he heard scrabbling, as if Jones was desperately trying to stop the boat from capsizing.

Don't want to go back in the water, do you? Ryan thought. It couldn't have felt good on his burns. And while Ryan didn't know if crocs could taste blood in the water the way sharks did, he wouldn't have bet any part of himself he liked they *couldn't*.

Jones stopped the boat from flipping over toward him. Ryan reached up and grabbed the gunwale. Yanking the boat toward him, he heaved himself up and over the side.

The *Doria* exploded with a sky-busting bang. Shock waves set the rowboat to rocking perilously. Broken planks, chunks of metal and possibly body parts cartwheeled overhead and pelted the water around them. The two men ignored it all, intent only on chilling each other.

Jones was all the way in the boat on his hands and knees. Ryan used his momentum to throw a straight right palm-heel. The would-be assassin managed to jerk his face far enough aside to avoid taking it full on the chin, but the evasion meant the heel of Ryan's hand grazed his right cheek and scraped along the bone hard. Jones gritted his teeth between peeled-back lips. But the agony of impact, salt and friction on his skinned flesh made him grunt.

His momentary distraction allowed Ryan to slam his right elbow down on Jones's knife hand. Fingers opened and let go of the Ka-Bar-style blade.

Jones pounded a left hammer-fist into the back of Ryan's head, making his vision swim.

Ryan rolled onto his back. He grabbed the shoulders of Jones's camo blouse and lifted.

Anticipating Ryan's intention to raise him and pitch him overboard, Jones grabbed a bench with his still-functional left hand, clamped his elbows hard against the side of the boat and began heaving himself forward with all his considerable and scarcely diminished strength.

Except that wasn't Ryan's intention. The treacherous chief did exactly what Ryan wanted him to. The one-eyed man was no weakling. But he preferred to do as much of his fighting as possible in his mind. Going strength-to-strength with an opponent when it wasn't absolutely necessary was macho posturing—a loser's game.

Instead he sat up hard, pulling Jones in the direction the other man was pushing. Jones twisted his body hard, trying to escape when he felt himself being drawn inexorably toward his foe. Unbalanced, Ryan fell onto his right side.

He planted his boot soles against his side of the boat and used the power of his legs to keep jackknifing and drawing Jones in. The chief got his left arm crooked around his adversary's neck and tried to crush his windpipe. Ryan got his chin down and blocked the move.

Ryan's idea, unless he found an opening right directly, was to drag both of them over his side of the boat and take his chances on grappling in the water. Jones was bleeding. Ryan felt blood warm and slick on his right palm. The CPO was hurt, painfully if not seriously. Ryan was not. After a life spent traversing the Deathlands, Ryan was actually more ready to pit his endurance against any other man's than his strength. He liked his chances here.

He felt the other man reach out with his right arm. Instantly he knew Jones was groping for his knife with his good hand. Meanwhile he felt the relentless closing of Jones's left arm squeezing his chin up and out of position to save his throat. Grabbing his opponent's left biceps with his left hand, he clutched for his other arm with his right.

His fingers brushed a sleeve. Before Jones could react, Ryan had his forearm in a claw grip. He pulled the captive limb toward him, away from where he reckoned the knife might be.

And Jones used his own trick on him. When Ryan pulled his arm, he didn't pull back. He pushed.

Instantly his right hand gripped Ryan's face and tried to pull his head up so he could close the fatal circle around his throat. Ryan reached up and clutched at the hand. It felt as if it were made of iron, and driven by hydraulics. He might have been draining out faster than Ryan, but fury gave him double strength.

And then the crocodile hit the boat.

Furiously struggling for his life, Ryan at first thought the impact was his opponent inadvertently kicking the far gunwale. Then he realized the small craft was rocking far too much for it to be that.

Bringing a great slog of water with it, a croc that had to have been a dozen feet long burst out of Dead Man's Creek and flopped into the boat with jaws agape.

The toothy trap snapped shut on the back of Jones's shirt.

Instantly the croc slid back into the water, its bulk pulling Jones inexorably along with it. Ryan let go of him to grab parts of the boat and hang on for dear life.

For a moment Jones kept his death grip on Ryan's head. The one-eyed man once again felt his chin slipping out of the way of the man closing his left arm.

Jones lost his hold. The croc peeled him away from Ryan and dragged him out of the boat.

But somehow Jones managed to clamp his right hand on the gunwale and hold on despite the immense weight of the crocodile trying to pull him free. His eyes stared at Ryan in desperation from his half-seared face.

"Please," he said. "Help me!"

"You and the croc deserve each other," Ryan said. He kicked the clutching fingers hard. Bones broke. Jarvis Jones howled as he was plucked away.

The waters of Dead Man's Creek closed over his cries.

Ryan lay in the bottom of the boat breathing hard for several minutes.

Then he gathered the oars and started rowing back toward the Sippi, never looking back.

"RECKONED YOU'D TURN up about now," J.B. called as Ryan—running on fumes—rowed the last few feet toward the cleared southern shore where the *Queen* lay aground, sheathed in red iron. "Now that the hard work is done and all."

The little beach was full of people, far more than the ones he'd left behind. Several folks he didn't know wearing knee-length shorts and T-shirts splashed into the shallows to help him from the boat when he suddenly could not hold his arms up anymore. "Thanks for helping me and all," he told them as they guided him up onto dry land. "But who in the name of glowing nuke shit are you people?"

"Funny you should mention that," said a tall gangly black man with an off-center smile in an off-center face who was standing nearby. "We're swampers."

"Swampers?" Ryan shook his head as if that might clear out the cobwebs. It only made the world spin around him and made him want to puke. He hoped he was just exhausted to the point of dizziness, and not concussed. "No disrespect or anything, but aren't you supposed to be chilling us?"

"They're friends," J.B. said. "Long story."

"Ryan!"

He lifted his head, which was showing a marked tendency to drop forward, to see Krysty leap from the tugboat's bow and come running toward him with red hair flying.

"Best not jump into my arms," he warned. "I'll fall right down."

She hugged him, but gently. She looked up at his face with green eyes glowing and said, "I knew you'd come back."

"What took you so long?" demanded Mildred, who debarked the boat more deliberately than her friend and walked toward the pair.

"It's a long story. What happened to the fireblasted boat, J.B.? Looks like a bridge fell on it."

"Funny you should say that," Mildred said.

"Long story," J.B. repeated, and then Krysty dragged Ryan's mouth toward hers for a kiss.

He didn't resist.

Chapter Twenty-Four

"So, let me get this straight, J.B.," Ryan said. "You're telling me this story about the Confederates building themselves an ironclad in the middle of a nuking cornfield might not even be *true*?"

"That's about the size of it," the Armorer admitted.

The *Mississippi Queen* looked as if somebody had tried to build a long tent on her deck out of railroad rails, but had neglected to pull them together at the top to close it off. Its rail had been covered in hunks of U-beams that had been knocked off the railway bridge by long-ago earthquakes. Random pieces of bridge trusses and other steel scrap had been stuffed in here and there to seal up the armor shell. Mostly. The front ob port had been left clear of major armor, but was covered in sections of decorative but strong-looking steel scrollwork, open enough to see through. Ryan vaguely remembered having seen work like it on the railway bridge. The wheelhouse entrance remained an open oblong. The whole thing struck him as half nightmare, half inspiration, and it was all held together with nothing but baling wire and sheer gall.

Ryan had spent the past hour sitting on the grass while Mildred stood over him and made him drink a lot of water, and then set about what Joe Trombone called "tinkering up his bruises," Joe being the long drink of water who had first greeted Ryan ashore. He was leader of the swampers who had helped J.B. carry out his insane scheme, along with a broad woman named Ermintrude. The whole time Krysty had sat by his side, not touching him, as she could see he was one giant mass of bruises, and that any contact would be painful. She did urge him to eat some crocodile jerky.

He was so hungry that the awful stuff tasted good to him. Thinking about certain of the monsters' recent meals actually made him feel better about eating it. On the one hand, the bastards had it coming. On the other, it felt like victory by proxy, of sorts.

He shook his head. "I have to admire your audacity, J.B.," he said. "Not to mention your unlooked-for abilities to bullshit people into carrying out your crazy schemes."

"He does remind one of Hernán Cortés, in ways," Doc commented.

Ryan was surrounded by most of the surviving members of the *Queen*'s crew, his companions, plus a whole horde of the swampers, who turned out not to be red-eyed cannie monsters with filed teeth, but folks who appeared to be normal, aside from having a general unhealthy look. They seemed glad for an excuse to take a break, and no wonder.

"Leaving aside that gentleman's less-appealing traits, of course. Such as his penchant for mass murder and torture," Doc added.

"You don't actually buy that crap about him burning

his boats and then conquering Mexico with just a handful of white guys, do you?" Mildred demanded. "You
come right out of that whole colonialist 'take up the
white man's burden' time—I mean, school of thought."

The old man smiled benevolently. "No, indeed. I
have read my Bernal Díaz del Castillo. I don't even
speak of Cortés's achievement in talking 100,000 na-
tive allies into doing the hard work of conquering the
Aztecs for him. The Aztecs themselves did the burden
of his convincing for him, by their treatment of their
neighbors. No, I speak of his ability, not just to fleece
his own men of their hard-stolen plunder, but to admit
as much to them—as desperate a crew of coldhearts
as ever cut a throat—and not just survive, but fleece
them *again*."

"Thanks?" J.B. said hesitantly.

"But his scheme isn't so crazy, is it, Mr. Cawdor?"
Nataly asked earnestly. "You see the evidence before
you."

Ryan grunted.

"Yeah. And I got to admit—you pulled it off. That
Arkansas story in back of it all may've been nothing
but a cloud of nuke dust. But it looks as if you've written your own legend here."

As if he somehow sensed the topic of conversation,
Myron Conoyer emerged from belowdecks, wiping his
hands on a grimy rag. "Isn't she beautiful?" he asked.

His wiry hair was a steel-wool disarray. His coveralls were almost black from grease. His face was
streaked with broad swatches of the stuff. Under the
crud his cheeks glowed pink, and his eyes were bright

with something other than incipient madness. He almost bounced on his feet and looked happy for the first time since his wife had died.

She's ugly as two feet up a stickie's asshole, Ryan thought. But I take your point.

"Yeah," he said, and smiled. "Yeah, she is."

And he meant that, too.

"You've done a triple-good job, all of you. The wiring-it-up thing is less solid than bolting the armor on, the way they do it on the New Vick ironclads I saw. But you knew that. Fact is, you're not much less protected than Baron Tanya is in the *Pearl*, except for the matter of sheer size. That's pretty ace."

"Couldn't have done it without the swampers," Arliss stated.

"Well, we were motivated," Joe said. "We're tired of soaking up rads from the ground and the air we breathe, and eating food seasoned with cesium salts. Also, the neighborhood's going to straight nuke anyway these days, what with the Vicks and the P'villes finally going for each other's throats."

While Mildred had cleaned Ryan up and examined him for major damage—and finding none, at least by his definition of "major"—Krysty had quietly confided that she and the others suspected some kind of internal discord among the swampers was adding to Joe and Ermintrude's urgency to get their respective groups out of the strontium swamps. Their new allies freely admitted that their two hundred or so people were only a fraction of the population in the inhospitable death zones.

That was surprising to Ryan. Then again, he had a keen appreciation of the value in the Deathlands of having a home territory that other people actively didn't want to try to take from you. Or even venture into.

Ryan stood. The effort didn't cost him as much as he thought it would. He barely even swayed.

"So how about it?" he asked. "How soon are we ready to sail?"

"Mechanically, she is as ready as she'll ever be," Myron said, beaming with pride and joy.

Ryan looked to Nataly and Arliss. While he was inclined to favor the new manic Myron over the suicidally depressed model he'd left behind when he jumped onto the *Yarville*, he wasn't sure he trusted his judgment anymore, although the man knew his ship, and her engines. Still, Ryan had gotten used to thinking of the first mate and master rigger as the responsible adults among the *Queen* survivors.

The two looked at each other.

"Reckon the man to ask is J.B.," Arliss said. "He's the man with the plan."

"What about it?" Ryan asked his friend.

"Well, we can fool with her and fool with her until the cows come home," he said, "and if some simp gunner on one of those big ironclads gets a lucky hit, one shell can still blow us all to Hell."

"Do you have to be so damned cheerful about it, John?" Mildred demanded.

"Now's the time for plain speaking, Millie. Cards on the table."

"Good enough," Ryan said.

Krysty had risen with him and stood beside him, still not touching, but close enough for Ryan to feel the heat of her well-curved body.

He smiled at her.

Krysty's return smile gave him a warm feeling. She knew just what he had in mind.

As usual.

"When can we leave, then?"

"You just got back, Cawdor," Joe said in his bantering way. "You in a hurry to clear out again so soon?"

"Yeah."

The swampers laughed.

"I'm saying the same as Myron," J.B. said. "She's ready as she's going to be. Aside from finishing up some."

"I see nothing to keep us here," Nataly added, "although it will take us a while to get our gear stowed back aboard."

"And supplies," Arliss stated.

"Right." Ryan nodded. He looked at the sun. It was already halfway down the sky toward the western weeds.

"Then I guess you folks might as well head back to your camps," he told the swampers. "Come back tomorrow with your boats and such belongings as you care to carry along. We'll go when you're ready."

"Right," Ermintrude said. Without further word the swampers turned back to the assortment of small craft they had arrived in, and in minutes were paddling back toward the derelict railway bridge.

Ryan looked to his companions. "Now. Tell me what still needs done, and I'll get to helping do it."

"You sure you feel up to it?" Mildred asked.

"I've caught my breath, Mildred," he said. "And after your fine ministrations, if I'm not fit to fight, I'm fit to fake it."

He looked around at the others. "And since you-all saw to contriving us a ride out of this hellhole, the only way I'm going to stay in it a moment longer than necessary is if I'm staring up at the stars!"

"So that's your secret weapon?" Joe asked.

It was full daylight. The sky was mostly clear, but it looked as if they might be in for a storm later. Wolf Creek was crowded with swamper boats as the people of the strontium swamp hitched them to the stern of the *Mississippi Queen*, along with the motor launch. To Ricky it all seemed to be taking forever, but Ryan did not seem concerned.

Ricky didn't have much attention to spare for anything but the Lahti L-39 Ryan and J.B. had uncrated and set up on its sled-like tripod on the shore by the tug's bow. The weapon was everything he'd expect something called an antitank rifle to be: a tremendously outsize longblaster, almost seven and a half feet long complete with muzzle brake, with a box magazine sticking out the top that held ten 20 mm armor-piercing cartridges and a pistol grip. It was an ugly monster, weighing in at over a hundred pounds.

Ricky thought he was in love.

"Will it penetrate ironclad armor?" Nataly asked skeptically.

"Some of it," Ryan said. "Their stuff's not consistent,

either—they use scrap, and a lot more varied than you did here. It's not dedicated armored plate or anything. It's what they could find that fit."

"Could you test it?" Jake asked.

"You know we only have twenty rounds for it," Arliss said. "We don't have enough to spare."

"She'll definitely do for keeping the patrol boats off our necks. Otherwise, we need to rely on armor, speed—and luck."

"How fast do we dare go?" Nataly asked Joe and Ermintrude. She would have the helm for their escape attempt. As Abner was the best hand with the small boat, the tall, lean, ponytailed woman was most accomplished at steering the tug.

Not that she or any of them had any experience driving the *Queen* with all that armor up top, throwing her balance all out of whack.

"Fast enough to outrun their patrol boats, if she'll handle it," Ermintrude said.

"She will," Nataly replied. "Even with all that metal piled on her, and drawing your craft behind, she'll likely be driving less of a load than the barge we were hauling when this mess got started."

"What about you, though?" Mildred asked. "We had to go superslow when our launch was towing us."

Joe and Ermintrude exchanged looks. "You were mostly riding those cobbled-together rafts," Joe said. "Any little thing was liable to upset 'em. Or just cause them to come apart."

"And we're double good at handling small boats," Ermintrude added, with more than a trace of smugness. "That rabbit-looking dude of yours, Abner, he's all right. But the rest of you—" She shook her head.

"Your funeral," Ryan said. "Right now we need to get back to work. I'm antsy to get moving, and this has already taken longer than I expected."

"It always does," J.B. stated. "You should remember that from Trader days. Even an outfit like his."

"Yeah," Ryan said. "But I don't have to like it."

"What about the blaster?" Nataly asked. "You want us to go ahead and load it?"

"Oh, no," Ryan said. "It's going in the cabin with us, and you will *not* like it when I touch the bastard off in there."

Ermintrude and Joe got back to overseeing the digging-out of the *Queen*'s hull to refloat her. They both took turns with the shovels, Ricky saw. It was a major job digging deep enough to let in enough water under the *Queen*'s keep to allow her to back off the shore, but the swampers were good at digging.

The rest got back to their various preparations.

An hour later Ricky carried one of the last of the cargo boxes down to the hold. They might as well have some return on this crazy trip, provided any of them made it out alive—Ryan and company as well as the tug's original crew. Ricky's group hadn't exactly been paid. In any event, regardless of Ryan's and J.B.'s, and even Nataly's, inclinations to ditch everything not absolutely essential to survival, with so much weight added to the *Queen*'s superstructure, they needed every ounce of ballast they could find to load.

From above came a muffled, indecipherable cry.

Ricky recognized Jak's voice. The albino was on watch atop the cabin. His sharp eyes were more use there than his slight frame was in hauling.

A babble of shouting broke out. Ricky hastily put down the crate of scavvy canned goods and hustled up the ladder.

Outside he saw the swampers in their boats pointing east and yelling. He looked that way.

A patrol blasterboat was motoring down Wolf Creek. It was just emerging from the shadows beneath the ruined bridge.

"¡Nuestra Señora!" Ricky yelped. He scrambled over the bridge-truss-armored gunwales and dropped into the shallows.

"Purple-and-yellow flag," Ryan was saying on the shore as he lowered his Steyr from his shoulder. "Poteetville."

"So the bastards found a way to get to Wolf Creek," Arliss said.

Joe splashed ashore from his little flotilla. "We've got to get moving!" he yelled. He sounded near panic. "They'll massacre us with their deck cannon."

Nataly stood by the big trench being dug around the *Queen*'s bow. She shook her head, her ponytail whipping her shoulders.

"It's still not deep enough. We'll be able to go soon, but not before they get here."

"Not a problem," Ryan said. He handed his Scout carbine to Ricky. "Take this and back me up. Everybody else, lie down. Find what cover you can."

Not that there was much, unless they wanted to

go retreat into the tall grass. Since both Jak and the swampers reported sign of stickies prowling around, Ricky for one wasn't eager to do that. He'd rather take his chances with a black powder cannon.

"You're just hankering to give that big old bastard a try," J.B. said mock-accusingly as Ryan swung around the hefty Lahti blaster and started to settle in behind it.

"It can't hurt to make sure the blaster and the ammo still work, right?"

"I guess we need to see if it's going to have any effect against a real boat," Jake said.

Ryan grinned like a wolf.

"Oh, I know what kind of effect it'll have on one of them. Now get down. Their bow cannon can throw a ball this far. Their gunner may get luckier than you are."

Most of the people on the shore hustled to lie down on their bellies and make themselves as flat as they could.

"Get on my right," Ryan told Ricky. "It ejects to the left. And keep back, because the muzzle brake will throw side blast like a bastard."

Feeling slightly miffed that Ryan thought so little of Ricky's armorer skill—so much of it learned from Ryan's own friend, the masterful J.B.—as to reckon he couldn't work that out on his own, Ricky settled into a seated position, side-on to the approaching boat, with his ankles crossed. He cinched his arm up in the Scout's sling the way he'd seen Ryan do. He made sure his left forearm was directly under the forestock, and that his elbows were braced against the insides of his legs. It was a stable firing platform, but mostly he wanted to make sure he could see all the action. He put his eye down behind the ocular.

"Fire in the hole," Ryan said. "Be warned, it'll get loud in three, two, one."

The Lahti went off. It made a sound so loud it felt to Ricky as if it would implode his head. The shock wave stung not just the bare side of his head but the whole left side of his body. It almost toppled him, although that might have been from surprise as much as the actual force.

The effect on the blasterboat, still three hundred yards off, was immediate—and drastic. The boiler simply blew up, or so Ricky guessed. For a moment the craft vanished in an enormous ball of steam. Fragments of the shattered cabin flew fifty feet into the air to rain down on the creek all around.

"Wow," Ricky said. He could barely hear himself for the ringing in his ears.

When the boom of the explosion reached them on the shore, it still wasn't as sharp as the echoes of Ryan's shot reverberating between the creek banks.

When the cloud cleared enough for the boat to be visible again, Ricky gasped at the devastation. The roof of the cabin was gone, except for a few wood tatters swinging from brass uprights. The boiler was a jagged, twisted shell.

"Don't see anybody left aboard," Ricky reported as he scanned the wrecked boat with the scope.

"Well," J.B. said, "the blaster works."

Ryan sat up and rubbed his shoulder. "Even weighing a hundred pounds and with the muzzle brake, she does pack a kick," he admitted.

"I see what you mean about not liking being cooped up with that monster," Nataly called as she picked herself up off the grass nearby.

Ryan shook his head. "Can't do that. Blow everybody's eardrums out the second shot, max. I'll go up top to fire, when we need it."

"But, Ryan!" Krysty exclaimed, coming up to join them. By that time the Poteetville boat had turned broadside in the current. What looked like smoke began to filter up from below its shattered deck. Ricky recalled Ryan's account of how the spilled firebox set the New Vick blasterboat he had blasted with its own swivel blaster the day before alight. "The cannon—"

They had armored the roof of the cabin to protect against what J.B. called "plunging fire." Since they were lower than the ironclads' cannon mounts, they risked taking a lot of that.

"We'll be moving along pretty brisk," Ryan said. "They'll need a lucky shot to drop one on me."

Krysty said no more, accustomed as she was to Ryan going into danger. She was also accustomed to how futile it was arguing with Ryan Cawdor once his mind got set.

As the P'ville boat floated closer, slowly rotating, the swampers began firing it up. A great racket and clouds of smoke rose from their muzzle-loading rifles and fowling-pieces.

"Shouldn't we try to stop them?" Mildred shouted.

"Why?" Ryan asked. "They want to waste their powder and ball, that's not our problem."

"But, ah, what about casualties?"

"Last night Joe and Ermintrude were telling me about a game the ville blasterboats play when they raid these swamps," Ryan said. "They like to catch swampers, find a nest of stickies in the shallows somewhere and toss the swampers to them. Then they pull out in the middle of the stream and laugh while the stickies have their fun."

Myron, who had been below making last-minute adjustments to his engines, stared at the blasted wreck floating by. Then he gave a resounding slap to the steel armor wired to the side of the cabin, and shouted in a voice loud enough to be heard over the now-sporadic blasterfire from the swamper boats, "In the blood of our enemies, I christen you, *Vengeance*!"

Then he covered his face and ran back into the cabin, obviously crying.

The stricken boat went turning past the aground *Queen*. Ricky saw pale flames begin to lick up. The shooting from the swampers petered out.

But the noise of blasterfire didn't. It went on, and on. Not loud. But deep. Like a monster thunderstorm some distance away.

"Ryan—" Krysty said.

"Fireblast!" Ryan growled.

He looked west. Then everybody did.

There were already clouds of cannon smoke visible, rising in the distance. Right about, Ricky judged, where Wolf Creek emptied out into the Sippi.

The thunder roared…

Chapter Twenty-Five

"We've got to go," Ryan said. "Now. Drop everything and get aboard."

"Are you put of your dark dusted mind?" Arliss demanded. "That's the sound of both damn ironclad fleets going at it hammer and tongs. Right outside the mouth of Wolf Creek!"

Ryan nodded calmly. "That's why."

"What do you mean?"

"I mean this way both sides will have something better to shoot at than us."

"He's right," J.B. said. "See, when the CSS *Arkansas* ran the Northern fleet, it did it all by its lonesome. All the ships were shooting at it."

He pushed his hat back on his head.

"I reckon, we got the advantage over her that way. And she came through fine."

"They're right, Arliss," Avery said. "It likely is our best shot."

"We may even be a little less likely to die," Jake added.

Arliss slumped. "Mebbe you're right. I can't see we've got much to lose by playing it this way, after all."

But Nataly shook her head. "No way. She's still stuck."

"Then everybody grab a shovel," Ryan said.

THE CONFLUENCE AHEAD of the newly renamed *Vengeance* was a hell-storm of fire, steel, smoke and noise.

"It looks like both sides are up in each other's faces," Avery said.

"Yeah," Santee agreed. "Looks like they picked today to settle things up, huh?"

Ryan could that see the fleets were close, possibly intermingled already. It was hard to make out details for the smoke. But he could see darts of fire from the relatively high cannon decks of the ironclads through the gray banks of smoke, and lesser patrol steamers maneuvering below most of the cloud.

"They're going to have their work cut out even seeing us," J.B. stated.

"Does that mean they won't shoot at us?" Avery asked hopefully.

The Armorer shrugged. "Just less."

Twelve people were crowded onto the bridge: the companions and the original crew's survivors, minus Myron, and Arliss, who was assisting the captain with the Diesels, and Suzan, who had panicked at seeing the inferno they were about to plunge into, and was back in one of the more intact cabins with a blanket over her head.

Ryan didn't see how her absence made any difference one way or another. It wasn't as if she was going to swat cannonballs out of the air with her palms. He couldn't rightly blame her, truth to tell.

I wish I had faith in the ability of old smelly wool to keep off the shells, if the makeshift armor can't, he thought.

"Better get your hearing protection on," Mildred said. She was already having to shout to make herself heard over the thunder of the battle going on hundreds of yards away.

But it wasn't because of the cannon dogfight they were about to become part of that she had badgered them into making pads of folded rag they could tie over their ears with headbands. It was because of the monstrous blaster, leaning to the left of the helm with its lengthy barrel angled out the front ob port through a gap in the scrolled-steel screen they'd put up. J.B. had backed Ryan's judgment that the worst of the noise would be diminished by having the muzzle with its brake well outside the cabin. But the backblast would still be hellish—capable of shattering eardrums, in all probability.

Ricky stuck his head out through the narrow gap between the chunk of scrollwork they'd pulled up to give some protection to the hatch to outside and the top of the entryway. He looked back.

"Swampers are giving us the thumbs-up," he reported, ducking back in. Mildred shot him a glare. He pulled his ear protector into place.

Ryan drew on his own. It muffled the sound but didn't deaden it. He could hear the others talk if they were close enough—as almost everybody crammed into the bridge or pilothouse was. They just sounded as if they were far down a well.

The *Vengeance* began to rock as she left the weed-masked mouth of Wolf Creek into the slow but powerful Sippi current. Ryan began to feel the blasts of cannon firing as the noise grew to thunderstorm proportions about them.

Not fifty yards ahead a patrol boat crossed their path from port to starboard, the dark smoke trailing from its stack creating a strain of stain in the pervasive light gray cannon smoke. A red-and-white banner whipped from the little mast at her stern. New Vickville colors. Its crew was busily reloading a two-pounder bow cannon and pointing excitedly at the mass of the nearest big ironclad: a P'ville frigate almost broadside to the current, meaning broadside to the smaller vessel, about two hundred yards northwest.

"Bocephus," Ryan said. He'd memorized ship silhouettes from both fleets during the dragging downtime of his "employment" with Baron Tanya, along with details of their armament and capabilities. Both sides, he'd learned, had pretty complete dossiers on their rivals' ironclad warships.

He wasn't sure how it could help, but he'd reckoned it might. *"Bocephus?"* Mildred said. "Really?"

The P'ville frigate fired its broadside: all of two six-pound smoothbores. That was another advantage their puny little homebuilt ironclad had over the *Arkansas*, on her legendary running of the Union fleet almost two centuries before: the Northern ships carried a lot more cannon than either of these modern fleets did, mostly heavier, and some rifled. The Confederate ironclad was targeted by a lot more, and more effective, blasterfire than they would be.

But the frigate's battery seemed neither small nor ineffectual when it was shooting almost right at a vessel.

One shot threw up a forty-foot column of water well off the *Vengeance*'s port bow as she started her turn south. The other hit the New Vick patrol boat in the foredeck.

That shot was apparently a shell. Ryan saw a red flash before the inevitable smoke blossom blotted out the scene. When it began to lift, the patrol craft's deck was a shattered shambles, with it and the front of the pilothouse already on fire. Its lone cannon had been blown right through the bow and into the river.

Several hundred yards ahead Ryan saw a huge dark shape appear out of the smoke: an ironclad "capital" ship. The others cried out in amazed alarm.

"That's the *Invincible*," he called out. He recognized her by her armored pilothouse perched at the front of her two-story cabin, which like her two sister P'ville heavy hitters carried eight eight-pound cannon. He'd always thought the extrusion was a stupe idea. It just made the ironclad a bigger target. And it *looked* double stupe. The ship was steaming almost due south, and just about to go broadside to broadside with the big New Vickville ironclad *Medusa*.

Steady, her focus likely as much to blot out the terror of their surroundings as to navigate them safely, Nataly steered the armored tug around her turn. She had called for Myron to reduce power in the Diesels to keep from capsizing the towed flotilla of swamper boats. Now Ryan felt the big engines begin to thrum more powerfully as she accelerated out of the turn.

The hammer of the gods struck the cabin just off the hatch to the deck. The *Vengeance* rocked perceptibly to the blow, and her whole substance shivered.

Avery gave J.B. a thumbs-up. "She held!"

"Glancing blow," the Armorer replied.

Oddly enough, once they were in the midst of the firestorm, Ryan realized the shooting was not a constant storm of steel and flame. Of course it couldn't be. The cannon took time to swab out and reload. From his time with the fleet, he knew that unless an ironclad was firing a virgin broadside—had not fired yet in combat, or at least recently—the cannon tended to shoot independently as long as they had targets. Or were ordered to continue.

But there were still a lot of cannon out there. There wasn't time to catch much of a nap between rounds, either.

He felt someone clutch his arm. It was Jak. The albino had been flitting about getting different angles on the scene outside—looking for threats to his friends, the way he always did. He barely seemed to brush up against the others when he did so, even if they were packed in there backside-to-business.

He pointed a white hand out the hatch. A New Vick frigate lay side-on to them, perhaps a hundred and fifty yards away. Ryan recognized her as the *Selene*.

Ryan held out his hand. That was the signal for Ricky, who also had the Steyr longblaster slung across his back, to hand the one-eyed man his navy longeyes.

Through the firing ports in the lower deck of the *Selene*'s cabin, their steel shutters raised for action, he could see crews frantically at work reloading. As he watched, one man finished and jumped back. A gunner yanked a lanyard.

Ryan reflexively lowered the longeyes and ducked as fire bloomed from the cannon's mouth. A beat later the cabin rang to the impact of a shot against a rail to port of the helm. Ryan felt as if the shock wave radiated through steel and wood to hit him, although he suspected that was an illusion of sound and vibrations transmitted through the deck.

"Fireblast!" It was time to discourage that shit. He gave Ricky the longeyes, grabbed the butt of the Lahti and deadlifted it. In a pinch, he could heft the whole blaster. It took effort to lever it up to aiming level.

He tapped Nataly on the shoulder. "Duck," he said.

She did, into a deep crouch that brought her head below the ob port's sill. She kept her hands on the wheel. That was enough; this wasn't a land wag, where you had to keep looking where you were going every second or risk a crash.

Ryan stepped past her, swinging the Lahti's barrel to his left to point at the frigate. At some point this blaster had its scope removed, but it didn't much matter, as the weapon spit out its heavy 20 mm projectiles at 2,600 feet per second, giving them a flat enough trajectory to hit pretty much where the blaster was pointing at that range.

Even with the smoke, it wasn't hard for Ryan to spot the blaster-ports. He aimed just above the lower edge of one, braced and fired.

The monster roared and kicked his shoulder like a mule. It didn't have the ground to suck up some of the recoil through its sled-like tripod this time. It hurt.

But it didn't kill him. Neither did the blast. He

switched his aim a few degrees left. The weapon was a gas-operated semiautomatic. It reloaded and cocked itself.

He fired again.

The yellow muzzle-flash of the colossal longblaster was followed instantly by a hell-red glare that filled the inside of the cockpit. Still holding the Lahti over the crouching form of Nataly, Ryan looked right.

He was in time to see the stern half of the *Invincible* explode in flame and fragments, then came the smoke, like a curtain closing.

Mildred slapped Ryan's shoulder. "Good shootin', Tex! Was that a carom shot?"

Ryan shook his head. He had actually heard her. Sort of.

"That wasn't my doing," he said, as he shifted to his left. Nataly snapped back into place as if she were on a spring.

"Glancing fire," J.B. called. "Hit the powder magazine."

"Not so *Invincible* after all!" Doc exulted.

And then the pounding began in earnest.

It was as if both fleets, though locked in deadly combat at dagger range in some cases, noticed this weird, armored thing intruding boldly and presumptuous into their playground. Two shots rang off the *Vengeance*'s armor almost simultaneously from opposite directions. Then three more, as fast as combination punches from a skilled boxer.

"Holding still," Avery said.

Ryan searched calmly for targets. He hoped his shots

had scared the gunners in *Selene* out of shooting at them anymore. At least until their petty officers beat them back to the task. Even with the monster power of the 20 mm longblaster, he had next to no chance of doing lasting damage to any ironclad.

He did put a shot through a firing port on *Clytemnestra*, off its port bow, and engaged with the capital *Conqueror*, which was actually behind the *Vengeance* and her train of small boats. Ryan wondered how they were doing.

But only briefly. He could do little for them, and they weren't *his* people. He wished them well, but that was most of it right there. He gave the big ship's blaster-port another shot, for good measure.

The 16-gauge wire wraps binding a rail to the front of the bridge parted with musical twangs audible even above the bombardment, and the residual ringing in Ryan's ear from his own weapon. He saw the rail fall away to angle across the bridge-truss rail through the hatchway to his left.

A New Vick patrol boat appeared fifty yards ahead and steaming right at them. Its bow cannon fired, a shout of yellow fire. The ball struck the bow armor in a shower of red steel-on-steel sparks and went moaning over the cabin.

Ryan was more concerned now about the patrol craft closing and grappling with them. His people could handle a boarding party. What none of them could afford was to be shackled to an enemy ship and stopped in the middle of this firestorm.

More impacts rang off the *Vengeance*'s armor. Ryan

scarcely paid attention to them. Except for the one rail, J.B.'s improvised armor was holding. For now. And again, there was nothing he could do but hope.

But he *did* know how to chill a steam-powered patrol boat. His next shot made the approaching vessel's boulder blow up so hard that when, moments later, *Vengeance* powered past her, she had slewed to the east and was sinking by the blasted-off stern.

Ahead of them to his right he made out the bulk of the *Pearl*. She was nose to tail with Baron Harvey's *Tyrant*. The two flagships were obviously hammering each other at almost hull-scraping range. Somehow in the scrum and the smoke they had swapped original directions, with *Tyrant*'s bow now pointing north toward Poteetville, and the *Pearl*'s bow toward her own home port.

Ryan blasted another patrol craft closing from their starboard. This one flew a Poteetville flag, he thought. The usual boiler blast put paid to her as a threat.

His next shot failed to hit the boiler of a New Vick blasterboat, because by chance her helmsman put the wheel over in a hard right turn even as Ryan's finger tightened on the trigger. The helmsman paid for it when the 20 mm armor-piercer smashed through the wheel and ripped his right arm off his body, just below the shoulder.

A frigate Ryan recognized as the New Vickville *Hera* steamed toward them almost bow-on, two hundred yards ahead, with black smoke pouring from her twin stacks into a now-cloudy sky. He realized with something like an electric shock that she was the last ironclad between them and open river.

"Holy cow," Mildred yelled. "I think we're going to make it!" Ryan aimed for the frigate's bow cannon and fired. He knew as the blaster cracked that he had pulled the shot high. He aimed again, fired again.

"Strike!" Ricky screamed from just behind him. He was watching Ryan's target through the longeyes. "You hit the gunner just as he was about to shoot! Wait, there's another—"

Somehow at this distance Ryan saw the blurred motion of a second brave sailor stepping up to seize the lanyard of the six-pounder bow cannon. He sighted on him and shot again.

As he did, the cannon's muzzle vanished in yellow glare and white smoke.

Ryan actually felt the shot punch through the unarmored decking, to his left up the walkway between rail and cabin.

Then he felt the shudder and the boom as the black powder shell exploded in the guts of the *Vengeance*.

Chapter Twenty-Six

Krysty felt like puking. We've been hit hard! she thought.

They were hit worse than she thought. In a moment throat-flaying smoke filled the bridge, redolent of wood, oil and seared human flesh.

The door astern burst open. Suzan appeared, her eyes and hair even more wild than usual.

"We're on fire!"

"Tell us something we don't know," Lewis said, coughing and waving smoke away from his face. It was futile. All he did was cause eddies in the choking stuff.

Myron came up from below. His hair was half burned off. His eyes stared crazily from a blackened face. His coveralls smoldered.

"We're breached and taking water!" he shouted. "Arliss is dead."

"What now, Captain?" Nataly asked.

"Didn't you hear me? We're done for! Finished! Kaput!" He began to laugh uncontrollably.

Avery reached out a hand and slapped him. The captain jerked his head back. He blinked twice at the boatswain. He seemed puzzled at being struck, and on the edge of tears.

"That's not really therapeutic," Mildred said.

"It shut him up," Ryan snarled. "That's therapeutic for us."

He looked to the first officer. "Steer us toward the *Pearl*," he directed. "Right up her ass. You can work the engines from here, right?"

Nataly looked from the tall, grim, one-eyed man back to the scorched and desolated figure of her boss. "I don't know."

"Do it," Myron said. His tone wasn't just sane. It sounded resolved. "Do what he tells you. And yes. We can work the engines from here."

"We prefer not to because the linkage is wonky and tends to jam up," Abner said.

Nataly was turning the wheel. The armored tug's nose swung toward the capital ship.

"Give her all the speed you got," Ryan said.

Nataly worked a lever beside the wheel. The Diesels' growl got louder.

"Engines sound rough," J.B. said. "Are they fit?"

Myron shook his head. "Both are running now. I can't promise more."

"Ryan," Krysty said, "what do you have in mind?"

"We're going to ram the bastard," he said, "and then we're going to hijack her."

"Are you out of your nuking mind?" Jake and Avery yelled in unison.

"We're on fire and sinking," Ryan replied. "If you've got a better plan, I'm all ears."

"But that's a *battleship*," Avery insisted.

"Pretty soon her cannon won't depress far enough to hit us," J.B. said.

The Lahti erupted with terrifying noise twice in quick succession. Even with the head-wrap holding cloth pads over her ears the reports were like daggers stabbing into Krysty's skull.

"That should keep *Hera*'s crew from playing with the bow cannon any more until we're in close to *Pearl*," Ryan said, pulling the big box magazine off the top of the blaster and replacing it with the full one. Their last one, Krysty knew. Not that that seemed to matter much now.

"Do you not understand?" Doc roared. Everyone looked at him except Ryan and Nataly. "We are going to fight them on *our* terms now!"

"He's right," Mildred said. "Crazy as a bedbug. But right." And she grinned.

"To hell with letting them hammer us with big weapons while we can do nothing about it!"

"Speaking of that," Ricky said hesitantly, "is anybody still shooting at us?"

"Mebbe not," J.B. said. The stern of the New Vick flagship was already looming like a house over them. On her far side her cannon and the *Tyrant*'s were still banging away at each other, close enough one cannon's flame could scorch its opposite number's crew. "Don't want to risk hitting the boss lady. At least, not in the midst of a fight they could still lose."

"Ryan! The swampers!" Krysty exclaimed. "What about them?"

"We've done all we could for them," J.B. said.

"Take over on the Lahti and empty the mag where you think she'll do the most good, J.B.," Ryan said.

"I'll go warn them. You couldn't have done this without them. Reckon we owe them that."

"I'll go," Krysty said.

"Krys—"

She silenced Ryan with a glare. She was precisely the only person on Earth who could do that. She was the only one not stone crazy who was likely to even *try*.

"As Ricky says, no one's shooting at us. And you know better than to try to shield me from danger, don't you, Ryan?"

"Get going," he replied. He hunched down behind the Lahti, angled its long barrel up at the rail of the rapidly approaching warship. "And hustle back here, triple fast!"

WHEN THE LAST spent 20 mm casing bounced jingling on the deck at his feet, Ryan tipped the giant longblaster forward out of the cabin.

"But, Ryan!" Ricky protested. He hated to see a good blaster treated that way, Ryan knew.

"It's just an anchor now, boy," J.B. said. He took off his ear-protecting headband and threw it out the hatch. The others followed suit. "Unless you want to hump it, your blasters and your pack up that ramp there." Before he'd opened fire again, Ryan had suggested everybody grab everything they meant to take with them.

"Ramp?" Nataly asked.

Ryan shouldered her aside. "I got it."

She looked outraged and tried to push him away. Mildred grabbed her in a bear hug from behind, pinning her arms and dragging her back.

"Let it go, Nat," Myron said calmly. "He knows what he's doing. He's the only one, but that's enough, now."

Ryan steered the tugboat for the stern just forward of the big rudder and the submerged screws. A gangplank was tied upright above the spot Ryan was targeting. It looked intact. He didn't think the *Pearl* had taken any major fire on this side. Except for his 20 mm rounds raking the rail and the cabin.

He heard the heavy steel scrollwork over the hatch scrape on the deck. "Just heave it over," he ordered without looking. He heard it clang against the chunk of bridge truss that armored the rail across from it.

"I'm back," he heard Krysty say. "Swampers cut loose. They're already rowing south."

"Godspeed to them," Doc said.

"Ace," Ryan said. "Brace for impact."

The New Vick flagship was armored to the waterline, but Ryan had noticed during his time with the fleet that the improvised plate there wasn't maintained as well as it might be. It was bright red with rust where it regularly came in contact with the water.

That meant it was weakened. At least slightly. He hoped.

The *Vengeance*'s bow smashed into the larger ship like a baby whale nuzzling its mother a touch too aggressively. She slammed to a stop with a grinding, screaming, rending crash.

Ryan heard thumping and tumbling and cussing from behind. There was a limit to how braced you could *get* for an impact like that, especially jammed in a little room that held mostly other people and overfull back-packs.

The tubby river tug was stoutly built, and her bow was armored. Ryan heard her frame creak and felt things break inside her. But she punched a double-big hole in the *Pearl*'s hull, smashing through the rust-brittled scrap armor. Water instantly began to gush into the New Vick flagship.

"All aboard," Ryan said.

"But how will we get up?" Jake asked dubiously. He was eying the water-slicked black-iron rungs hammered into the hull as a ladder of sorts to her deck, a story overhead.

"Got," Jak said. He slipped out the open hatch before anyone could tell him otherwise. Not that Ryan meant to; he'd planned on Jak opening the way for the rest.

J.B. pulled back the lever to cock his Uzi. "I'll cover," he said. Stooped slightly beneath his backpack and slung shotgun, he followed the albino out. The others trailed behind.

Nataly took Myron by the arm. "Come on, Captain. It's time to go."

But he shook her off. "You go. I'm staying."

The cabin was getting hot. As he turned away from the wheel, Ryan could see the evil glow of fire down below from the open hatch.

"But the ship is lost!" the first officer said pleadingly.

"No. Trace deserves the Viking funeral I could never give her before. And poor Sean. Me too, for that matter. Plus, I might just be able to do the rest of you some good with my famous final scene."

Nataly blew out a long breath. "Then I'm staying with you."

"No! I'm ordering you to go."

"I won't!" Her voice was tearful.

Suddenly the potbellied captain had a blaster in his hand, a Russian 9 mm Makarov, of all the rad-blasted things.

"If you don't go yourself, I'll shoot you in the leg," Myron declared. "You don't want to make your shipmates carry you, do you? Not a fine officer like you?"

She turned and bolted out the hatch, sobbing like a lost child. Outside, Ryan heard full-auto fire stuttering. J.B., on his submachine gun. Apparently some *Pearl* crew had shown their heads above the rail too close to Jak for comfort.

As Ryan bent to shoulder his pack and sling his Scout, Myron tipped his little black handgun to his brow.

"It's been an honor serving with you, Cawdor. And thank you."

Ryan nodded. "You too," he said. And left.

THE GANGPLANK SLAMMED down with a thump. It came almost to the deck of the *Vengeance*, now well stuck in the bigger ship's stern.

Sometimes the gods smiled, Doc thought, even on the likes of us.

At the top of the ramp he had just dropped to his friends, Jak spun away, his white hair flying, and dived clear of the ramp's upper end as blasterfire rang out. Wood splintered from the gangplank.

Roaring, holding his ax in both his mighty hands, Santee ran up the ramp with surprising speed.

Doc drew his rapier from his belted sword stick, and with sword in his right hand and blaster in the left, charged up the ramp after the giant Indian. He was no less sick than any of them of suffering one-sided abuse at the hands of tormentors untouchable behind the iron walls of their warships.

As he had told the doubters among their crewmates: this was *their* kind of fight now. And if the odds still lay against them—as Mildred would say, what else was new?

To the left of the ramp Doc saw Santee, swinging about with his ax. Blood flew from its head. To the right Jak slashed and rolled with his knives.

As he neared the top, Doc heard a shot crack from nearby. He saw the big man's body jerk, then at least three more shots rippled out.

Santee reeled back a step. He dropped the ax.

Then, drawing in a breath that seemed to inflate his chest to twice its normal enormous size, he charged his adversaries.

A sailor jammed a socket bayonet mounted on the end of a carbine into Santee's stomach. He blasted its single shot into the man.

Bellowing, Santee spread his arms, then he swept them together, gathering up the man who had bayoneted him with two of his mates, like a mother bear scooping up her cubs. Then he hurled himself and the three sailors over the rail to splash into the water below.

Doc came onto the ramp. He saw no opponents to his left. He spun right. A trio of sailors, one with a bayonet-mounted Springfield carbine, one with a Winchester repeater, and a third with a cutlass, were trying to bash or stab the elusive Jak. He eluded their savage sallies, but was finding no opening to riposte.

Doc lunged and thrust the rapier into the kidney of his nearest foe, the man with the bayoneted longblaster. The man shrieked as if he were on fire and fell thrashing, drawing Doc's arm with him.

The cutlass man spun and cocked his arm back across his chest to cut at Doc. The old man obliterated his bearded face with the charge in the LeMat's stubby shotgun barrel.

The last sailor raised his repeater to shoot Doc down. His dark eyes went wide as Jak's matched pair of butterfly knives pierced his stout neck from opposite sides from behind.

Sheets of blood erupted to briefly mask his face as Jak thrust the blades forward and out through his gullet, severing carotid arteries and jugular veins alike.

Blasterfire erupted from behind Doc. He tore his slim blade free of the wounded man and turned. More sailors were swarming onto the deck from the big cabin. One fired a carbine over the rail at the ramp. Others aimed blasters at Doc.

He and Jak jumped nimbly to press their backs across the scrap-armored side of the cabin. The shots went wild.

That was one advantage, to make the best of the bad,

of Doc's condition: on those occasions when he didn't feel as old as he looked, he also did not *move* like a man who looked that old. He leveled the LeMat and returned fire from the longer .44 barrel.

More shots sounded from below. Before he could duck back, the man who had leaned over the rail to shoot slumped over it, dropping his blaster into the Sippi.

Then Doc's comrades stormed onto the ironclad's deck.

Chapter Twenty-Seven

Mildred nodded in satisfaction. Her shot had caught the man who had blasted Suzan right between the eyes. Exactly where she'd aimed.

It was too late to do poor Suzan any good. The middle-aged woman, running up the ramp, had simply fallen straight over the rail into the river when she was shot. Mildred didn't even know where the bullet had hit her.

"Move it, Mildred!" Ryan shouted from just below her. He had his panga and his SIG out, and blood in his blue eye. "Admire your marksmanship later."

When you're right, you're right, she thought, lowering her arm and hustling up the gangplank. She heard Doc start blazing away with his revolver. A moment later J.B.'s M-4000 shotgun joined the chorus.

Everybody but Ryan was there ahead of her when she puffed her way onto the deck. No living enemies remained. At least not when Jak stood up from the body of the man who'd been shrieking and carrying on.

On the water below, Mildred heard the Diesels roar. She felt crunching through the soles of her combat boots, heard tormented metal screech on metal.

She looked down. The *Vengeance* was backing away

from the *Pearl*. Already she could see the doomed tug was riding deeper in the water, and canted to her port.

Dark smoke poured out the ob port and hatch. But still, an arm appeared through the front port. It turned a thumbs-up to the ironclad's deck, then disappeared.

Ryan was still on the ramp behind her. Mildred realized she was blocking his way when he made a fast motion. He wouldn't hit her, but he'd push any of his companions out of the way if he had to.

But the rangy one-eyed man wasn't going anywhere. He was aiming his SIG up and along the deck to his left.

"Eyes forward!" he shouted.

RYAN WASN'T SURPRISED when his sight was filled by the ample bulk of Baron Tanya Krakowitz of New Vickville. Even though her cannon crews were still trading spitting-distance shots with their rivals aboard the *Tyrant*, she knew somehow where the real threat to her flagship lay.

She was dressed in her tailored admiral suit, which like her stateroom was surprisingly restrained: enough gold braid and bird poop to signify that she was in charge. But no more.

She stopped dead as blasters pointed at her face.

"Cawdor!" she exclaimed. "I should have known."

"You know when I said I considered myself separated from my earlier employment?" he called. "I lied."

"No shit." She gave her head a little shake. "I knew I never should have trusted you. But how could I help myself? I always knew you were this bloody good."

She nodded at the Mossberg shotgun she carried in patrol position across her hips.

"Well, it looks as if we got ourselves a good old-fashioned Sippi standoff here," she said.

"It doesn't work that way, Baron," Ryan replied. "You so much as try to twitch that scattergun up, we'll blast you out of your shoes. No, what really happens now is, you drop the blaster, put your hands up and come peaceably with us. You behave yourself, and I'll let you go when we're clear."

"You're hijacking my ship?"

Ryan jerked his head toward the *Vengeance*, which was still backing clear of the ironclad. He wasn't sure where Myron meant to take her. Much less whether she'd survive to get there, before the fire or the water won the race to claim her.

"It's our only ride out now," he said. "So, yeah. Let's go."

"Me? Your hostage? When pigs fly."

She dropped the shotgun to the deck. Then with startling grace she sprang to the railing. Before even Ryan could react, she launched herself in a dive for the surface of the Sippi.

"'When pigs fly,'" Doc murmured. "At the risk of seeming unchivalrous, that seems curiously apt."

"Good form, though," Avery commented.

CANNON FIRE ERUPTED off to Ryan's left as he led his storming party forward down the passageway toward the *Pearl*'s bridge. The stout wooden walls and scrap-steel armor muffled the sounds. But they weren't hard to identify.

A lone sentry with a Springfield carbine stood watch by the hatch. His eyes widened when he saw the smoke-smudged, blood-spattered band bearing down on him, bristling with blasters.

Ryan aimed his SIG toward the middle of the sentry's forehead. The sentry was a kid, maybe fifteen years old. If he shook any harder, he was in imminent danger of losing some parts.

"Feel like being a hero?" Ryan asked, his voice soft but deadly. The sentry shook his head.

"Then get out of here!" Mildred told him.

"First, lay the blaster down easy," Ryan added.

The kid obeyed, vanishing down the ladder on the passageway's port side.

At Ryan's nod, J.B. hauled open the hatch. "*Hera* reports herself fully engaged with *Devastation* and *Bocephus*, Captain," a female officer was saying. The steel shutters of the portside and forward ob ports were raised, allowing in a weak spill of daylight. The starboard shutters, the ones on the side facing the *Tyrant*, were closed. "*Clytemnestra* reports *Conqueror* withdrawing, but *Glory* is now firing on her from—"

Ryan stepped in with blaster leveled in both hands. The briefing stopped.

The ship's captain was a fine figure of a middle-aged man, if a bit of a bulldog in build. He had a shock of snow-white hair, coal-black brows over blue eyes, and a chin so manly it could double as an anvil.

It was set in resolve now. "What is the meaning of

this interruption?" he said as he spun to face the intruders.

When he found himself staring right up Ryan's handblaster barrel, he didn't even flinch.

"We're taking command now," Ryan said. "Surrender your ship and we'll—"

"Surrender the *Pearl*? The pride of New Vickville? To a renegade traitor and a gang of filthy pirates? Over my dead bo—"

Ryan fired a single shot.

"Does anybody else want to negotiate?" he asked, as Garza folded to his own command deck with both bright blue eyes turned upward toward the hole in his forehead. Ryan turned his handblaster left and right, in case anyone wanted to take him up on his offer.

Instead the other six people on the bridge promptly raised their hands.

"Cover them," Ryan ordered. He lowered his blaster and stepped to where a pull cord hung from the control to a steam-driven horn. The brown-haired female warrant who had been delivering the situation report stepped hurriedly out of his path.

He sounded the horn, three quick times. Pause, then three blasts more. And then one more time.

"But that's the signal to abandon ship!" exclaimed the portly first officer. "What does that mean?"

Ryan let go of the cord. "It means abandon ship," he said. "You know that. So it's time for you and all the rest of you to abandon the rad-blasted ship."

"But—"

Ryan gave him a look.

The commander's face paled. "All right! Everybody, to the lifeboats!"

"What about the *Tyrant*?" the warrant officer asked. "She's still firing on us!"

Indeed, Ryan could hear the noise and feel the trembling of a ball coming in and a ball going out.

"Our problem now, girl," Mildred said. "Git!"

"Are you going to let them go?" Jake asked, as the warrant followed the rest of the bridge crew out the hatch. "Just like that?"

"It's not like they're going to do us any harm," Ryan said.

"But what about Santee? What about Suzan?"

"What about Myron?" Nataly wailed. She covered her face and began to cry again. Somehow Ryan doubted she was calling for avenging him, though. But rather, wondering at his fate.

And suddenly Ryan knew what the captain intended.

"Nothing's going to bring our friends back now, Jake," Avery said, patting his shipmate on the shoulder as Ryan hurried past him to the port on the starboard side of the bridge. "Just let it go."

Whether they used gears or clever counterweights to raise and lower the shutters—too heavy to shift by hand—Ryan didn't know. But the crank turned readily and lifted the heavy plate readily enough.

He heard people gasp as he leaned far out and looked astern.

The shots were coming few and far between the ironclad flagships. But as he watched, a lone orange flame spurted from the *Tyrant*. A single shot replied from

Pearl. From the smell of the dense smoke, there was fire aboard both ships.

But the smoke had cleared enough that he could just make out the red pup-tent form of the *Vengeance*, flames pouring out of her cabin now, driving full speed at the far side of *Tyrant*'s hull.

She disappeared from view.

Whether it was the fire or Myron finding some way to trigger it, the several hundred pounds of black powder stashed in the tug's hold went off at once. From the fine timing, Ryan judged the latter.

From the yellow flash and the knife-sharp sound, it *was* enough to detonate like a high explosive.

The enemy ironclad actually rose perceptibly from the water.

And then a second, vastly louder blast knocked her at least four feet into the air. The sound of her back breaking was not as loud as the second detonation. She settled back down amid a cloud of smoke and steam that instantly shrouded her midsection. Before he pulled back from the port to avoid possible flying debris, Ryan thought he saw her settle in the middle, with bow and stern angling up.

She was finished, he knew that much.

"Whoa," Ricky breathed.

"Magazine explosion," J.B. said. "Ace job of driving."

"It would appear," Doc intoned, "that our captain attained the Viking funeral he desired, for himself and his lost loved ones."

"And then some," Mildred said.

Nataly just wept.

"What now?" Abner asked, as Ryan pushed his way through the crowd back to the helm.

"We steam south out of this place," Ryan said, studying the controls.

"You know how to pilot this thing?" Jake asked.

Ryan leaned toward a speaking tube. "Engine, bridge. All ahead, full."

He waited for what seemed like forever. After he had concluded that the engine room crew had fled their posts like sensible people, he heard, faintly, "Aye-aye, sir!" rattle out from the horn.

He felt the vibration as *Pearl*'s screws began to bite water.

He turned to the others. "Yeah. I can pilot her."

"Didn't the engine crew hear the abandon ship?" Jake asked. The perpetually gloomy navigator actually sounded skeptical that what was happening was happening.

"Do I look like I know?"

Nataly wiped tears from her reddened face. "Ryan, she's holed and probably sinking. And from the smell I'm almost sure she's on fire."

Krysty came up beside Ryan and slipped her arm around his waist. He put his arm around her and smiled down at her.

Then he turned his face south. That was where their future lay, and he always tried to keep facing the future.

Whatever it held.

"Then we ride her until she won't go any farther," he said. "And then we'll play whatever cards we happen to hold at the time. Same as we always do."

"I have an idea," Mildred said. "Next time, let's not sign on for the adventure cruise, okay?"

EXHAUSTED FROM HER crosscurrent swim, Baron Tanya Krakowitz of New Vickville hauled herself to her feet in the shallows of the Sippi's eastern bank.

She saw *Pearl*—her flagship—steaming south with black smoke trailing from her stacks. Behind her, and now to the north of her, the *Tyrant* was sinking with her bow and stern jutting from the water and her middle underwater.

"Cawdor, you magnificent bastard!"

Her cry startled a bittern, which exploded from the tall grass to her left that had hidden it and went winging majestically across the mighty river.

"This doesn't end anything. Our paths will cross again."

She raised her hand to her brow in salute, then she gave the departing ironclad the finger.

No longer a baron after that major goatscrew, she turned to make her way inland. In her mind, she had already started a brand-new life.

Again.

* * * * *

Available August 4, 2015

THE EXECUTIONER® #441
MURDER ISLAND – *Don Pendleton*
On an uncharted island, a psychotic hunter stalks the ultimate prey: man. His newest targets are an international arms dealer—a criminal who was in CIA custody when his plane was shot down—and Mack Bolan, the Executioner.

STONY MAN® #138
WAR TACTIC – *Don Pendleton*
Tensions between China and the Philippines are on the rise, and a series of pirate attacks on Filipino ports and vessels only makes things worse. Phoenix Force discovers that the pirates are armed with American weapons, while Able Team must hunt down the mastermind behind the attacks.

OUTLANDERS® #74
ANGEL OF DOOM – *James Axler*
The Cerberus fighters must battle Charun and Vanth, alien gods intent on opening a portal to bring their kind to earth. If the alien forces succeed, an invasion from a barbaric dimension will lay siege to Europe…and beyond.

COMING SOON FROM

GOLD
EAGLE ®

Available September 1, 2015

GOLD EAGLE EXECUTIONER®
SYRIAN RESCUE – *Don Pendleton*
Tasked with rescuing UN diplomats lost in the
Syrian desert, Mack Bolan is in a deadly race
against time—and against fighters willing to
make the ultimate sacrifice.

GOLD EAGLE SUPERBOLAN®
LETHAL RISK – *Don Pendleton*
A search-and-rescue mission to recover a high-
ranking defector in China leads Mack Bolan to a
government-sanctioned organ-harvesting facility.

GOLD EAGLE DEATHLANDS®
CHILD OF SLAUGHTER – *James Axler*
When Doc is kidnapped by a band of marauders
in what was once Nebraska, Ryan and the
companions join forces with a beautiful but
deadly woman with an agenda of her own...

GOLD EAGLE ROGUE ANGEL™
THE MORTALITY PRINCIPLE – *Alex Archer*
In Prague researching the legend of the Golem,
archaeologist Annja Creed uncovers a string of
murders that seems linked to the creature. And
Annja is the next target...

Nothing is stable…not even the ground underfoot

Read on for this sneak preview of
CHILD OF SLAUGHTER
by **James Axler!**

"Help me!" Even as he shouted, he knew it was in vain. Even if Ryan and the others were directly overhead, they could never hear him through a layer of rock.

Taking a deep breath of the chilly, damp air, he fought to get control of himself. Calm thinking and resourcefulness were the only qualities that ever saved a person in the damnable Deathlands.

"Perhaps my tools…" Doc reached into the folds of his frock coat, seeking the holster of his LeMat revolver, with no success. Next, he rolled onto his right side, searching around him for the blaster or his ebony swordstick. He did the same on his left side, finding a hard rock wall within arm's reach, but no revolver and no swordstick.

Just then, Doc heard a scuffling sound in the direction of his feet. "What now?" He pushed himself up on his elbows, staying low enough that his head wouldn't hit the ceiling. "Rats, I suppose? Some other burrowing vermin come to feast on my flesh?" He reached around for a rock to throw but found nothing. "Begone, vermin!" Noise would have to suffice. "I shall not be your dinner yet!"

The scuffling came closer. Doc peered toward it but saw nothing in the pitch-blackness.

"Begone, I say!" He drew up his legs, pulling away from whatever was there. "You won't find me an easy prey, I promise you!"

Suddenly, he heard a different sound from the same place, a distinctive sound that could not be mistaken for any other.

Giggling.

Doc's mouth fell open. The question was no longer what was over there; it was who.

Doc's heart hammered in his chest. He meant to snap out some words of defiance to try to intimidate his giggling visitor.

But before a single word could leave Doc's lips, the visitor scrambled forward. Hands grabbed hold of Doc's ankles and wrenched his legs straight with an iron grip.

Then a voice, high-pitched and girlish in the lightless void, said, "You're mine now. All mine."

Doc gathered his bravado and snapped, "Now see here!"

But those were the only words he got out before the person—or thing—in the night dragged him from his stony cell.

And then, all of a sudden, there were many more hands, coming from all directions. And all of them were grabbing at Doc.

Don't miss
CHILD OF SLAUGHTER by James Axler,
available September 2015 wherever
Gold Eagle® books and ebooks are sold.

James Axler
Outlanders®

"You can't hide from the truth because it will always find you."

Almost two centuries after the nuclear catastrophe that led to Deathlands, the truth comes out: aliens were behind the nukecaust that reshaped, remolded and forever changed the face of the earth and its inhabitants. One hundred years after Deathlands, anarchy is in retreat in the newly renamed Outlands. A rigid and punishing hierarchy of barons rules the oppressed populations of the fortified villes. Now the baronies have been consolidated in a Program of Unification and are protected by highly trained and well-armed enforcers. Kane, once a trained enforcer for the barons, finds a new destiny thrust upon him, pitting him against the powerful alien forces directing the world's fate.

**Available wherever Gold Eagle®
books and ebooks are sold.**

GOLD
EAGLE®

GEO2015

Joan of Arc's long-lost sword. A heroine reborn. The quest to protect humanity's sacred secrets from falling into the wrong hands.

Rogue Angel is sophisticated escapism and high adventure rooted in the excitement of history's most fabled eras. Each book provides a unique combination of arcane history, mystery, action, adventure and limited supernatural elements (mainly the sword). The series details a young woman's transition from an independent archaeologist who hosts an American cable television show to an action heroine with a surprising connection to Joan of Arc and a role in French mythology.

Available wherever Gold Eagle® books and ebooks are sold.

GOLD EAGLE®

GERA2015A